Son of Woman

Spear Books

Sugar Daddy's Lover Rosemarie Owino
Lover in the Sky Sam Kahiga
A Girl Cannot Go on Laughing All the Time Magaga Alot
The Love Root Mwangi Ruheni
The Ivory Merchant Mwangi Gicheru
A Brief Assignment Ayub Ndii
A Taste of Business Aubrey Kalitera
A Woman Reborn Koigi wa Wamwere
The Bhang Syndicate Frank Saisi
My Life in Crime John Kiriamiti
Black Gold of Chepkube Wamugunda Geteria
Ben Kamba 009 in Operation DXT David Maillu
Son of Woman Charles Mangua
A Tail in the Mouth Charles Mangua
The Ayah David Maillu
A Worm in the Head Charles K. Githae
Twilight Woman Thomas Akare
Life and Times of a Bank Robber John Kiggia Kimani
Son of Woman in Mombasa Charles Mangua
My Life with a Criminal: Milly's Story John Kiriamiti
The Operator Chris Mwangi
Birds of Kamiti Benjamin Bundeh
Nice People Wamugunda Gateria
Times Beyond Omondi Mak'Oloo
Lady in Chains Genga-Idowu
Mayor in Prison Karuga Wandai
Son of Fate John Kiriamiti
Kanina and I Charles Mangua
Prison is not a Holiday Camp John Kiggia Kimani
Confessions of an AIDS Victim Carolyne Adalla
Comrade Inmate Charles K. Githae
Colour of Carnations Ayub Ndii
The American Standard Sam DeSanto
From Home Guard to Mau Mau Elisha Mbabu
The Girl was Mine David Karanja
Links of a Chain Monica Genya
Unmarried Wife Sitwala Imenda
Dar es Salaam By Night Ben Mtobwa
The Sinister Trophy John Kiriamiti
Kenyatta's Jiggers Charles Mangua

Son of Woman

Charles Mangua

Spear Books

NAIROBI • KAMPALA • DAR ES SALAAM

Published by Spear Books
a subsidiary of
East African Educational Publishers Ltd.
Brick Court
Mpaka Road/Woodvale Grove Westlands
P.O. Box 45314, Nairobi

East African Educational Publishers Ltd.
P.O Box 11542, Kampala

Ujuzi Educational Publishers Ltd.
P.O. Box 31647, Kijito-Nyama, Dar es Salaam

First published 1971 by
East African Publishing House

First published by Spear Books 1988

Reprinted 1994, 2000

ISBN 9966-46-552-9

Printed in Kenya by English Press Ltd.
Enterprise Rd., P.O. Box 30127, Nairobi

to my father

1

Son of woman, that's me. I am a louse, a blinking louse and I am the jigger in your toe. I am a hungry jigger and I like to bite. I like to bite women — beautiful women. Women with tits that bounce. If you do not like the idea you are the type I am least interested in.

Maybe you have heard about me and again maybe you haven't. Either way you have missed nothing. To you I am the crank from downstairs who is not worth knowing. So what?

I am the son of woman and I'll repeat it till your elephant ears ache. Never had a dad in my blinking life. My whoring ma could never figure out who my pop was. A very short memory — that's what she had. It was one of the scores of men who took her for a bed-ride but she wasn't bothered to remember who among them I resembled. That's my mother. Nothing bothered her. Didn't bother to get married either. All she did was collect a quid from the punks who came for a tumble. That's me. I was conceived on a quid and mother drank it. Poor mother. God rest her soul, she is dead.

Yes, I am the son of woman. I ain't no brother to the son of man and I ain't no brother to nobody either. If I had a brother probably the punk wouldn't like me. Maybe you wouldn't like me either if I told you a few things about myself. So what? Nobody asked you to like me. If you don't like me take a short-cut to bed and snore your silly head off, but if you like me, I'd advise you to take the first opportunity to consult a psychiatrist. You are sick.

"Damn you and damn you again, you onion-eating pale-faced son of a coolie. Who the hell do you think you are?" I am not thinking about you, my friend. I wouldn't say such a thing about you. I am thinking about this Indian magistrate who put me in jail. Merciless bastard, that's what he is. God! I can still see him. He is sitting on his ass and chewing some leaves. Damn him again.

I am the son of woman and I've said it before. If you are bored, plug your ears. Don't get any funny ideas that there was something between my mother and the holy ghost because she never saw a ghost in her life. She never saw the inside of a church either. The only time she saw a ghost was when the cops picked her up from a ditch and put her in the can because she was dead drunk. She confused the cops for ghosts on account of the hooch and the poor lighting in the cell.

I have inherited a few of her qualities and that is why I am cursing this magistrate. She was always cursing some man who'd taken her personal goods and refused to pay the bill at the specified time.

"Horrid, that's what they are. All men are horrid," she used to say to Miriam, the whore next door. "They smile when they take you and at the end of the month they run to avoid you. They go to fish in fresh waters. Laughing, cheating bastards, that's what men are. They want everything for free." She'd curse men and then go looking for them.

I remember this vividly. I was just a lad at the time and very green at that. I had a little back room but I always heard them when they came in. They came roaring drunk and singing drunken tunes but I didn't know what they came for. There was always the talk of money, but all I knew about money was that it could be used to buy sweets. I liked sweets. I've always liked sweet things. Perhaps you do.

One day, when I was still too young to understand, it happened. My mother died. She was run over by a car when she jumped off a moving bus to confront a fellow who owed her some dough. She was dead drunk again. Miriam, our next door neighbour, took me to her house. She was a prostitute too. God! Even as a kid I had to go through hell.

There was this little girl Tonia in the house. She was the daughter of this Miriam and she was my age. We were both eleven. When there was nobody in the house Tonia used to ask me to do to her what the men did to her mother. When I confessed that I didn't have the vaguest idea what the men did to her mother Tonia gave me a wallop. She used to wallop me just for kicks. I hate being walloped by girls — even little ones. Later on I found out. I had to, otherwise Tonia would get fresh on me. It wasn't so bad once I learned. Tonia stopped beating me after that.

Skip the years, mate. I am now thirty but there are times when I feel twenty-one. Me, I don't believe in one woman. Inheritance again. I like to have a bird here and another there just in case one of them happens to lay an egg when I am in the tumbling mood. If you are the type that sticks to one woman, you should have your apparatus examined. You are blind, my friend. You are probably blind to the

8

fact that the beautiful frill you possess only sticks to you because you
furnish a contrast. This explains why cute dames more often fall for
ugly mugs. If you are this type of mug we all join hands in sympathy.
If I were you I'd be nice and faithful but don't get me wrong. I am riot
like you.

I am one hell of a fellow. My name is Kiunyu. Dodge Kiunyu,
known to my friends as Dod. If you don't like my name, just don't.
I don't blame you because I don't like it myself. The priest who
baptised me must have been nuts. Most priests are nuts anyway.
I can never figure out how this crank invented this name for me. He
must have been thinking about the bishop's car instead of the holy
waters he was pouring right into my eyes instead of my forehead.
Very devoted priest, this fellow was. At least he didn't have a one-track
mind. One priest among many, I must say.

Everybody in this goddam place is clamouring for education.
Me, I am not. Take it away. I have had some but I don't want it. I am
a rebel. It has done me no good. Maybe I'll end up becoming a thief,
so what? Damn exciting life until you are caught. Most thieves are
caught anyway and I'd hate to think myself one. I have gone for two
days without food and by God I'll have to pinch some from somewhere
tonight or tomorrow. I simply can't survive on my bitter saliva while
mugs are feeding meat to dogs. It ain't fair. I've got to eat something
and I don't care how I get it. If you know how, you are wiser than
I am.

As I walk, I am counting my old friends. Friends who are not
friends any more. They were friends at university. During my five
years at Makerere I made plenty of friends. Then we came out. I had a
B.A. Honours in Geography. Lousy subject this Geography. Jack of
all trades and master of none.

I took this job with the Ministry of Labour and Social Services.
I was a Labour Officer, and a good one at that. I was doing fine but
got no promotion. I didn't humour my boss and I believe I was
supposed to. Anyway I didn't humour him and consequently I didn't
get a promotion. Fellows who I knew to be mugs were getting ahead.
Not me. A fellow I'd always detested on account of his stupidity, lack
of guts and lack of bodily cleanliness became my boss. He was the
type that thought that his hat was more important than his head. A
punk. They must have been nuts to promote him. I just couldn't get
over it. The fellow didn't brush his teeth and he insisted on summoning
me to his office just to infect me with some of his foul breath. It was
real Chinese torture listening to this fellow telling you what to do and
what not to do. That was the beginning of the end. My end. I couldn't

stomach the blighter and I didn't beat about the bush in letting him know it.

In my dingy office the most intelligent companions were evil smelling cheating bums bothering me for jobs. I sympathized with them but there were no jobs going. All they had to do was register.

I was getting bored. Bored stiff. I started applying for jobs. I wrote at least two applications a week. Nothing doing. I always got regrets. I was called for three interviews but again I flopped. In whatever I tried I flopped. My friends were pinching my girlfriends. My fianceé left me high and dry and got married to a butcher. A butcher! My ass! Fancy that. A blinking butcher. Whenever I imagined him acting husband in bed I'd go to the john and leak.

The devil take his soul. The bitch was pretending to be mine and mine alone while secretly letting the bloody butcher work some overtime on what I considered my goods. The thought that I was having a tumble with a woman who'd allowed the butcher to put his dirt in her made me puke. I mean it really. I did it in the bathroom. Yellow stuff that left my mouth bitter and dry.

I started feeling sorry for myself. I was really sorry for poor me. Folks were laughing at me. Others were sorry for me. I hated them and hated myself. The only company I enjoyed was my own. I'd brood and muse and curse and spit. There was something wrong with me. I tried to figure out what, but two and two always made five. I couldn't get four. I noticed some change in my countenance. In case you haven't seen me I am a handsome cuss. I mean it. I've got what it takes if you know what I mean.

I decided to see a psychiatrist but changed my mind. He would merely bother me. Loneliness was the best thing for me. One by one my friends dropped me like a hot cake and I was not invited to the usual weekend goat eating, beer drinking parties. I had this depressing feeling of inadequacy and my office became dingier than before. Job seekers grew fewer and fewer on account of my bad temper. I had to do something.

I started to hit the bottle. When I say hit the bottle, I mean hit the bottle. No half measures. I simply drank myself silly every evening and went to the office late with my constant friend, Mr. Hangover. He bothered me but I couldn't get rid of him. I realized the stupidity of it all and to punish myself, I hit the bottle harder. Funny enough I made friends again; drinking friends. Different friends. People who'd forget you as soon as you were out of their sight. Friends who would cut your throat if by so doing they'd gain something.

Then there were the women. I had plenty at my disposal. I was

dishing out money and drinks right and left and naturally running
down my savings. It was during this time that I met Doris and others.
I was just carefree but rather unhappy at heart. Somehow I knew I was
going downhill but I wasn't bothered. I even caught V.D. but
instead of pulling the girl's ears I gave her money to go and see a
doctor. Being charitable pleased me. It pleased me to see women
pleased when I bought them drinks — and I bought plenty. There is
no bar in Nairobi I have not set my foot in and if there is then it is not
worth a visit.

After six months I was broke. I had only my salary to drink on
and that was that. My savings were completely finished. Gone. I had
somewhat recovered my composure. I was thinking seriously about
life. The job did not look so dismal and I was going to marry Doris.
She was my blessing. Together we would set up a home and breed
brown kids. Brown like myself and as beautiful as Doris. God be
praised.

I remember that fatal day very vividly. I was driving to Limuru
and some cops who stopped me pointed out that my road licence had
expired. They were damn right and they were prepared to let me go if
I bribed them. That was how I became a jailbird. It was the first day
of my present life. I didn't bribe them though. I merely got fresh and
we had a fight. It's seven months ago but the memory is dew-fresh.
I was tipsy as hell and I can still hear myself addressing the cops.

"The devil take your soul, you foul-faced ill-smelling bow-legged
cop. I ain't going to give you no bribe. Why don't you ask your dumb
superiors to redesign your uniforms for you? You wouldn't be sweating
like pigs. Gosh! You'll soon sweat blood if your ass doesn't burst
out of your pants." I was real fresh but I got the surprise of my life.
Cops are not that dumb. The bastard hit me. He hit me real hard.
I reeled backwards and then lashed out. I clouted him bang on top
of his silly mouth and hurt my knuckles against his teeth. You should
have seen the poor devil. Never saw a cop look so murderous. He came
at me and gave it to me hard and proper. Nearly broke my arm, the
stupid fool. Twisted it till I saw the innocent clouds turn pink. With
one final effort he hurled me to the ground. He felt his lips. He licked
them and spat blood. He called me something nasty.

I rolled on the ground to ease the pain in my arm till his
companion gave me a kick in the ribs and asked me to raise my arms.
He slipped on the bracelets in spite of my curses and yanked me to my
feet. He searched my pockets and came out with my car keys. Locked
all doors, checked them and then rechecked them. Gave me a kick on
the ass and shoved me forward.

"Move on, bull fighter," he says to me. "We leave your bus here.
We shall feed you for a while at the police station. Good meals we
provide. See how you manage on fried water. Move!" Fancy that!
A cop promising to feed me. I'd rather be fed by a snake. They both
feed you on poison. Not much difference — between cops and snakes.
Both can be very vicious. In their protection I didn't feel so good.

I take a look at the bow-legged cop who gave me the wallop and
I smile inwardly. I understand why the bastard lost his goat. He's got
a tooth missing. He doesn't look beautiful with this big tooth missing.
Hasn't improved his appearance any. I smile again because I can see
his tongue sneaking between the gap and licking the bleeding gum. I
reckon that this fellow had a right to wallop me. Maybe I'll get even
one day.

That was seven months ago. I remember the incident vividly.
They prosecuted me and found me guilty of assault and causing actual
bodily harm. Put me in the cooler for six months and the damn
magistrate would not accept a fine. Six months, no fine. Six good
months in the can among stinking criminals, lechers, sodomites,
burglars and lots of other filth. God!

It's a month since I left the cooler. I have been hanging around
for a whole month without a job. My friends are scared of me. They
don't like my looks. Behind my back they refer to me as a jailbird.
Jailbird! Me! Gosh! I am a jailbird — so what? My old girlfriends
don't want me. Fancy that. They actually sympathize with me. My foot!
They make me laugh. A pain in the neck — that's what they are.

I am thinking about this girl I was going to get married to. This
Doris girl is a receptionist at the New Stanley Hotel. I met her through
this tutor of mine at Makerere. He came to the New Stanley, met
Doris and got amorous. I met her in his room when I paid him a
courtesy call and I liked her ass. When he left I took over.

Doris gave me a few tumbles and I liked the tumbling. I have
had tumbles with all sorts of women in all sorts of places and believe
you me, I know the difference between a good so-and-so and a hollow
ass. This Doris is different. She sort of doesn't let you have all of it.
You are left with a feeling that there is some secret hidden depth where
you have not been allowed to reach. Some sweetness further down the
street which you have not been allowed to taste. It doesn't matter how
hard you try, you don't get there. If you are an explorer like me, you
want to keep trying. You must discover what is in darkest Africa and
so did I.

It was all very funny. First it was greed. Greed for a tumble. I got
it all right but I couldn't help begging for another. I got that one too

12

and I became a slave. I couldn't help myself. Doris was my master and mistress. Then she told me a fib. She told me that she was going to have a baby. She was merely testing my feelings but I believed her. I believed her because I am allergic to rubbers and I don't use them anyway. They make me droopy, that is what they do. I hate them. Doris hated pills and I don't blame her. Nothing exciting in them, if you see what I mean.

We were going to get married. She had to provide the money of course but then I got fresh to the cops. I'll never forgive them on account of Doris. She was married after I'd been wallowing in the cooler for four months God have mercy on her. She had no baby in that little tummy of hers. She'd told me a fib. Women are always telling me fibs.

It was four weeks ago that I went to see her — the day they opened hell's gates and let me out. I'd bathed myself and had my beard barbered twice but I reckon I still looked like a jailbird. I had my arms open and I was striding like the King of Siam when I saw her at the old reception counter and was I beaming? Gosh, man! My heart was beating like a ram and the look on my face was the real personification of joy. Happiness unbound. I was grinning like the cat that swallowed the bird.

This Doris catches a glimpse of me approaching like a batman and her mouth pops open. Her bosom sags and she looks around as if she wants to run. I check my stride and approach slowly but deliberately. I am all excited. I want to fly at her but I dare not.

"Hi, kid, guess who. This is Dodge. I've dodged my way out of Satan's jaws. Mighty glad to see you again, my human doll. You look like the flowers in heaven." I extend my hand and she responds in a feverish manner. I feel something ooze out of me. I am getting confused and embarrassed. To save my face I grab her and administer one quick kiss on the cheek. That did it. She rubbed her cheek where my lips had touched as if I'd put some prison dirt there and faced me.

"No, no, Dod." She always called me Dod and I liked it. Sometimes it sounded like Dad. She extended her left arm and spread the fingers in front of me. Sure as hell it was there. A gold wedding ring on her finger. A wedding ring — my foot! I couldn't get my silly eyes off the ring. I stood there dumbfounded and dazed.

"So?" I enquired, shrugging my shoulders slightly and feeling very unsure of myself.

"I know it's a shock, Dod, but I got married. I am married, Dod. I have been married two months. I — I had to. Do you understand? I had to. I had to restore faith in myself. Friends deserted me when they put you in. They referred to me as a criminal's girlfriend. I couldn't bear it, Dod. I simply couldn't. At times I prayed for you and hoped that some miracle would open prison doors and bring you to my arms. Other times I wished I'd never met you. I could have waited, Dod. I could have waited but I felt that it would never be the same. I kept telling myself that I was wrong but I couldn't believe myself. It was terrible. I was lonely and sad. My life was hollow. I didn't know where I was going or where I was coming from. Then it happened, Dod. It happened. Don't look at me like that because it can't be undone. It has already happened. I am married now. It's all different, Dod. Yes, Dod. I am sorry but you must understand. It happens to people you know."

"Who is the fellow?" I asked. Her face furrowed and her complexion changed. She said seriously.

"He is my husband. Let that suffice. Please."

"Do I know him?"

"Yes. You know him, Dod. He is your friend. He was your tutor at Makerere. He's the one that led you to me. That same man is my husband."

"God Almighty! You mean Dugan! That short stout bald headed bad tempered fellow is your husband? Jeez! You must be out of your mind. Of all the news that falls on passing ears, what could have possessed you to choose a middle-aged pink-faced Englishman instead of me, jailbird though I be? Gosh, Dory, I'll murder him for you. By Jingo I will. I wouldn't let you. I wouldn't let you be ruined. No, no. No, thank you. Where is he?"

Then I had it. I am always having it even from women. Unlucky fellow, that's me. She called me a poor conceited worthless opinionated blackguard who spent my beggarly life smearing other people with dirt while I was dirt itself.

"How dare you breathe such words about my husband? I'll have none. Not from you. Please leave me now. I have work to do. Don't try to see me again even when you've learnt to have respect for others. Please go," she hissed.

There and then I spat. I spat on the floor and walked out. That's me. I simply can't stand women hissing at me. Women should not hiss at all. At least not at men. I couldn't be bothered if they spent their whole goddam life hissing at each other — but at me! Oh no. For that I shake my head. That's why I spat.

My shoes are number ten. They are long, broad and brown. I notice with disgust the red familiar dust on them as I walk towards Eastleigh. They are always dusty, my shoes. I can't afford shoe polish

14

and the shoe-shine boys wouldn't even lend me their brush. I am slouching at a slow unsteady pace because I have lost the nail of my big toe. The thick bandage does not help. The blinking toe is beating drums. Wet pus is making the inside slippery. God! I hate myself at times. I hate pus. Ruins my appetite, it does. Gosh, my toe hurts. I must see a doctor soon. I am all confused.

I have walked and cursed for a mile and a half. I have fathoms to go. I mean furlongs. I wish I was sinking fathoms instead of walking furlongs. I am hungry but that is nothing compared to my toe. I never realized that it was such a long walk from the centre of Nairobi to the Eastleigh slums. My old car has grown a beard. The damn thing wouldn't start and it is growing moss and lichens at Tigoni Police Station, where they dumped it after dumping me in jail. It is the only real friend I had — my car I mean — and it is the only thing I own that has a roof. The road licence expired a couple of million years ago and I can't get a friendly soul to buy the damn car even as scrap metal. That's me. Plain broke. Broke as a dry twig. Broke as hell. Not a thing. Nothing. Damn it. And I am a graduate. That's what I am. A graduate. University of London Geography Honours at Makerere and I can't get a job. That's how helpful education is. Very helpful. Gosh! I am hungry.

I am there now. I mean I have arrived at Eastleigh. It's two-thirty and the sun is melting my head. I have little hair on my dome because the first thing they do when you are received in the cooler is unhair your head. Tin roofs are shimmering everywhere and the smell of dust, dirt and prostitutes is offending my nostrils. A plane is taking off at the airport and it is raising a sandstorm along the murram runway. It sounds like ten thunders. What a place? Gosh! I am hungry.

There is a prostitute standing there and there is a prostitute standing here. There are prostitutes standing everywhere. Maybe some are not, but they all look alike. They are hungry for money. It's written on their faces. Can't help them. Not me. I don't have a cent. Not one thin cent.

As I pass this respectable-looking house a Johnnie emerges from inside buttoning his trousers. A middle aged Somali woman is at his heels angrily demanding the tumbling fee. She is talking in Swahili and English at the same time.

"*Toa pesa* Johnnie. *Lipa*. Twenty shillings. *Mzungu* pay. Twenty shillings you pay. Not *bure*. Not free. Give." She got hold of his collar and yanked him — an ill advised move. He whirled round and slapped her hard with the back of his hand. She kissed the ground and started screaming — "Thief! *Mwivi!* Johnnie thief!" and the

Johnnie took to his heels.

I don't know where the people came from. It's hard to believe that those small houses sheltered so many people. They came out like hordes of desert locusts and the poor English soldier was cornered like a rabbit. The cruelty — God! They kicked him and kicked him and kicked him. He lay lifeless on the ground and yet they kicked him. Everybody wanted to kick him. Another half-dressed Johnnie burst out of a house and fled barefoot towards the army barracks. Everybody shouted something or other but nobody pursued him. The prostitute he was having a tumble with came out of the house and started pissing behind the house. Horrid. She didn't mind whether you were staring at her or not. Gosh. These women have no respect for their asses. Makes me wonder whether this is the type of woman God designed for man.

As sure as hell there is going to be trouble here. The beaten up Johnnie is not stirring. He is a bleeding mess. The English soldiers will sure take some revenge. They'll beat up men and rape women. I must get the hell out of here. Might get raped by a homosexual. You never know English soldiers.

I walk past several blocks and turn to the left. The house I am looking for is on the far side, one row from the airport barrier. I have never been here before but I got very precise instructions of how to get there. Judy is always like that. She makes sure that you find her.

As I look to the right, the number is staring at me, 1564, written neatly in charcoal with "welcome to my den" scribbled below.

I am now approaching the den. I don't feel so good on account of my toe. It will be the second tumble in a month. I have come all this way for it, heat or no heat, toe or no toe and now I want to turn back. I don't like this den. I am holding a brief discourse with myself but I am still slowly walking towards the den. I am in two minds but I can't stop walking. Something is pulling me. I hear a scream somewhere behind me and I walk fast and knock at the door. Nothing happens. Not a sound. I can hear more screams and I knock frantically at the door. Then I hear it. I hear the bed creak. Light footsteps are approaching the door. I control my breathing. Sometimes my lungs are very stupid. They just don't control my breathing.

The door opens. I have prepared a smile for Judy but I get a surprise. Women are always surprising me. This one is not Judy. She is a halfcaste. A cross between a Chinese and an African. A real dish. She is as different from Judy as I am different from you. The smile dies on me and my brain is not working very fast. This is

16

unusual. I am a quick thinker.

"Yes?" she blurts out, raising her eyebrows and inspecting my anatomy. All the time I am looking at her tits. Real medium rare her tits are, and I make a mental calculation that they are better than Judy's. I like tits. I like to put them in my mouth and think of babyhood.

"My name is Dodge — Dodge Kiunyu and I like your tits. I am looking for Judy — Judy Waira. Does she live here?" She eyes me with disgust and is just about to bang the door shut when we hear another scream from the direction of the fighting place I'd just scrammed from. She hesitates.

"She is not here," the Chinawoman says. I say Chinawoman because she is more Chinese than African. Never saw an African with bulging oblique eyes.

"Does she live here?" I ask politely.

"Yes, she does but she is not here now." I notice that she is not as hard boiled as she makes out to be. This Kimono-like nightdress she is wearing is thin and vaguely transparent. It doesn't show much but I can see all that I want to see. She is wearing pants all right and I can see they are blue. I go for pink but blue is tolerable especially when the woman wearing them is this woman in front of me. I am secretly praying but don't ask me for what. You should know.

"Forgive my disturbing your mid-day nap but would you know where I can find her? I had an appointment for three o'clock." She looks at me queerly.

"A business appointment?"

"Yes, and no," I tell her. "Friendly business if you like." She smiles archly and then sneers.

"Free trade eh?"

"Again yes and no. Simply business without trade."

"You broke?" God! Her white teeth are killing me and she is showing them tits of hers to advantage. The light afternoon breeze is blowing her nightdress against her thighs and I start seeing shapes. Blast! And she is asking me — what the hell was she asking me?

"You are, aren't you?" she asks again.

"Oh, sure. I am. Oh—wait. You asked me whether I was broke?"

"Uh."

"Sorry. I am not. I mean yes and no. We are all broke in a way. We can't have all we want. We are all broke and yet we are not. Hey, can I come in for a while? I don't like this screaming from over yonder. Gets on my nerves, it does." She thought for a while and then smiled. This really gets my goat. Prostitutes are always thinking or letting on

17

to be. They don't want you to take them for granted. The only time they don't think is when you show them a brand new currency bill. The bill does the thinking.

"Eh, O.K. You may come in for a while. I am not sure that Judy will be back today."

"And where the hell is she?" I ask her as I pass through the door. The interior of the den is dark even at three — reason being that the only window has these carton slabs to serve as curtains. She moves over and removes one of the slabs and immediately some light filters through. I like to see myself during daylight, besides, this dame here is an eyeful. If you have any imagination you'll agree with me that a cross between a Chinaman and an African is bound to be an eyeful. And they are so rare.

She sits down on the bed as if she's not heard my question. There are no stools or chairs and when she says have a seat I don't know whether she is offering me the floor to sit on or the bed. I hesitate and she motions the bed. I am feeling uncomfortable, the reason being that the perfume she is wearing starts to drift to my nostrils and it sure dilutes my blood. My heart doesn't beat steadily either. Very stupid, this heart of mine. I sit huddled up for fear that some part of me might start trembling and repeat the question.

"She went to a movie with her boyfriend," she answers.

"At this hour?"

"They left at eleven o'clock. Movie is one thing. There are other things."

"You are telling me," I echo, pretending to be disappointed. I am not. I am looking at this dame's tits through the corner of my eye and smiling the crocodile smile. If I could make this dame, Judy could go nut-cracking for all I care.

This Judy promised me a tumble. One for free. I used to know her when I had the dough and she must have unloaded a thick wad off me. I met her three days ago and I told her I was broke and flat out. She gave me a quid out of kindness and actually persuaded me to come to this den of hers for a free so and so in memory of old times instead of which she gallivants away with this other mug, and leaves a cute Chinawoman in her place. The fellow who said that life is nuts knew his words although he was nuts himself. It takes a nut to say life is nuts. It ain't nuts.

"Do you also live here?" I ask. She shakes her head.

"I only came here this morning because I have a friend at my house. She has her boyfriend with her and they want some privacy. They haven't met for a long time. I had to leave my room to them."

18

"And will they wash the sheets?"

"That's a silly question. What did you say your name was — George or Gorge?"

"Dodge, my dear girl. Dodge not Gorge. What do they call you? Honeypot I suppose."

"Something similar."

"And that is not telling me."

"Annie. It sounds like honey, doesn't it?"

"It sure does. Now that you mention it, I remember that I haven't tasted honey for centuries." I teased. "It's a beautiful name. Almost as beautiful as you."

"And your name is gorgeous. I'd have preferred Gorge though. You'd better go home now. Nobody's screaming."

"I'll start screaming," I tell her. She gives me a look that would open the mouth of a meditating Yoga King. I give her a shy close look.

It was difficult and it was easy. I used delaying tactics and something in heaven came to my aid. There was this roar of thunder and yet another. Annie is the type that get scared when the heavens clash. Thunder gets into her stomach. I was licking my lips as she unconsciously drew closer to me. Then the rain. Some women simply go soft when it rains. The rhythm of the falling rain brings music to their ears. The humidity makes them sleepy and lax and they want you to sing them a lullaby as they snuggle and cuddle close to you. The stage is set. No resistance. Softly please. Gently my friend. You have a free ticket to Hongkong. So did I with my Annie. A trip to Hong-Kong and back.

It is night and I am walking back to town. Back to the centre of Nairobi. I am not sure where I am going. I have nowhere to go. I have no house, no friends. I am a jailbird. Thrice I have slept at the railway station and on several occasions I have kept various watchmen company throughout the night and the stones near the fire are as good a place as any to rest one's wearied bones. When I remember what I used to be, I curse this big star above me because it looks like the star under which I was born. It blinks at me and my toe starts up all over again. I hate toes.

I am thinking but I don't know what the hell I am thinking about. Painful process, thinking. Some part of me is happy. Real happy. I close my eyes and I see Annie peeling off this subtle Kimono-like nightie and my heart kisses my lungs. Gosh. The softest miracle ever to come into contact with a male — and the works? Boy oh boy! If you haven't screwed Annie you've never had a screw. You're going through life with blinkers on. Gosh! I am hungry.

2

It's eight o'clock and it's bitter cold. Very unusual for January. My fingers are frozen, absolutely frozen. Rubbing them together doesn't help. It never does. Tonia is by my side and we are going to school. It's about one mile away from home and we have to walk it. We are always walking, Tonia and I. We don't have much else to do.

There is a hole in my khaki pants and there is a white patch on the hole. The patch is getting worn out too. Miriam fixed it for me the second time two months ago so that I can use the pants for going to school but there's something wrong with my ass. Keeps wearing away patches. Perhaps there is something wrong with my sitting posture. There are lots of things wrong with me.

Today is Friday and it's our fifth day in school. Tonia's mother has been trying to hammer into our silly heads, the importance of education and the comforts she has to deny herself in order to send us to school. How depressing. Miriam never denied herself anything in her whole blinking life. The only thing she denied herself was our presence while we were at school. Our presence was a real headache to her. Sent us out she did, every time some fellow paid her a visit for an hour or two during which the door would be locked and the curtains drawn and then the fellow would walk out looking somewhat weaker and ashamed. A damn nuisance men are really. Some would come when it was raining and Miriam wouldn't know what to do with us. At such times we were a real pain in the neck to her. One day when I was reluctant to go out on account of the heat outside which wasn't conducive to curing my aching head, she poured a flagon of God's drink on my head and asked me to go dry myself. Very clever this Miriam. Knows how to temper heat and cure headaches. Damn her.

The only thing we learnt at school yesterday was the importance of having our nails clean and not to have foul breath. The teacher's breath was most foul. Hadn't cleaned them damned teeth of his after

20

his last encounter with onions. He must have taken dry smoked fish for dessert and later tried to eliminate the gaps between his teeth by smearing avocados. Very remarkable he is — this teacher of ours. He's even got an artificial plastic carnation in the buttonhole of his coat and laughs at his own jokes which we are too stupid to understand.

His name is Jack, this teacher of ours. Whenever he says Jack you always hear Jock which is what some people call their draught oxen. Looking at him, he reminds you of an ox. No horns, tails or humps but all the same, an ox. Fat like an ox, our Jack is, but only slightly more stupid. A remarkable fellow.

On Wednesday we spent half the morning pouring water in the classroom to drown the dust. Very dusty our classroom is. You blow your nose and the mess that comes out is half dust. Perhaps there won't be much dust today on account of the cold. Dust is better than cold anyway. You can wash it off or blow it off your nose but you can't wash cold. Chills your blood, the blinking cold does, and when there is a hole in your pants directly under the ass it doesn't help to ease the situation. No part of your body wants to get chilled, not even your ass.

Tonia is wearing a nice new little light blue dress on account of being daughter of her mother which I am not. My mother is dead. This Tonia keeps asking me whether I like her dress and I grunt something to that effect. She thinks she is a perfect lady at eleven and a half — we are both eleven and a half but she looks down on me as if I was six. Looks down on me she does, on account of this hole in my only pair of pants.

Miriam cannot afford to buy me clothes. I am not her son. Don't get me wrong though. I would not like to be her son. No, sir. Not by a long chalk. Oh no. Miriam should not mother anybody. My mother should not have mothered me either. This I'll swear and you can go to hell if you don't agree with me.

Miriam took possession of everything we owned. She wears my mother's clothes and cooks in her pots. She sold a few of the things that she didn't need, got drunk on the proceeds and then rented the house — our house. That is why she is so kind to me which accounts for the hole in my pants and Tonia's new dresses. Gosh! Women can be kind. Miriam's kindness is very remarkable. A gold-digging, oversexed, fat-assed whore, that's what she is. No kidding. She's real bad, this Miriam who is also my guardian.

I was telling you about Wednesday. After drowning the dust Jack started teaching us a, e, i, o, u. We sang a, e, i, o, u, the rest of the morning so that by lunchtime I was so bored that it would have been

a relief to play with green snakes. The most boring half morning in
my eleven and a half years' lifetime. A very interesting teacher, our
Jack. I am hoping and praying that I'll never have to repeat a, e, i, o,
u. God! I wish my prayers would be answered — I really do.

On getting to the school compound we find that there are only
a few kids around. We join this group leaning against the mud church
wall and I start chatting with a girl on my left. She is real cute but
she talks too much. When I tell her that I am cold she rubs my cheeks
and they glow. Me, I like little girls with warm hands. They make
your cheeks glow, they do. Tonia does not like this little girl I am
talking to.She grabs my hand and says "Come!"

I don't feel like going so I ask: "Go where?" Tonia pulls harder
and repeats more loudly, "Come". I am not feeling so good. I don't
like to take orders from little girls. Tonia wallops me once in a while
but I ain't no dog and she ain't my master. All the same I decide to obey
Tonia but I ask her again, "Where are we going? It's cold you know."

"Never mind," says little Tonia.

"But I mind," says little me.

"Do you want to go back?" Tonia asks.

"Not particularly but where are we going?"

Tonia pushes me back and yells in her little cooing voice, "Go
back then. Go. I'll tell mother." Fancy that. She'll tell Miriam.
I don't know what she'll tell about but whenever she tells something
about me Miriam gives me a hiding. It doesn't matter what. Whenever
she accuses me of something, I get a beating. These beatings are
becoming too frequent for my liking. Sometimes she pinches me with
those coarse hands of hers and it doesn't improve my cheeks. Very
coarse, those hands of hers. Worse than sandpaper, I am not kidding.
They are real bad, especially when they pinch your cheeks.

I ease back and start talking to my cute little girl. Her name is
Lucy and her mother works for the City Council. She sweeps drains
and what-have-you. Respectable, though filthy as a profession. Earns
a living, Lucy's mother does. Better than whoring with charcoal
sellers.

Little Tonia follows me and stands behind me. I don't see her
because I am whispering something to Lucy and I am not aware of her
presence till she grabs me by the collar.

"What shit are you cheating now?" Tonia asks me and I turn to
face her. I am so annoyed that tears are almost welling up in my
eyes. I am struck dumb and I am shaking all over. My knees are
knocking. Stupid knees, my knees. They are always knocking.
Murderous rage, that's what I am in.

I look at Tonia and spit at her. I spit right on top of her flat nose and she lets go my collar. I am thinking that it would be unseemly to have a showdown with Tonia so early in the morning but she doesn't. Slaps me she does, this little Tonia, and slaps me again. She pins me against the wall and spits right in my right eye. The great worm in my brain turns on his back and I lash out. I go slap, slap, slap, slap, kick, and my little Tonia takes to her heels. Lucy is thanking me for the good performance when this boy with a round head comes along. A real bully, this boy, and he is wearing the devil's smile.

"Come and fight me," the roundhead says. I don't say a thing because I don't like his fists. They are too big.

"Are you coming or shall I drag you by the hair, you girl-fighting lousy lily-livered mongrel?" I am thinking that this roundhead is the devil himself and I don't like devils. And he is smiling, this roundhead. Teeth like maize grains he has.

"Go to," I say to the roundhead instead of which he darts at me and smashes his dome against the wall because this stomach of mine he was aiming at had already moved. I moved to the left swift as a lover's wink and unwittingly occasioned the ramming act that the roundhead's dome was performing on the wall. A good smash it was, woe to the harmless wall. Damn stupid to start a war on the wall.

The roundhead doesn't feel so good. He shakes his head and focuses his hippo eyes and sees me.

"Rat!" the roundhead cries and springs at me like a cat. This time he gets me but he is too annoyed to use his fists. He squeezes me between his hands, intent on squeezing the life out of me. All the time his foul breath is offending my nostrils. I get one hand free and as I try to raise it to grab his hair, one of my fingers goes "poke" right into his right eye.

"Aao!" the roundhead yells and lets go. I go smack, smack, smack, push, and the roundhead starts kissing the ground. Lucy is congratulating me again when the teacher comes around — this Jock, I mean Jack. Our Jack. We all hurry into this big dusty hall which is both a church and a gymnasium and as we are walking, whimpering roundhead edges his way close to me and gives me a dig in the ribs with his elbow.

"Another round at lunchtime, what say you?" he asks.

"What?" I ask him.

"A boxing session and God have mercy on your teeth." He winks maliciously at me.

"Thank you very much and may your maize teeth fall out," I

retort as we get in this big dusty hall. I make sure that I don't sit anywhere near master roundhead. When he moves to the benches on the right, I move to the left just to keep away the germs. Real infectious our roundhead is. Poor roundhead. The following morning he was run over by a fire brigade's vehicle while on his way to school.

We all felt sorry for him. All except me. He'd given me a wallop on the way home and promised me another the following day. I was scared to the white patch of my pants and spent the whole night praying. I was praying that master roundhead be run over by something the following morning and by Jingo my prayers were answered. The fire brigade did it for me. I felt that the Almighty God loved me. At least He had listened to my prayers and I was glad. Later I was very sad. I knew that I was responsible for this catastrophe but I didn't tell anybody. Not even Tonia. Tonia was too self-important. Carried her neck high she did, and shouted "shut up!" whenever I opened my sweet mouth to speak to her. Fancy that. A girl my age shouting "shut up!" at me.

Me, I don't like Tonia. I don't like her one little bit. I don't like her hair, her ears, her eyes, her mouth, the mucus on her nose, her teeth, her neck, her tummy, her legs, her feet and I don't like her blinking ass. I don't like her dresses, her shoes, her pencils, her books and I don't even like her whoring mother. I don't like Tonia. Gosh! I hate her.

Our Jack is teaching us A B C D. He has invented a tune for singing the alphabet and that's all we have done for the past two days. We have just sung the alphabet. Of course, we can't write it but we can sing it. Today is the third day that we have been singing this song and Jack reckons that we know it well. To make sure that we know he now wants us to sing the alphabet backwards starting with Z. He asks us whether there is anybody who can do it satisfactorily and the tall boy who raises his hand starts: "Z Y X V S T," and Jack tells him to sit down. He adjusts the false carnation in his button hole and calls out: "Anybody else want to try?" Nobody volunteers so our Jack points at Lucy.

"Give it a try, will you?" Lucy merely giggles and hides her face between her hands. Very shy this little Lucy. She goes on giggling and Jack is still pointing at her. Reminds you of a tired ox, our Jack does. When Lucy continues to giggle he wags his tail — I mean he scratches his head — and points at me. He points at me because I am sitting next to Lucy and my hand is halfway up because I want to help her.

"Z Y X W V U S T R P Q," my mouth is saying and Jack

24

asks me to shut it up and I do. He is always asking you to shut up this Jack. He is like Tonia.

I am wondering where I went wrong when Lucy tickles me. I am very ticklish so I let out a loud "Wao!" and Jack looks at me in surprise and finally tells me that the alphabet does not start with a Y anytime even if you are saying it backwards. Lucy laughs aloud and Jack throws a piece of chalk at her. Then he goes to the board and writes the alphabet backwards. We all sing after him.

The house is locked when we get home. It is locked from the inside because there is no padlock on the outside. Tonia knocks but there is no answer.

"Mummy! Mummy!" she calls out. There is no answer. Miriam must be sleeping like the python that swallowed a goat. She is always sleeping during the day. She sleeps more during the night. "Don't disturb her," I say to Tonia but she does not listen to me. She knocks harder, all the time calling, "Mummy, Mummy, Mummy, open up." The door is opened a crack and Miriam is wearing her night things. She also wears a frown that would have scared the devil himself. We have seen the frown before.

"You are lice and I hate lice. Go away," she says and bangs the door shut again. She is a very loving mother, this Miriam. She loves us, she does. God loves her and that's why she is very kind. Very kind.

We saunter away speechless because we are not very stupid. This is not the first time that this has happened. One time it was raining but we had to stay out. We understand. Tonia is very bitter about this but I don't care a fig. I am not Miriam's daughter. My happiness is my tummy. Once my tummy is full, which is rare, my heart is full. I am a simple fellow, that's me. Too simple. Fill my tummy and I'll give you all the treasures in my kingdom. They are plenty, my treasures. They include my khaki pants with the white patch. I love them, my pants.

We are sitting under this jacaranda tree and it does not give enough shade. Its little leaves are gone. Gone with the wind. The sun has baked them and when they are this ripe yellow colour, the wind picks them. Most of them have of course dropped right under the tree and we are sitting on them. Tonia is very clever. She had pulled up her little pink dress and is sitting on her little green panties because she does not want to soil this little dress. Very ladylike our little Tonia. Very much like her mother.

We are staring at the row of shanty houses in front of us. I am wondering why we must always have dust and flies. Dust and flies, smoke and evil smells, that's what we've got. Nude hungry children and dirty whoring mothers — that is the order of the day. This is Eastleigh. Most famous place in Nairobi for advanced prostitution. Ninety per cent of the kids are fatherless. They are bastards. I hate the word. I hate the word bastard. Jack calls us poor little bastards and the damn fool is right. That's what we are. Bastards. God! I hate myself.

We have our eyes focused on the door of our shanty mudhouse when this burly-looking smiling gentleman comes out. He is combing his hair with his fingers and his eyes are blinking on account of the strong sunlight. He looks round like a thief and starts to walk away. He notices our keen eyes on him and walks in our direction. I have a good mind to run but before my mind is made up he is standing in front of us. He looks at us as if we were vermin but doesn't say a word. He just stands there scaring the pants off me. He puts his hand in his pocket and comes out with a shilling. He looks at it and then drops it without a word and walks away.

When he has gone a few steps we look at each other, at the man and then at the shilling. As if by a signal we both jump. We jump for the shilling. Tonia rolls me over and the shilling gets buried by these dry jacaranda leaves. We are both chasing frantically for the burly man's shilling but it's no longer there. Tonia is calling me bad names and blaming me for the precious loss but I am not listening. She is always calling me names but I never listen. I don't care a fig.

Then I see it. I catch a glimpse of it under the leaves near Tonia's right foot. She is almost stepping on it. By God she'll see it! I am hoping she won't. I am praying very hard. I go in front of her and pretend that I have seen it. She dashes at me and I roll back. I keep rolling till I have the shilling in my hand. She doesn't see me pick it. She is still looking for it. Poor Tonia.

I start walking towards the house and she suspects something.

"Have you got it?" she asks. I shake my head because I don't like telling lies but Tonia is not satisfied.

"You've got it," she says. Again I shake my head and Tonia does not know what to believe. She makes a final search and decides to give it up as a bad job. She comes to join me and we walk to the house together. I am smiling like the cat which swallowed the canary. I am absolutely satisfied with myself and am even starting to like myself. Tonia smells a rat but so what? Tonia is always smelling a rat. She's always calling me a rat. It's a hell of a good name when you have a shilling in your pocket.

Miriam has dressed in a hurry and she is now making the bed. There is no smell of food. No food has been cooked in this place. It's not the first time either. It has happened many times before. When Miriam has a male guest she doesn't bother to soil her nails with pots and pans. She takes us to the little tea kiosk near the charcoal seller's dump and buys some tea and dry bread for us. We like this because it is not always that we have bread but we never have enough of it. Two dry slices and a mug of tea each is all that Miriam can afford for our meal. Thereafter she goes away and comes home at midnight drunk and buzzing like a bee, tagging a man at her heels. Very thrifty, this Miriam. Knows how to save her money, she does.

We are walking towards this kiosk and I am licking my lips. We are going to have tea and bread. This tea kiosk would be a nice place if there weren't so many flies hovering all over the place and sometimes dropping into your tea. They are always dropping into your tea, these flies, and you've got to fish them out with your finger. Real dogs in the manger these flies.

Miriam is looking beautiful in spite of herself. She has these long earrings that are dangling to her shoulders and is wearing some lipstick which is too red for her black skin. She is wearing a light blue blouse that shows her breasts to advantage and a tight brown skirt that has a big chocolate heart in front. Seeing her from far off one would think that she had cut a heart shaped hole in her skirt. Her skin is shining and fresh on account of the soap lather that she smeared on herself just before we left. She is also wearing this cheap Sudanese perfume that speaks out to men. If she wasn't fat, she would be a beauty. A real beauty.

She orders tea and bread for us and tells us to go home when we have finished. There are some men who are winking at her but she pretends not to notice. She looks straight ahead and pays the bill. Very modest, this Miriam is. Real modest. Modesty is her name.

She collects the change and scrams. She doesn't even bother to look back at the winking gentlemen. She walks haughtily like a new-born queen in the direction of the bus stop. I look at Tonia but she is too busy gulping her tea. I take mine slowly and feel the shilling in my pocket. I am grinning to myself.

We finish the tea and the dry bread and Tonia rises to go. I can see that she hasn't had enough but I let her walk out. When she is out I ask this thin-faced kiosk keeper to give me four buttered slices and two mugs of tea. I give him the shilling and I almost kiss it as it leaves my fingers. He supplies the order quickly and I pocket the change. Twenty cents, my change was. Enough to buy twelve sweets. Twelve round ginger sweets.

Tonia comes back to find out what I am doing and I smile at her.

"Fall to," I say. "This time the wheat stuff has some butter on it."

"Who bought it?" she asks.

"Father Christmas, my dear girl. Long beard and all. Came down my chimney he did. You'd better start or the flies will eat all of it."

"Did Father Christmas drop a shilling?" she asks.

"Go and ask him. When you find him say I said thank you. Eat, Tonia. Aren't you afraid of earthquakes?"

"No, but I'll eat. I saw Father Christmas coming out of our house. Dropped a shilling he did. Oh! you hypocrite, we should have shared that shilling."

"That is what we are doing," I tell her. "You are eating your share."

"Not all of it. You are real mean. Most boys are."

"I've got to be like other boys, haven't I?"

"They don't all talk with lots of bread in their mouths, or do they?"

"Next time they buy you tea and bread, have a close look at their mouths. If they are unlike me, they'll let you have all of it. I am happy today."

"Get wings and fly. How I would thank God."

"Is that a prayer for me?" I ask. Didn't know what she meant. No kidding. Talks in parables sometimes, Tonia does.

"Yes it's a prayer for you. For you to fly away. Away never to return and good riddance it would be surely."

"You are stupidity itself," I tell her. "What would you do without me to buy you buttered bread and sweets later?"

"I'd be glad to be rid of you, sweets or no sweets. I give you sweets more often than you give me. You are gloating because of a mere shilling while you are feeding on us. Mother could afford more things for me with you out of the way."

I am starting to get annoyed, which is rare. Tonia keeps reminding me that I don't belong there and that I am feeding out of her mother's hand. She's a real pain in the neck. One of these days I'll go from here and find refuge on Mt. Kenya where the old gods are supposed to live. I can't stand Tonia's tongue. I have tried but by jingo I have failed. I have failed miserably but I can't help but be in her company. Her company is the worst torture. Continual torture to my young immature brain. God! She hates me, little Tonia does. She thinks that I am standing between her and nice things. She thinks that Miriam would be able to afford four slices for her at the kiosk if I didn't exist. She hates me.

We finish our meal but instead of going home to quarrel we walk towards the shops because I have promised Tonia some sweets. She really wants her share of the shilling. We get there in less than no time on account of our full stomachs and I ask this fat Indian shopkeeper to give me sweets for twenty cents. I point at the glass jar containing round ginger sweets and he gives me twelve. On second thoughts he gives me an extra sweet and says "Merry Christmas!" I accept the sweet with a smile although of course it is nowhere near Christmas. It's April now.

"Thank you very much," I say to him and we walk away. Tonia extends her little hand and I count six sweets into it.

"What about the thirteenth sweet?" she asks still extending her hand. I have a good mind to kick her hand and send her six sweets to the four winds but I control my temper. I am always controlling my temper.

"It's my Christmas gift from a kind friend," I tell her.

"No," says Tonia. "It was given to both of us. Split it into two."

"How?"

"Use your teeth," she says.

"All right," I tell her. "Have all of it. The Christmas gift was meant for you." She has no shame, this Tonia. She actually grabs it from my hand. I look at her and make a mental note that her name should have been "Gluttony." I put a sweet in my mouth and try to whistle. I can't on account of the sweet so I challenge Tonia to race me to the house. She scowls at me and tells me that she is not the dead roundhead to go competing with me. I decide that she is horrid company and I race myself all the way to the house. When I get there I look and notice that Tonia is also racing herself and I burst into laughter.

We go inside and Tonia goes to her bed. She lies on her back and says "Come."

"What for?" I ask her.

"Come. Let us play."

"Let's go outside then," I tell her. She shakes her head and looks at me playfully.

"Right here on the bed. Let's play our old game. My mother does it with the men."

"Oh! no. Not for the love of God. No. It's stupid and I'll not play it. It's shameful. No. I wouldn't. Let's go out and hop. God, Tonia, you must be out of your mind."

"It's too hot for that. Come over." I protest like mad but I don't know how it happens. In spite of myself we are playing this old game when the door bursts open. Miriam rushes in and stands looking at us

with her mouth open and her eyes flying out of their sockets. She
doesn't say a thing. She is too shocked for words. She just stands
there and stares like a cow. Looks like a cow she does. All she needs
is a tail and she'd start eating grass.

We scramble off the bed and dash into the other room because
Miriam is blocking the door. We know we are due for a king size
wallop. I open the window and I am squeezing myself through when
Miriam dashes into the room to squeeze the caloric out of us. I just
manage to slip through as she tries to grab my feet and I fall to the
ground. A mad dive it was. Hit the ground head first and lay down
there stunned. Then I feel my limbs go limp and there is this funny
darkness and bees are buzzing all over the place, then out. I pass out
there below the window and I don't even know it. I am dead to the
world.

When I come to, Miriam has this wet cloth on my face and it's
already night. The lamp is burning feebly where it hangs on the wall
casting dubious shadows that look like walking ghosts. There is no
sign of Tonia.

I shake myself and try to focus my eyes instead of which bees start
buzzing again. I relax and stare at the hurricane lamp and the blinking
lamp stares back at me. No kidding. Miriam lets go my head and I
reckon I go to sleep again because when I wake up, there is no one in
the room. I yawn and try to sit up. As I do so I let out a loud fart and I
feel better. I sit up in bed. I can't hear a single sound. The lamp still
burns dimly and depresses my spirits. I get out of bed and start prowling
but I am afraid to make a noise. I am wondering what happened to
everybody else when the door to Miriam's bedroom opens and she
stands arms akimbo looking at me.

"Are you all right now?" she asks.

"Yes," I stammer.

"Go to bed then. There is no dinner for you." I ease back to my
little bed and cover myself from head to toe. I can't stand the sight of
Miriam standing there arms akimbo staring at me. I hear feet
approaching and the lamp is taken off the hook. My heart is in my
mouth and I am just about to piss on myself because Miriam hasn't
moved away. The blankets are pulled off my head and I find myself
staring at the lamp again.

"What were you doing when I came in?" she asks. My throat is
dry and my saliva glands have gone dead. I can't speak unless I croak.

"What were you doing?" Miriam demands fiercely.

"Playing," I tell her.

"Playing what?"

"A game. A new game we learnt in school. It's called "Press ups.""

"And how is this presses or whatever you call it played?" she demands.

"One pushes up the other pushes down."

"In that posture?"

"Posture?" I am feeling very stupid.

"Yes, posture. Is the game played like that in school?"

"Almost similar with minor modifications. We don't like it," I say.

"You are lying. That is not what Tonia told me. Games like that are not played anywhere. There are no such games. That is vice. You have brought vice to my house and infected innocent Tonia with your filth. You are like your mother. Always filth and more filth. It's in your blood. You will leave this house tomorrow. Tomorrow morning you must go. You can go and live with your grandmother back in Nyeri if she is not dead. Go you must." She walks away and bangs the door of her bedroom shut. I am left to the night and my poor little head to bother me. Poor me.

It all happened a long time ago but my memory is as fresh as a fresh shave. Those were the days indeed. When I reflect, as I have been doing, I laugh and cry. Sometimes I do both simultaneously. So what? You can laugh and cry if you damn well please. Nobody is stopping you. Go ahead and yell your head off.

This old watchman I am sleeping next to keeps poking his fire and telling me a lot of filthy nonsense about his youth. He waits till I am just starting to snore and then starts talking. He keeps on repeating the same words if I don't say "uh" and his voice is starting to give me the creeps. I wish I had somewhere else to sleep but I haven't. Since I had that wonderful time with Annie this afternoon, I have had no rest. I have been chasing for food and a place to sleep and I haven't succeeded either way. I turn to the watchman.

"Hey friend. Do you know of a place where one can safely grab some grub? I am famished."

"It is never safe to pinch," the blighter tells me. "If you are a thief walk from here this minute before I clout you on the head with my club."

"Easy mate," I tell him. "I was merely joking." The blinking watchman is not satisfied. He has decided that he doesn't like my company any more. He stands up, adjusts his heavy overcoat and holds his club firmly.

"Walk from here this minute," he says fiercely. I can see that he is not kidding. He means to clout me. I get to my feet slowly and look pleadingly at the fellow.

"You are making a mistake, friend. I merely ———."

"I don't make no 'mistakes and I ain't your friend." He cuts me short. "Walk from here this minute." Blimey! Just fancy that. A watchman sending me away from his fire to brace the solitary cold of the night in the streets of Nairobi. Gosh! Is my company so low that even an old watchman won't accept it? Damn it. There is something wrong somewhere. I simply can't live like this.

I am walking away in all directions because I have no fixed direction. I am wondering why I left Judy's den. I could have pleaded with Annie and she might have agreed to take me to her place because her friends were leaving at eight. I could have spent the night there. Damn fool. That's what I am. I am getting foolish in my old age.

I limp away and I am cursing mankind. I am also cursing my big toe because it's throbbing again. A damn nuisance, this big toe of mine.

The cold is penetrating right to my belly. It's very empty, this belly of mine, and a damn nuisance too. I can't get a thing to put into it. Haven't done so for days. I am thinking about Annie licking my lips and pitying you. I am pitying you with all my heart. Poor you. How very sad.

I can't walk any more. My limbs are failing. I must rest awhile. I am out of breath. God! I am hungry. I lean against a dustbin and close my eyes. God's sleep says hello and I smile.

3

There is this South African Boer who is yelling at us as we queue in front of the railway ticket office. "Git outa de way!" he is shouting. "Make way for memsaab. You Kaffir, move back." Where he comes from it would be a crime to be found in the same queue with natives. Very tolerant fellows, these Boers. Never knew what the word queue meant.

This Boer has a typical oversized Italian belly, Spanish black hair which is thinning on the sweating crown of his dome, a German round

32

head, Norwegian blue eyes, French nose, porpoise mouth, Krushchev
ears and a bushman's accent. You can almost hear the click. Attached
to his right hand is a wan underfed reedy female who staggers after
him like a native dog. She is as flat as a wall where her breasts are
supposed to be and has these knock-kneed legs which are as straight as
stove pikes. If it wasn't for her ass, one would mistake her for a sexless
creature from Mars.

The Boer confronts this fellow who is selling tickets and gets two
first class tickets to Nanyuki. He leads his staggering female by the
hand and they disappear under the subway. Gosh! What a contrast.
You look at the woman and immediately you think that there is famine
in Kenya but when you look at the fat Boer you know that he is the
cause of the famine. He has eaten all the food and then proceeded to
squeeze all the calorific juice out of her. Very heavy feeders, these
Boers. Bloodsuckers.

The damn queue is not moving. We've been standing on the same
spot for four centuries. Kamau is holding my hand. He is tall, black and
strong and wears a serious frown when he is not smiling. A very
funny man this Kamau. He has the look of a brute and the smile of a
passionate lover at the same time.

He comes from Nyeri, this Kamau. He is going home to see his
folks and Miriam managed to persuade him to take me along and
deposit me with my aged granny. She gave him a free tumble and he
felt obliged. He is now taking me home, not because he likes me but
because Miriam promised him something. Gosh! This queue is
static. I ain't an impatient cuss but I wish the damn queue would move
anyway. That's the trouble with queues in this goddam country. They
just don't move. Some Boer or some other privileged punk walks to the
front and gets served while you stand and get so impatient that you
could piss or puke. Damn the railway, the trains, the railwaymen and
what have you. Damn them all.

The following day after the fatal game Tonia went to school as
usual. Miriam asked me to remain behind while she went to make
arrangements to ship me home. She was gone the whole day and I had
to skip my lunch. All the time I was cursing Tonia for having put me
into a mess and later blaming the whole works on me. She told Miriam
that I knocked her down on the bed and that she was all the time
fighting me off. I don't like Tonia. She's too damn good at telling fibs
even at her age. She is the cause of my banishment, the cause of the
pain in my neck and the cold in my ass. It's damn cold and there's a
hole in my pants.

When she came from school she did not say a word to me. Not a single word. She kept aloof and went behind the house to play with grasshoppers. She was hungry too. I sympathized with her later when I sneaked behind the house and found her crying. She was looking at a bee in its normal course of collecting nectar and I reckon that she was jealous of the bee. She looked at me with those pitiful big eyes of hers and I felt like crying too. I mean it. I nearly cried.

In the evening it begins to rain. Huge heavy drops that hit you on the forehead with a bang. A real wet bang. Me, I am indifferent to rain. Tonia goes to rest on her bed while I stand at the door watching the gracious drops. Within half of no time there are pools of God's drink and streams of muddy water winding strenuously towards the sewage dump. I stand and watch the raindrops fall on the pools outside. Very fascinating these raindrops. They drop and drop and every time a drop hits the surface of the pool, it forms a crater with outward spreading waves. The whole pool is a conglomeration of craters and waves. Very fascinating. Reminds you of a photograph of the moon, a nutmeg grater or a picture of measles.

Miriam showed up just before it got dark and to my surprise she wasn't drunk. Very unusual. Kamau graced her heels and I had to get out of the way when he was ushered in. Miriam lit the lamp and spread out her arms.

"This is my joint," she said. "You are welcome."

"Uh," Kamau nodded.

"Not much of a place. Please sit down. This is the boy," she said pointing at me.

"Uh," Kamau nodded.

"Looks like his mother, doesn't he?" she asked.

"Uh," Kamau nodded again. Miriam proceeds to tell my story which I am sure she has told before. Kamau is not interested. He keeps saying "Uh" and looking at her tits most of the time while she explains that it was necessary to get rid of me in order to protect the morals of her innocent Tonia. She made me sick, she did. She is always making me sick, this Miriam. A most remarkable woman. Maybe you know by now.

They withdraw to her bedroom for some thirty minutes and we simply sit there, Tonia and I. We pretend to be deaf to the creaking of the bed and the grunting noises that drift to our ears. Very nauseating this creaking bed. Needs real greasing, it does. Their pig noises don't help either. You can hear the creaking above the loudest grunt. Gosh!

After thirty minutes the two emerge from the bedroom. Miriam walks out and starts to leak. She is pissing on a pool of water and it sounds as if the rain hasn't stopped. Sounds like a real water tap. I plug my ears. That was long ago but I can still hear the water tap.

Early next day Kamau comes for me. Miriam had packed my things and tied them in a bundle. All my earthly possessions were tied in that little bundle and I was leaving all my mother's things behind. They all belonged to Miriam now. What was mine by right now belonged to Miriam. I bequeathed the whole damn lot to her — may the devil blast her soul.

We walk out of the house and as we do so I feel hot tears on my cheeks. Fancy that. I was really crying. Whimpering like a lass. Miriam is soothing me but that makes it worse. I don't like her dirty claws on my shoulder. Reminds you of a monster you read of in a book.

"Don't cry, Kiunyu," she is pleading with me. "Things will work out right for you. You'll miss nothing by going to the country. It is better there. You'll have plenty of air to breathe away from the muck of the city. The city is no place for boys with healthy minds. It breeds filth and more filth. We shall miss you greatly but God is alive. He will help you. He will show you a different way of life. A better way. We are beyond help and that is why we must remain. Don't cry therefore my little one. Your grandmother is very kind-hearted."

This speech reminds me of Jack our teacher. He was always saying things like that. It nearly makes me vomit. Can you fancy Miriam making a speech like that? Full of goodness and all caressing my shoulder with her polished claws. Jeez! Wonders are many. Miriam is one of them. A damn wonder.

Tonia did not say goodbye to me but she waved as we disappeared towards the bus stop. I waved back and again felt tears welling in my eyes. I don't like her one little bit but I know I'll miss her. So what? I am always missing somebody.

It's two hours since we got off the bus and joined this damn queue. We are catching a train to Karatina from where we shall walk ten miles to Kaheti. I have never been to this place before but it's where this granny of mine is supposed to live. Kamau will take me there. It's a hundred miles from Nairobi and a hundred miles from anything I know. Yes, by Jingo. I am the young tree which is uprooted to be transplanted a hundred miles away. No kidding. If this damn queue does not move, I'll start growing roots. No sir, I won't. It's moving now.

It's cold and damp as we go under the subway to platform number two. The whole goddam place is littered with human beings, males and females of course — some fat, some thin, some dirty, some clean, some smoking, some taking a whiff of snuff, yelling babies, suckling babies, people with lots of luggage and people with nothing

on them apart from tattered items of apparel clinging to them. There is
a kid with a hole in his pants and he looks at the hole in my pants as
we walk past and he smiles. I smile back at him. We both understand.

We are sitting on the hard benches of this third class compartment
and Kamau has lit himself a Crown Bird. He is smoking contentedly
looking out of the window scanning the landscape. It's very green,
this landscape and I have never seen anything like it all my life. I have
never been out of Nairobi and not very much out of Eastleigh at that.
For me it has always been shops and slums, streets and mud roads,
evil smell, prostitutes and flies. Now before my eyes lies this expansive
stretch of God's country inhabited by trees and green grass, beautiful
insects, rats and fresh air. I open my mouth and inhale a lungful. It feels
good. It's good in the country.

I look around and decide that God is very rich. He has everything.
He owns this beautiful country and I am also thinking how many other
beautiful countries belong to Him. He must be very happy to sit on
that golden throne and look down with a grin on this green grass
around. From wherever He is, He can see this goddam slow train that
is belching black smoke like a puking drunkard. Gosh! I feel hungry.

I am thinking that although I am not a Moslem I am always
fasting. I fast quite a lot especially between meals. One of these fine
days I may decide to become a Moslem and maybe when I get old and
rich I'll go on a pilgrimage to this place they call Mecca. Fancy that.
Me going on a pilgrimage. My first pilgrimage will be to hell. I'd like
to meet old man Satan and his woman. Gosh! I have a headache.
Sitting in this train one would think that there is an earthquake. Shakes
you like an earthquake, this train does.

"How do you like the country?" Kamau asks me.

"I like it. I like it very much. I'd like to be out there playing on the
green grass. I'd like to chase those butterflies feeding on morning
dew. I'd like to do all sorts of things out there," I reply.

"You will have plenty of it soon. It will bore you after a time."

"Nothing bores me. I am like that," I tell him.

"That's what you think but you are too young to know. One
month of maize and beans and another month of maize and beans and
more months of maize and beans. That is what they eat out here. After
a time you will wish you were a cow so that you could eat grass for a
change. I ain't no expert on diets but I know that maize and beans is
one hell of a meal." Kamau laughs and looks at me. "Toughens your
jaws though," he adds.

This does not sound very exciting to me so I fix my eyes on this black smoke that the locomotive is vomiting into the atmosphere. As I look I start thinking about volcanoes but then decide that I don't know a thing about them. Not a thing. All I know is that they are horrid creatures that spit fire. I reckon that trains and volcanoes are just about the same and wonder what would happen if a train met a volcano. It would be one hell of a meeting with lots of fire thrown about.

We are several miles from Nairobi and we are moving fast. This train does not tire. We have only had one stop at a remote station where the train took a drink. We are now pulling into a big station and I ask Kamau what place it is.

"You can read the big signboard. This is Thika," he tells me.

"Thank you," I say, "but I do not know how to read." He scowls at me and then looks at his boots.

"I thought you'd been going to school. Didn't you learn how to read and write?"

"I can read the alphabet forwards and backwards but really I can't read words. Our teacher Jack has great faith in the alphabet. We had to sing it all to a tune which Jack borrowed from 'God save our gracious Queen'. It sounded horrid when sung backwards but Jack liked it."

"It sounds as if he was a very good teacher," Kamau says.

"I don't know. He called me a lovechild one day and declared that he had little sympathy with bastard brats. I didn't understand his fine words but I understood his sneer. He is both good and bad. Hey! What are those animals out there?"

Out of the window I can see this herd of small beasts staring at the train when they are not nibbling at some leaves. They are a light brown colour with a dull white tummy and a black stripe and a short white frightened tail which looks very funny when it wags.

"They are gazelles. Thomson's gazelles. I don't know why they are called Thomson's. Might be some fellow who used to rear them on his farm. Again it might be the same fellow that discovered Thomson's Falls. I wonder why they are not called Kamau's gazelles. Sometimes I am as wild as the wretched beasts."

"Is that why you are not married?" I ask him.

"Whatever gave you that idea? I am married and have kids much older than you. I am going home to see them."

"Do you have little boys I can play with? I don't like girls."
"Why?"
"I don't know. Little girls are moody don't you think?"
"I don't think so. At your age girls are more intelligent than boys."
"No, that is not true. I have not met one intelligent girl of my age.

When they are not moody they are giggling, silly and shy. They think they are grown up at the age of ten."

On the other side of the carriage, sitting on a hard seat like ourselves, is this medium stature handsome gentleman who can't keep his eyes off the beautiful female on his left. When she is not looking he steals a glance at her and devours her with his roving pleading brown eyes. A very loving gentleman. I have my eyes on him and he doesn't like it. He wriggles and fidgets as if in a dream and casts his eyes down like a chastised dog. Every time he looks at the girl I look at him and when he notices me he casts his eyes down. I reckon that this is one hell of a game and I am sitting on top. He tries to stare me out but nothing doing. I stare back at him as if he was the eighth wonder and he dips his eyes. He does it like a perfect dog and I start wondering whether he has a tail. I come to the conclusion that his tail is wagging inside his pants on account of the girl. Life is funny.

We have gone past Fort Hall and are approaching Sagana. I have been firing questions at Kamau and I guess by the look on his face that he doesn't like my questions. He pretends to be dozing but he has his eyes on the girl too. I reckon that Kamau is funny too.

I close my eyes and try to sleep but in case you are not aware, a train rocks you to sleep and rocks you awake. You are half awake and half asleep, if you see what I mean. Right now I am three quarters awake and I have my eyes on the girl. I guess I am funny too.

Kamau prods me with his elbow and I wake with a start. I must have slept at last. I rub my eyes and gape out of the window. It's about four thirty in the afternoon and I am hungry. I decide that there is nothing I can do about my stomach so I shrug my shoulders. Kamau stands and starts to gather his things.

"We have arrived, Kiunyu. This is Karatina. Don't forget your little bundle."

We get off the train and walk towards the market place where we are supposed to get some means of transport home. It's all very exciting. I am going to see granny.

Walking in front of us is a tall dark-coloured benevolent-looking middle-aged man. He walks with long slow deliberate strides and is carrying two suitcases. He smiles at me sweetly and I notice that he looks like me. He must have noticed the same thing because he looks at me again, curiously this time, and seems to make a mental calculation. This gives me the creeps. Frightened me he did. I don't like people who resemble me. Any one of them could be my father which is a constant reminder that I am a bastard.

There is a throng of people at the market and the place stinks.

The stench is the opposite of that normally exuded by prostitutes. It is the smell of sweat and filthy armpits added to rotten bananas, snuff, onions, smoked fish, live chicken, cucumbers, oiled skins, sisal bags, oranges, tyre sandals, cheap alcohol, oiled hair, diesel exhaust, cabbages and mud. It's one hell of a combination of different smells and scents whose total effect would be to make you puke outright. Foul and filthy air is what these folks are breathing and what I am breathing now and I don't envy myself. Kamau lets out a loud fart and it doesn't smell good either. He must have eaten something rotten.

On the other side of the market is a big truck with the inscription: 'Kaheti Traders'. We edge our way towards it and Kamau tells me that we are lucky.

"This lorry will take us right to Kaheti. Muiga, its owner, is a friend of mine. He'll take us for free."

There is this wiry, shaggy haired, very broad-nosed fellow with big gaps between his teeth whistling his head off and shouting, "Kaheti! Kaheti! Kaheti! Anybody going to Kaheti here? Passengers for Kaheti — bus for Kaheti is here".

Gosh! What a blasted villainous liar. He calls this ramshackle of a truck a bus without blushing and he is not even counting how many people are getting in. You don't even have to speak with him. All you have to do is mention Kaheti and he will literally push you into the truck. There are about thirty people already standing or sitting in the lorry together with their luggage and there is hardly any space left. The fellow is not perturbed. He continues to whistle and yell his head off, at the same time loading more people into the truck. There are other trucks and there are similar fellows yelling their heads off calling different place names depending on their destination. It's all one hell of a big noise which reminds you of frogs in season.

Kamau points at the yelling gentleman and says, "That is my friend Muiga. Wait here while I talk to him." He moves and taps Muiga on the shoulder and they shake hands. They talk for a while and Muiga starts shouting again. Kamau comes over to where I am standing and asks me to hop into the truck. He lifts me because I can't get in under my own steam and goes back to talk to Muiga.

It's five thirty when Muiga thinks that the truck is full although it was actually full by four. Kamau has been invited by Muiga to sit in front and the rest of us, about sixty head, are at the back of the truck. The truck moves forward with a lurch and Muiga is dodging his way between other trucks completely oblivious of the human cargo whose souls are in his hands.

At Tumutumu the truck stops. Kamau and Muiga get out and without explanation they move away to a little shop on the left and go in. They are housed in there for some thirty minutes and when they come out they are staggering and laughing like the wicked of Sodom and Gomorrah. Muiga is speaking like one possessed and you can see with your eyes closed that he is suffering from chronic verbal diarrhoea. I'd rather be locked amidst a cohort of madmen than listen to Muiga's shit. It's real shit, I am telling you.

It's dusk when we get to Kaheti. There is enough light to see by and there is not enough light to see by. From what I can see, this is not much of a place. Three quarters of it is a Consolata Catholic Mission School and the rest is a row of dust-covered shops. Half the shops are closed while in the other half shopkeepers are trying to make last minute sales before it gets too dark. There is no electricity here. Any light you see is from a hurricane lamp dangling at the end of a rope. Gosh! This place gives me the creeps. It's real ghostly this place.

Muiga collects five shillings from each passenger and grabs Kamau by the hand. Kamau in turn grabs me. We move to the last building on the row which is a bar. We get in. There is this reedy rat of a barman with a funny moustache who is as drunk as Miriam on weekends. He smiles affably at Muiga and leans across the counter to speak to him.

"What is our local millionaire drinking tonight? Good native brew or lousy beer?"

"You drunken eel. How can you take care of your business when you are as drunk as our local padre?"

"Go ask the padre. He will give you a sermon on the defects of sobriety. Give it mouth, friend. Local stuff or clean beer?"

"Good local stuff for me and lousy beer for my friend. He is from the city where they can't stomach filth. Give me the filth." The barman proceeds to open a bottle of Tusker which he hands over to Kamau. He then fills a one pint bowl with some stuff that looks like porridge contained in an oil drum behind the counter and hands it over to Muiga. Muiga takes a sip, unbuttons his shirt and spits on his chest.

"This is a good brew, Titus. Real good brew, my dear Titus. Finger millet is a hell of a good grain. Very nutritious. Very good for your health. All you have to do is take this stuff and you'll grow a tummy. Don't need food either. This is food itself. Real good food. Don't need to bother your wife about supper. She can eat it and get fat. You know women eat a lot. They are always eating. When you are working they are eating. They are always nibbling at something. That reminds me of rabbits. Women are like rabbits and rabbits are like

40

women except between the sheets. Ha ha. This stuff is real mellow. Whoever invented alcohol was a crank anyway. Hey Kamau! What is the little brat drinking?" Muiga takes the last swig and gives the bowl back to Titus. "Get me another drop, Titus. Fill it up to the brim and then give this little man a pint of milk or any soft drink he prefers. What would you like eh? Hey, what is your name?"

"Kiunyu," I tell him.

"That sounds like salt. What would you like for a drink?"

"Milk please."

"Sorry there is no milk, Muiga. This is a bar and not a dairy. We stock drinks but no baby stuff. The boy can have Fanta," says Titus.

"Is that all right for you, Kiunyu?" Kamau asks.

"Yes. It will be fine," I tell him. Titus gives me a bottle of Fanta and I drink it out of the bottle since he does not give me a glass or a straw. I am getting fed up with this joint. Muiga is still suffering from verbal diarrhoea and Kamau is content to sit there and empty bottle after bottle of this Tusker stuff oblivious of my presence. I should be talking to granny, whoever she is, and not sitting here with an empty stomach and drunks for company. This is not the place for the likes of me. It is for drunks and I am not one of them. I am a nice little orphan boy with lots of brains, torn pants and a belly that is making noises.

At nine o'clock I start dozing and Kamau shakes me up. He is so drunk that all you need is to hit him on the head and he'll start laughing. He is taking the last half pint in gulps while explaining to Titus and Muiga that he has to take the brat to his granny. If I hate anything, it's somebody calling me a brat. If I had the strength I would strangle Kamau and thereafter piss on him. I know I would.

Kamau says goodbye to his friends and motions me to rise. Titus looks at his watch and frowns.

"You know, Kamau, it's not all that late. How about one on the house before you go? It will improve your snoring."

"Tomorrow, Titus. I am juiced out of my mind and I have the brat to take to his granny and a wife and kids to meet later. I really must go."

"So long but come again. In future you can call me Oates. Titus Oates. It's what the padre calls me on account of my lies though I don't have the vaguest idea who Titus Oates was. This padre here is a crank."

"They all are. Bye for now, bye Muiga. I'll see you in the morning. We should really slaughter a goat and give ourselves a treat but I'll confirm in the morning. Come on, Kiunyu. We are homeward bound."

"Say I said hello to your ladyship. I haven't set eyes on her for many days but don't wake the kids. They wouldn't know why you are so drunk," Muiga says and proceeds to order himself another bowl of drink.

We ooze out of the place and are immediately enveloped in darkness. Kamau grabs me by the hand and drags me along as he staggers on the narrow path. I am very annoyed because I have to stagger like him since he is holding my hand. He starts belching and then hiccuping and before I know it he is puking. He is still holding my hand as he pukes. Gosh! I feel like puking too.

After an arduous mile in the dark we come to a cluster of mud huts and Kamau points at the one on the far right.

"That is Wangui's hut. She is your granny." My heart is jumping because I am all excited. I am as excited as a rat. Granny has not been told that I am coming and I am wondering how I'll be received. She'll get a big surprise. We get to the hut and Kamau taps on the door. No answer. He taps again but then we notice that it's locked from outside.

"Where could she be?" he asks himself. He drags me again and we move to the nearest hut. He taps on the door and we can hear some noise from the inside. An old woman opens the door and looks at us with curiosity.

"What is it?" she asks.

"We have been knocking at Wangui's hut but it is locked. This boy is her grandson. Would you happen to know where she is?"asks Kamau.

"Yes, but she's where you can't find her. Through the will of the gods she joined her ancestors a fortnight ago. She died of old age."

4

Thank the padre and thank him again. Sometimes I thank him and sometimes I damn him but I thank him more often. A very nice fellow, this padre. His name was . . . . What the hell was his name? I remember. Father Burton. He caned me several times for calling him

Further Button and threatened to slit my tongue in pursuit of "better
pronunciation" which according to Father Burton is a great virtue.
A very conscientious fellow, Father Burton. An easy-going priest born
in Ontario, raised in Colorado, graduated in Australia and consecrated
in Rome. He had been to nearly all the countries of the world except
Hawaii where a priest friend of his had once been raped. He thought
that women on that island were a damn sight too sexy for his health.
What he didn't know is that his friend had not actually been raped but
had been overcome by the symmetry of the swinging hips and straw
skirts and later blamed it on the woman. So what? I don't blame the
priest.

When it became apparent to Kamau that this granny of mine had
popped off a wee bit too early, he didn't know what to do with the
likes of me. Almost got sober, he did. He dragged me by the arm again
and said in disgust, "What the hell does a woman want to die for after
I've taken all the trouble to bring her grandson home? A hell of a time
for her to choose and what in the name of the gods do I do with you?"
I had no answer so I kept quiet. I had no idea where we were going and
I didn't care. Thank him anyway. He took me to his house and left me
to the humble care of his wife while he staggered to bed to snore away
the beer. She gave me what cold grub was left over from their dinner
and later spread a rug on the floor for me to rest my small bones.
I rested my bones — very soundly in fact.

"We are going to church," Kamau said to me in the morning.
Obediently I followed but instead of going to church we went to this
same Titus place where Kamau got drunk last night. Titus was
sweeping the place up. Looking at him one would think that he was
doing so in his sleep. Looked like a real tired skinny wizard — untidy
clothes, shabby hair, dirty claws, unpolished boots, half open eyes, a
sagging mouth and a running nose. His name should have been Titus
Flattoes on account of his flat feet. He had not slept at all. Spent the
whole night getting juiced on his own drink, the poor devil. Very
funny, fellows like Titus. He was ready to start again on the native
brew.

They held a brief conference and Titus burst out laughing. It was
apparent that he was giving Kamau some advice. After the conference,
Kamau joined me and said, "Now we are ready for church." We
walked towards the mission and on getting there we turned left to the
padre's office. Kamau knocked and a female voice answered.

"Come in."
We went in and Kamau said, "Sorry to disturb you, Sister, but
I thought I would find Father Burton here."

"He will be here in a moment. What is the nature of your business?" the Sister asked. Kamau explained briskly.

"It's this child. His name is Kiunyu. He has no parents, relatives or friends. He has nowhere to stay and nothing to eat. I thought kind Father Burton might help."

"Where did you get him?"

"In the streets of Nairobi. A friend told me that his grandmother was some old woman I happened to know from Kaheti and I volunteered to bring him to her. On getting here last night, we found to our horror that the old lady had passed away. I can't simply take him back to the streets of Nairobi. It would be a great shame because he is a good lad. I don't know what to do with him."

"Take him to your wife and family," the sister said. "It's part of every Christian's duty to help the afflicted."

"But I am not married, Sister. I have no family," Kamau lied. "If you will excuse me, I'll consult a friend who is waiting for me at the chapel and see whether he'd be kind enough to take Kiunyu into his family. I'll be back presently."

I knew it was a lie but I didn't say so. Kamau walked out and left me standing in front of the smiling Sister. I have never seen him since. He disappeared from the map. Now he is just a name. A forgotten name. Maybe just a dream.

Somebody gives me a dig in the ribs and I grunt. I open my blinking sleep-laden eyes and there is this cop staring down at me. I am still leaning against the dustbin where I took repose on account of my company being disagreeable to last night's watchman. Chased me away from his fire he did, thinking that I was the thieving kind. Poor blighter.

It's a hell of a time for a cop to be on the beat because judging by the cold and the amount of light in the skies it must be around six in the morning. The pain in my toe has stopped but my tummy is still a vacuum. I am inwardly cursing this cop for disturbing my beauty sleep and I don't like the way he is looking down at me. He reckons I am a beggar and I reckon that he is going to treat me like one. I hate cops.

"What did you do that for?" I ask him.

"What?" he asks contemptuously.

"Disturb my sleep," I answer him.

"This is nobody's sleeping place, you bum."

"And that is precisely why I am sleeping here. It's no man's land."

"Sorry friend. You are allowed to beg during the day but you are not allowed to feed off dustbins and make a public pavement your sleeping place. You haven't paid rent for it, buddy. We do not condone vagrancy. Get going before somebody thinks that you are loitering with intent."

"And where am I supposed to go?" I ask him.

"Begging if you like. I don't really care where you go but get the hell out of here before they come to remove the rubbish. Somebody might mistake you for a piece of garbage not forgetting that we have a place for the likes of you. Our strong rooms are not full."

"I am allergic to those lousy cells of yours so I reckon I'd better beat it. Tell me — what are you supposed to do when you are on the beat apart from disturbing honest sleepers?" I ask him as I scramble lazily to my feet. He looks at me impatiently and then smiles. He looks very good natured when he smiles like that.

"One word before you go. If you are going to sleep on the streets make sure that you don't do it in my beat. You look like a fellow who'd get a job if you tried hard. A fellow like you should not be walking the streets or maybe you are cracked."

"Maybe I am. Thank you very much for your kindness. I'll be on my way," I tell him.

"On your way then but if I catch you again, you will walk a different way."

I start walking away but then I remember something. I walk back to the cop and say, "Hey, friend. Maybe you can spare a shilling for a dying fellow. I am destroyed with hunger. Three long days and no humble bite. Please."

He looks at me as if I was something the pig rejected and wags his tails — I mean his finger — at me.

"I don't mind beggars but I object to their begging from me. Why don't you go begging from somebody else?"

"It's too early I guess, please. Just a shilling."

"Go get damned!" he yells and scrams fast, leaving me standing there. I debate on my next move whereupon I put my hands in my pockets and start walking the streets.

At half past nine by the Khoja mosque clock I am sitting on a bench in Jeevanjee Gardens. I am counting the number of black ants that climb over my boots and wondering what they feed on. Very industrious creatures, these ants. Busy the whole day long doing one thing or another. I wonder what I should be doing. I get onto my feet and walk along Government Road and envy these people who are having coffee outside the New Stanley Hotel. I linger around and decide to go in. Doris is at the reception desk talking to a female redhead who has a typical American accent and fat legs. I wait till they have finished and I walk to the desk.

"Hello, Doris. I reckon you are surprised to see me," I say.

"No, I am not," she says. I raise my eyebrows. I notice that she doesn't like my looks. She'd rather play with last week's accident corpse than entertain my company. I brace myself and hit the nail bang on the head.

"You wouldn't believe me, Dorry, but really I have come to beg. Oh, no, don't wear that surprised look. I'll explain. Firstly, I am broke. Secondly, I am hungry. Thirdly, I have no friends. Fourthly, I am just about to give up the ghost in hopeless despair. Fifthly, I trust that you are still kind hearted and sixthly, I have come to beg. No kidding. Ten bob will keep me going for two days and it's all I ask for. I am sorry, Dorry, but I have been reduced to this. A lowly beggar. Don't stare at me like that. It's me. This is Dodge. Dodge that used to be. Dodge that was but now is no more. No pity, please. Just a little help. Ten shillings."

In spite of herself, I notice, she has been touched. Women are very funny creatures. One time they are hostile and other times they are touched. This Doris looks at me as if she'd like to mother me and I notice that her big eyes are not very dry. She looks at me through the wet film that is forming in those eyes of hers and shakes her head. Makes me feel uncomfortable, she does. I don't like to look at women when there is a wet film developing on their eyes. A queer fellow — that's me.

Doris fidgets with her handbag and finally gets it open. She peers into it and the next second there is a wad of notes in her hand. She peels off a fiver and extends it to me. A real pink five quid note that starts my eyes dancing.

"Oh no," I protest. "That's too much!"

"Take it, Dod. You'll need it." She looks at me so piteously that I want to cry. I really want to cry. Jesus! As I take the note she squeezes my hand. A warm gentle squeeze that really brings tears to my eyes. I can't stand it. She is looking at me and I am looking at her and we are staring at one another. I can't keep my eyes off her. I murmur a feeble thank you and start walking backwards holding the note firmly in my hand.

As I pass the coffee boozers, I feel as well fed as they. There is nothing like money in your pocket. Fills your tummy and moves your legs and gives you lots of confidence.

I walk across the street and start walking towards Queensway.

46

I brush shoulders with a swell piece of female wearing these tights and I say "Hi, lady" but she hasn't got the courtesy to say "Hi". It doesn't worry me one little jot. Females are very unpredictable creatures except when they are predictable and that is rare. If you don't agree with me, you don't know women.

I get into this joint they call the 'Hole in the Wall' and flash my fiver at the cutie selling at the counter.

"Yes please?" she asks, eyeing the fiver with those gluttonous eyes that every strumpet wears.

"Pilsner," I say.

"Cold or warm?"

"Medium," I tell her.

As I pour the beer into a mug, I am kicking myself. I am kicking myself because I should have ordered something to eat instead of this beer stuff. I take a sip and lick my lips: It feels good. I take another sip and then I gulp. I belch and smile at this cutie who is staring at me as if I was her long lost brother. She smiles back and gives me the change. I count two shillings and sixty cents and give it to her.

"That's for your bottle," I tell her. The smile she gives me would have melted the south pole. I like women when they smile like that. Warms you up it does. I am looking at her tits and making a mental calculation that they are not very bad. They are a wee bit on the small side but I reckon that they are a good contrast to my usual bouncing favourites. A good contrast.

I order myself another hooch and ask her when lunch would be ready.

"I can get you something to eat right now. Mutton and chapati is ready." I tell her that I would very much like mutton and chapati and would she please get me some.

"At your service," she says and beckons one of the waiters. She gives him the order and he disappears into the kitchen swinging his green uniform. I look at the various faces around the joint and decide they are not worth looking at. They are either drinking tea, eating samosas or having a beer. There is no interesting woman except this cutie at the counter so I turn to her. I grin broadly and open a line of conversation.

"Hey," I say. "You didn't tell me your name."

"Neither did you," she says.

"Dodge. Dodge Kimnyu, best known to my friends as Dod. What's yours?"

"Call me anything but if you do not like to offend me, call me

Nancy. Nancy Muthoni. Are you new to Nairobi?"

"Yes and no. I used to come to this joint seven or eight months ago when a girl called Faith was serving at the counter but then I died. I have just risen from the grave. When did you start working here?"

"Two months ago. Why?"

"I was just asking. I was hoping that I might meet Faith but I assure you I am not disappointed."

"Meaning what?"

"Curious eh? Don't men tell you that you are cute?"

"Only the cheating bums who'd tell their eighty-year-old granny that she looked fifty. There are many like that."

"Well, I reckon I am one of them because unless I am deceived, which is rare with me, you are what I would sincerely pronounce as beautiful."

"And I wouldn't believe you or take any notice of your words."

"Sorry Miss, but you'd have to take notice before disbelieving. What the hell are they doing with my mutton and chapati?"

"Dressing it, perhaps. Tell you what. You are not bad looking yourself."

"Thank you very much but I have heard it before. Unlike you I believe it. There are mirrors you know."

"You're telling me," says she.

The waiter brings my food and I eat it very deliberately. I go back to this Nancy girl and I ask her whether they have rooms to let.

"What do you want a room at this time for?" she asks.

"None of your business, sister. If there is a room just say so and I may later tell you why I want it." She looks over her book and tells me that there is a room. I ask how much and she says that the best rooms are ten shillings exclusive of meals. I say that this is okay by me and would she please show me the room.

Another waiter is summoned and after I finish my third drink I am led upstairs into a dingy room and I say thanks to the waiter.

First thing I peel off my clothes and have a real refreshing cold bath. I go back to the room and lie on the bed. I am feeling good. Real good. No wonder I go to sleep.

It's about three when I open my blinking eyes again. Somebody is shaking me and I thank God when I discover that it's not another cop.

"Hey, what is this in aid of?" I ask Nancy who is standing over me.

"Sorry to disturb you but I was passing outside when I noticed that your door was ajar and on peeping in I saw you sound asleep. It's not a safe thing to do when you have money in your pockets."

"Thank you very much."

48

"I am going off duty now. I'll be back at eight tonight."

Funny things happen. I did not expect this one but it happened. Nancy gave me a lay — she did. You may not believe me but it's the goddam truth. Some of these town women are so experienced that they nearly twist your little man out of joint. Gosh, what a joint.

I take another bath just for kicks and I ease out into the street. I am not feeling bad. I have not been lacking where females are concerned. Yesterday I had Annie and today I have taken Nancy. Life can be funny.

I walk down towards the Machakos bus stop and I get to Gikomba. There is this street that turns to the left and leads to this place where they dump junk. There are stacks and stacks of scrap metal ranging from scrap buses to discarded marmalade cans. I look around and then walk to the office.

"Yes?" inquires the Indian boss eyeing me with disgust.

"I've got some junk to sell," I tell him.

"What junk?"

"An old car. An Austin A.40 that has nothing wrong with it but which is now junk as a result of several months of disuse. It's at Tigoni Police Station."

"You'd have to bring it here before I can quote a price."

"But I can't. The battery is down and the damn car has not moved for centuries. Approximately seven months to be precise. It would have to be towed."

"Sorry, but we only buy scrap when it gets to our yard. If your car has to be towed you will have to make the arrangements."

I go back to the 'Hole in the Wall' and get myself drunk. It's good to get drunk when you do not know what to do with yourself. Right now I don't know what to do with myself. I wonder whether I should go to Eastleigh and buy Annie a drink because she is a nice kid but I decide against it. There are lots of nice kids around. Plenty of them. More women than men — that's what we have in this city. All you have to do is buy drinks and ward them off.

The following morning I hold a meeting with myself. I don't have enough money to get a tow from Tigoni to Nairobi. I'd really like to bring my junk to Nairobi because I figure that I might get some twenty or thirty quid out of the heap. Lots of dough for a fellow like me.

I can't make up my mind what to do so I saunter to the museum. It's a hell of a walk but I am well fed. My big toe is behaving itself and I like the morning sun. I pay a shilling entrance fee to this old gentleman who has a wart on his nose and I get into the museum. Very fascinating this museum. Lots of preserved dead beasts that really look alive. There is an Indian lady next to me who has used a lot of coconut oil on her hair. You can smell the coconut from way off.

I go upstairs and I start studying the displayed different species of butterflies. I come to the conclusion that butterflies are very beautiful creatures but I don't like the Latin names with which they are labelled. They are too long. Butterflies should have poetic names.

I move over to the prehistoric section and admire the grinning skull of some African caveman. Very strong jaw this fellow had and his teeth are somewhat frightening. I wonder what a monkey's skull would look like and I decide that it would really look like this caveman in front of me. Life is funny. I would really like to see a caveman's penis out of curiosity but I suppose that I was born too late. I get fed up with these dead creatures and get out of the place and cross over to the snake park. I pay two fifty and walk in. The small crocodile I used to know has grown somewhat and the iguana has a longer beard. Old mama tortoise still stinks and the chameleons are still basking in the sun. I move around and feast my eyes on the snakes. Some are beautiful while others are ugly but they are snakes. I can't figure out why God created snakes. If He wasn't omnipotent I would definitely say that He must have been out of His mind but I won't say it.

As I walk away towards the city centre I am thinking about snakes. All the time I am praying that they don't visit me in my dreams. It would be horrifying. I have a knack of dreaming about those things that I don't like to dream about and I'm telling you, I am not very happy about the snakes. There was this horrifying movie "Dracula" which I saw in Kampala — it gave me hell for a whole week. This blood-thirsty Dracula attacked me the first night with his bared fangs and proceeded to suck blood from my neck. You should have seen me when I woke up. I was scared as hell. The second night I dreamed about the fellow again. This time he was an African dracula and he sucked my blood from my tummy. I couldn't stand it any longer. Third night I shared a bed with Kisa, a snoring friend of mine, but Dracula came again. I put up a fight and grabbed him by the neck. We wrestled all over the bed. Lord! I nearly strangled Kisa to death. I hate dreams and I hate snakes. I detest them both.

I get back to the town centre and I hit on a definite idea. I am going to Tigoni. It's some fourteen miles away and therefore cheap by bus. I don't really care whether I get my heap towed to Nairobi but at least I can set eyes on it. I'd like to look at it and think what good service it used to give me. As I walk to the bus stop, I am thinking that I am a mug — a real lousy heel but so what? You sometimes feel like

50

that yourself — or don't you?

I get to Tigoni at twelve thirty. I am inspecting the car and getting thoroughly bored with the cobwebs that spiders have been excreting all over the machine and I decide that I don't like spiders. There are other junk cars next to mine and I wonder what the cops did to the owners of these other cars. Perhaps they put them in the cooler as they did to me. That is cops all over. They are lousy bastards. If they fail to put you in the cooler, they are failing in their duty.

A cop comes from the central office and advances towards me. I look at him twice and then I stiffen. It is the same cop I clouted on the kisser and who later walloped me and who was the cause of my stay in the blinking jail. He has one very white false tooth in place of the one I knocked out. He looks younger now.

"Yes?" he says to me by way of greeting.

"Yes," I say to him.

"Uh, what can we do for you this time?" he asks.

"Nothing," I tell him. "I am merely admiring my car."

"Why don't you get the junk out of here? In one and a half months' time, it will be auctioned."

"Who will auction it and on whose authority?" I ask him.

"Government will. They don't need your authority to do that. We do it every year. Unroadworthy junk cars that are not claimed by owners are impounded and sold to the public. If you want your junk better remove it when the going is good. Besides, it makes the police station very untidy. This, my friend, is not a graveyard for cars. It's a police station."

"Thank you," I tell him and I start walking away.

"Where are you going?" he asks me.

"It's none of your business where I go and where I don't go chum, but if you must know I have an itch in the anus and I want to signify the fact to a physician. Maybe I have tapeworms."

I reckon he doesn't like this crack at all. He produces a dirty hanky from his pocket and proceeds to blow his nose furiously. I walk away smiling to myself.

I pass Tigoni Butchery and I come to Tigoni Garage. It's not much of a place this garage and the only vehicles that they seem to repair are Landrovers. There is a goggled fellow welding a radiator and his friend is lying on his back repairing something under a Landrover. I look around and decide that this is one hell of a garage and the fellows are not interested in customers. I start walking out of the joint and the goggled gentleman notices me. He takes out his goggles and shouts after me.

"Hey! Did you want something?" he asks.

"Yeah!" I say. "I want plenty."

"What?"

"Maybe you can help me and maybe you can't," I tell him. "I have an old Austin A.40 lying at the police station. It has not been touched for over six months on account of which it has now grown lots of moss and cobwebs and the battery has a nil charge. I would very much like to tow the little bus to Nairobi where some Indian has promised to buy it. At present I have very little money on me."

He squints and seems to remember something.

"Is that the light green Austin A.40 number KAF 106?"

"Yes," I tell him.

"Somebody told me that it was going to be sold by public auction because the owner has disappeared. Are you the owner?"

"Yeah."

"Why did you abandon it? It looks a good car to me and I was preparing to buy it when it got auctioned, do a few repairs here and there and sell it for more. It will sure need plenty of repairs."

"I didn't abandon it as you may suppose. The bastards sent me to jail for clouting a lousy cop and I have just come out. I can't afford to have it repaired neither would I be able to run it. I have to sell it."

"How much is the Indian giving you for it?" he asked.

"Seventy-five pounds," I tell him without thinking.

"What!" he exclaims. "Is the Indian your brother or something? I assure you that with minor repairs I can sell that car for more than twice that amount. You don't have to give your property to thieving Indians you know. Sell the damn thing to me. I'll give you eighty pounds for it."

I pretend to be reluctant although I think I have struck a gold mine. I was only banking on twenty to thirty pounds if I sold the car as scrap metal and now this fellow is offering me eighty. I would be mug number one to refuse it. I roll my tongue in my cheek and think up my answer carefully.

"Thank you very much for the offer but since you expect to sell the car for approximately twice that sum don't you think it would be fair if you gave me — say — one hundred pounds?"

"No. It would not be fair and that is the money I have in cash. I don't like debts and I'll therefore not offer more than I have in liquid cash. Sorry, friend, but you either accept eighty or take it to your Indian for seventy five. Please yourself."

"Okay, I see your position. How about eighty-five pounds?" I ask.

"I said eighty and not a cent more. Make up your mind."

"I reckon I haven't got much of an alternative. I'll take eighty and it's a deal."

"Right. Where is the registration book of the vehicle?"

"The cops have it."

"Here at the police station?"

"Yes," I tell him.

"Right. We can conclude the deal here and now."

"Sure," I say.

He calls somebody on the phone and I gather that he is asking for money. He is sweating all over as he bangs the telephone back on the cradle and he literally drags me to the Landrover outside.

"Let's go get the car," he says, out of breath. Gosh, the fellow is crazy.

It's four thirty when I get into a country bus bound for Nairobi. I have eighty quid in my hind pocket and I am singing this hymn about the Lord moving in a mysterious way His wonders to perform. Although I am not what you'd call a devout Christian, I am thanking the old man. I have nobody else to thank except Him. I am licking my lips and feeling like a million dollars. I am beginning to believe this fellow who said that worries are only temporary. He was a lousy philosopher but so what? On this occasion he talked sense.

When we get to Machakos Bus Stop in Nairobi, I walk back to the 'Hole in the Wall' and ask Nancy whether my room has been rented by another customer and she says no. I say I would like to rent it for another night and she says that I can do so. I pay the dough and I get the key to the room. I give Nancy a come-over-kid-if-you-are-game smile which also says a lot of other things and walk upstairs to this dingy room where I spent last night. I count my money for kicks and blow a kiss to nobody. I proceed to peel off my clothes because I reckon that it's a good idea to drown the dust of poverty in the bath.

I've had a real refreshing cold bath which has left a few needles on my back and an itch on the right thigh. I look at the door and stretch myself on the bed. I stare at the ceiling and feel generally in love with everything. I look back on my life and decide that life is nothing. All you got to do is be alive like I am. You touch your cheeks and you feel that they are your cheeks and you know you are not dead. That's all there is to it and that's life. Very funny. I am remembering that day a long time ago when Kamau disappeared and left me at the mission. It was one hell of a bad day for me. He was a very nice fellow, this Kamau. Very kind and loving. Miriam must have given him a free tumble for getting rid of little Kiunyu and that's me. He can thank himself.

This Sister is smiling at me and I am looking her all over because I haven't seen a white woman this close. She keeps peeping outside expecting Kamau to turn up anytime and whenever she hears footsteps outside and it's not Kamau she gets sort of disappointed but hides it behind a smile. I notice that she is smiling with her mouth but not her face and that my presence is making her uncomfortable.

A priest turns up. This is Father Burton and I am seeing him for the first time. He looks very pleasant. The Sister tells him what little she knows about me and he frowns. He pats me on the shoulder and I nod my head foolishly. I really felt foolish.

After a week they have now accepted the fact that Kamau has disappeared from the map and that I have to be taken care of. They have checked with Titus and he has told them a lot of lies and they have confirmed that granny is dead. I am accepted as a homeless orphan and I am to be brought up out of mission proceeds. I am too young to understand all these things but I do know one thing. I know that I am nobody's child and that life is too complicated to understand. I do not understand a thing. When they start teaching me this holy religion of theirs, I do not understand. I do not understand why they teach me and I do not understand why Father Burton wears a collar and funny long robes and I do not understand why Sisters are called Sisters and why they keep their hair covered. There is an old one called Mother and the others are always bowing to her. Mother Margarita, that's what they call her.

They put me to school but it is a different type of school. Half the time we are learning to read and write and the other half we are learning to sing in some foreign language. My classmates seem to like the singing part but they are not helpful when I try to find out what the hell we are singing about.

"What's the meaning of this Gloria and Maria that we are always singing about?" I ask the class prefect.

"You ignorant nit. Don't you know that Maria is the Mother of the Son of Man and Gloria is the Goodness of the Father?"

"You mean Father Burton?" I ask him. He opens his mouth and eyes me as if I had told him that a fly was a gorgon.

"You should be punished for that. I'll tell on you. You have clay in your head and mucus on your nose."

He points a finger at me and that is the end of my search for further knowledge. I decide that when we are singing in this different language about Maria, Gloria, etc. we are actually singing about

54

Mother Margarita and Father Burton and that they are married since
one is the mother and the other the father of the same son. I start
wondering what their son looks like and why he doesn't stay with
them.

Three years later I am a very important young man at the mission.
They have made a true Christian out of me. I am assisting the Father
before mass, holding his robes, lighting his candles, ringing the big
bell on Sundays and doing other odd jobs like polishing the chalice
and polishing floors. I am prefect of my class and I am damn clever.
I am always getting top marks and I therefore stay in the front row.
My classmates call me "Mission boy" in my absence and when I
overhear them I fight with them. I like fighting boys but I dare not
touch a girl. They are so fragile, these little girls and they remind me of
Tonia. Wicked Tonia.

I went to Mangu High School on a mission ticket. The idea
behind all this free education was to prepare me for a monastery or
some other place of holy orders. Father Burton was very anxious that
I become a priest in my later life. I liked the idea very much. I liked the
idea till the year I was doing my Cambridge Overseas School
Certificate. There was this Christian friend of mine from Thika who
invited me to stay with him during the three day mid-term holiday.
I accepted the invitation and Mwaura — this friend of mine — assured
me that it would only be a few minutes' walk to church on Sunday
morning.

The unexpected happened. His father was a jolly engaging man
and I didn't have the guts to say "no" when he offered us native liquor.
Thtat night I was drunk for the first time and I laid a woman for the
firse time. I dare not tell you how I felt but you will possibly understand
whn I tell you that the following night I laid another woman and on
Sunday evening I did not want to leave for school. I had been promised
a lay. When we got back to school, I'd already made up my mind that
I wasn't going to be anybody's priest and that what the church forbade
was wholesome and juicy.

I went to Makerere University College on a Kenya Government
bursary and broke my ties with the mission. At Makerere I drank if and
when I could afford it, chased women, and read when there was
nothing else to do. In brief I did those things that you would not like
your mother to hear of. I had no mother to think about. After five
long years of this life, plus books, I was thoroughly fed up and on
graduating I promised myself that I'd never study again. The only
things I'd read would be novels and the only things I read are novels
and occasionally the newspaper. I don't really read the newspaper.

55

I merely go through the headlines till I get to the page with classified ads. When I am satisfied that there are no suitable jobs going I embark on the junior crossword puzzle. Very interesting, this junior crossword. Sometimes it puzzles me.

I am lying on this bed and I am getting fed up staring at the damn ceiling and remembering old events. It's a thing you can do all your life and get nowhere. I reckon that I am getting nowhere and decide that a beer would do some good. I get out of bed, rinse my eyes after a king size yawn and transport myself downstairs.

There are very few people down here and I select a table for myself. I ask the waiter to supply me with a Pilsner that is neither cold nor warm and he's back presently with the bottle and I proceed to consume its contents. Within half of no time the bottle is empty. I look at the empty bottle and start to feel poetic. I order another and while I drink it I compose some poetry in my mind in honour of the bottle. I take pen and paper out of my pocket and start to write.

> *A bloodthirsty louse, this blinking Master Dodge*
> *He held me by my slender neck, this lusty Master Dodge*
> *I couldn't scream, I couldn't shout and I couldn't duck*
> *He carried me he did, to his cabin full of muck*
> *And stripped me, damn him, of all my evening clothing*
> *A curse upon him, for his shameless snooping*
> *He stared he did, at my nude small opening*
> *His thin trembling fingers caressed my cold solid hips*
> *And with a final tilt pressed me to his dry fevered lips*
> *I couldn't possibly resist, I gave him all the goods*
> *He worked on me he did, lousy Master Dodge — ouch!*
> *I couldn't stop him or stop myself till the very last drop*
> *He let go my bottom and pushed poor me away to flop*
> *Exhausted and drained and that's why I lie here*
> *A discarded empty bottle that was once full of beer.*

A tricky poem, I thought. I would like to read it to some dame for kicks but there aren't any dames in this place who would appreciate poetry even if that poetry was lousy. That's dames all over. They are not interested in a lot of things but don't get me wrong. When they get interested in a thing they really get interested. Right now, by the looks she is giving me, I reckon that this Nancy behind the bar is very much interested in me. So what? Forget the dames and skip one week during which I have done nothing except think about nothing. I mean it. There is water in my head.

I am nicely dressed in a light grey suit and I am walking along Harambee Avenue towards Shell House where I have been called for

an interview. I am wondering what I will say on my behalf when they
ask the questions interviewers always ask and I don't seem to be
getting anywhere. I ask myself a lot of likely questions but I have no
answers. Whenever I have an answer, it would not get me anywhere in
my cause. I am not pleased with my slow thinking this morning and
I curse myself for the self-inflicted hangover. I am feeling scared.

As I go up the lift to the fourth floor, I make up my mind
quickly. I decide to use the old method of mentally stripping the
interviewer of his clothes and imagining what a poor figure he'd cut
sitting on his naked arse. Hairs under the armpits, protruding stomach,
a scar on his chest with small hairs growing round it and his manhood
shrunk right inside itself. If you can look at the boss and in your
mind see him thus, then you are damn sure to pass the interview. As
it turns out you actually interview him. I grin as the lift stops and
decide that I am going to give somebody one hell of a time.

Three people are sitting behind a polished mahogany table and
I am asked to take the only seat on the opposite side. On the left is an
African wearing horn rimmed spectacles who squints at me as if I was
something the cat brought in and in the middle is a smartly dressed
Englishman smoking a pipe and smiling at me as he goes over some
papers. The gentleman to the right looks like himself. Top executive
and all that. He wears his hair American style and does not seem
interested. If he had a toothpick I think he would start picking his teeth.

The gentleman in the middle introduces himself as Eric Scott the
Personnel Manager and then proceeds to introduce the others as
Thiga and Kennedy. I am asked several formal routine questions just
to establish my identity and I note that Kennedy is looking at me
suspiciously. Maybe he doesn't like my short hair. In case you have
forgotten, they unhaired my head when I was holidaying in jail for
which I thank them. I don't really need a comb.

"There were two jobs advertised, Mr. Kiunyu. One in Sales and
the other in Public Relations. Your application does not indicate
which one you are interested in. Is that right?" Mr. Scott asks.

"Yes and no," I tell him. "I did not make a definite choice but
I did recount my experience in public relations as a labour officer, my
private studies, my three months at the Kenya Institute of
Administration on a public relations course and the industrial relations
article I contributed to the Employers' Journal while I mentioned nothing
concerning sales. This, in my opinion, is indicative of my preference."

"So you want to be considered for the Public Relations post?"
Thiga asks.

"That's what I have been trying to say," I answer.

"You obtained a lower second class honours degree in Geography?" Kennedy asks.

"Yes."

"How good is that?"

"By which standards?" I ask him.

"By any standards," he says.

"It's as good as any," I tell him. I am one who believes in the golden rule of stupid answers for stupid questions.

Half an hour later I am walking back to the 'Hole in the Wall' and I am not pleased with myself. My imagination did not work right. I couldn't strip the three of them. I'd figured on being interviewed by one person. The way Mr. Scott finally said, "Thank you very much, we shall get in touch with you soon," made me feel that I'd flopped. I am always flopping — so what? I'll sit and wait for their damn letter. If it's a regret, I'll get myself drunk and then lay a woman just to let off steam. If I am accepted, I'll get myself drunk and then lay a woman to congratulate myself. Whatever they decide my reaction will be the same. You might think that there is some basic difference between letting off steam and congratulations. There isn't. Either way you are letting off steam.

I get back to the 'Hole' and give it a glance. Nancy is smiling at me but I am not in the mood for smiles. I'd like to kick somebody or call them shit just for kicks. I am in one hell of a truculent mood.

"Hi, Dodge, you are looking very smart," Nancy says to me.

"Thank you very much, kid. You could have spared yourself the compliment. I looked at myself in the mirror," I tell her. She doesn't like my tone but this does not worry me. Sometimes I don't like women to like me.

"Goodnight," I tell her and I start for the stairs.

"Are you going to bed at this hour of the morning?" she asks.

"What would you do if you were me?"

"I wouldn't want to be you but if I was, I'd be working somewhere. Too much sleep dulls the intellect."

"That's funny coming from you. I hadn't noticed the brilliance of your intellect. Honest I hadn't and I reckon I was simply blind. I am starting to see the light."

"Why don't you go right up the stairs and sleep till doomsday? Sleep is all you are capable of. Always sleep and more sleep. Sleep during the day, sleep during the night. You are always sleeping."

"Thanks again, kid. One of these days I'll pay you to be my tutor. Goodnight again. If you want a tumble, I wiil kindly oblige. I am a kind gentleman where cost is not involved. I will leave the door open; goodnight."

I go to my room, strip off my coat and tie and rest on the bed. I am thinking about the interview. The more I think the more I feel that it will be another regret. I miss out on everything and this instance will not be an exception. I am getting depressed. Very depressed. Gosh! I get out of bed and walk to the top of the stairs. I shout at Nancy and ask her to bring me two bottles of beer and a packet of fags and I ease back into the room. Presently, she's up with the beers. She opens one and carefully pours the whole lot into a one-pint mug.

"Here is your sleeping tablet," she says extending the mug to my outstretched hands.

"Thank you," I say sarcastically. "You are very nice. One of these fine days I might decide to marry you." She makes a face at me.

"Thank you for the offer but I am already engaged to a real man who works with his hands. I think you'd bore me."

"I don't envy the fellow. It's obvious he doesn't mind left-overs. I am different."

"That is real rude you know. Even if you really despised someone you shouldn't call her a left-over, in her face. You have no decency in you. I'll see you later."

I can see that she is annoyed and I feel sorry for her. I shouldn't have said that even as a joke.

"I am sorry, Nancy. Wait a minute. There is no hurry. Honest, I am sorry. Of course I was only kidding. You know me now. You know I was merely joking and besides you know that I am damn fond of you. That's why I was joking. Please come. I want to tell you something."

"What?"

"Come."

"Okay, I am here. What do you want to tell me?"

"Sit down."

"Well?"

"I am an unhappy man, Nancy, and you are the only friend I have."

"I am flattered," she says lightly. I edge closer and put my arm round her.

"I mean it," I say softly. "I am not kidding. You are my only friend."

"All right but so what? Am I supposed to stand on the table and wave a flag?"

"You don't understand," I tell her softly, squeezing her gently and pulling her towards me. My mouth is somewhat dry and my heart is beating out of turn. I am a very excitable cuss.

"On the contrary I understand. You are worked up about something and you are all nervous. I would not be surprised if you cried a little when I leave. All this show of affection is escapism. You want to escape from yourself. You want to make love to me and if I say no it will break your heart. It will be another failure. It will bring about self-pity and you will want more drink. You mistook me the first day we met simply because I was mad enough to go to bed with you. I'll never forgive myself for that. I'd like you to understand that I am not that type. I try to be decent."

"I am not very indecent myself and I hope that I am not blowing my trumpet. I used to be a very decent fellow once but as you see, I am getting sentimental in my old age. I'll simply have to pull myself together and live without friends since you, the only friend, are not well inclined towards me. It is sometimes good to have no friends," I tell her. She looks at me as if I was her little brother.

"You shouldn't feel like that," she says. "Whoever is not your enemy is your friend. You have many friends."

She left twenty minutes later.

"You are a greedy bastard," she says as she gets dressed. I am not thinking. I am not thinking about her or this job with Shell. I am simply not thinking. My head is empty. No kidding. I am a real bum when it comes to thinking.

When I get this letter from Shell a week later I do exactly as I said. I get myself drunk and then go tumbling. You see. I always keep my promises.

5

I walk in the nude to the dressing table, open the curtains a little and look at myself in the mirror. I turn up my nose at what I see. What I see is me but I don't know what is me. I simply don't know. I find myself speaking to this fellow in the mirror who is me — Dodge Kiunyu esquire or whatever you like to call me and I wouldn't care. "Your name is Dodge," I say to myself. "What else are you? Are you a mere name? Where are you going and where have you come from? Where are you going, Master Dodge? Where? Tell me. What have you been doing all your goddam life? What have you done for yourself? What have you done for mankind? Nothing. You have done nothing Mr. Kiunyu and that is a lousy name. You have done nothing. All you have done is cause misery. That's all you have done. Cause misery. You are a miserable rat, a damn lousy rat. That's what you are, Mr. Dodge. A rat."

I pull my ear for kicks and then let go. The ear has done me no harm. What has caused all the harm is me. My whole me. I go back to the bed where I have hung my clothes on a rail and start dressing.

I have to vacate this lovely flat which I have been occupying for the last three months. I am sorry but I have to. It's very sad. I will be on the streets again. Gosh! The letter from the landlord gave me seven days within which to pay the rent or quit. I don't have the money so I reckon I will have to quit. That would not help much because the letter further says that the landlord's lawyer will institute legal proceedings against me towards the recovery of the two months' outstanding rent. I reckon they will hound me all over Nairobi till they get their pound of flesh. So what? This is not the first time I have been hounded and by worse wolves.

I got the Public Relations job with Kenya Shell all right. This gentleman . . . what was his name? Yes, Mr. Scott. This Scott was very kind. He offered me the job and there were lots of attractive side benefits going with it apart from the fat pay. Fat to me but not to you because you have not been a jailbird — so don't get me wrong. I worked for a month in Public Relations and some top hat thought that my talent would be more profitably utilized if I was in Sales Advertising. I was thereupon transferred to that department and welcomed by my new boss — a middle aged retired sea captain by the name of Abel Hook.

Abel Hook was a most fascinating gentleman. He would look at me and smile sweetly and whenever I put a cigarette to my lips he'd flick his lighter before I could strike a match. We were sharing the same office and the same table and so Mr. Hook was always flicking his lighter because I smoke like hell. Whenever we were leaving the office together he'd rush and open the door and hold it for me to pass and do me all sorts of favours. You've never met such a gentleman.

One evening Mr. Hook invited me to his flat for a drink. He also invited another friend of his working with the Broadcasting Corporation and an Indian from Zanzibar. It was then that I learnt why Mr. Hook had left the navy. The trouble was his ears. Something had gone wrong with the balancing mechanism inside the ear and movement made him go to sleep. On the same grounds he wasn't allowed to drive. He would go to sleep when driving.

We had eats and lots of wine and the party was getting lively. Mr. Hook wrapped his scarf around the Indian fellow whose name I forget because the latter kept complaining that it was cold. Then something funny happened. At first I thought that drink was the cause but I was proved wrong. Mr. Hook pulled the Indian and sat him on his lap. They started whispering what I later discovered to be love words but my boss told me that he and the Indian sometimes talked Japanese. The broadcasting gentleman started patting me on the shoulder as we talked and I started to smell a rat. He gave me such a loving, pleading, hot look that all the drink left my head. A man only gives such a look to a cherished woman and I don't even look like a woman. He must have been nuts but of course he wasn't. He was a downright queer and so was my boss. My boss had invited me to this four man party so that this other fellow could make a pass at me. Fancy that! I said, "Thank you very much, Mr. Hook, for such a delightful evening but really I must get going. I would not like to miss the last bus."

At first he didn't hear me. He was too drunk to realize that he was caressing the Indian's hair and that he was all flushed. When he understood he jerked himself awake and said, "Oh, no, no, Dodge. Peter will take you home." Peter was the broadcasting friend and he stood up to accompany me out and give me a ride home. I didn't say

a word, I simply walked out but Peter followed me. I turned left
and walked briskly aware that Peter was somewhere behind me. He
called, "Hey, Dodge! Not so fast. My car is the third from the beetle
on your left."

I was having a fast debate. I was wondering whether I should
let the fellow make another pass at me so that I'd have a good excuse
for socking him or whether to spit in his face and call him shit. I did
neither. I had a job to keep and he was a friend of my boss. I simply
told him, "I am very sorry but I like to walk. I want to take a walk
to the bus stop — I'll see you sometime."

"Oh no. Oh no," he pleaded. "I must take you home. We can
go to my house and have one more drink while we watch television.
The night is still young. What do you want, going to bed at nine?
Let's go to my house. Just one more drink."

"Thank you very much but I hate television and I have had too
much to drink already. I need a breather walking to the bus stop.
Sorry but I must go. Goodnight."

I left him standing there. He was mumbling to himself. He was
mumbling something to the effect that his friend Hook was deceived.
I left him mumbling. If I hadn't had a job to think about, I'd have left
him mumbling a different tune — but I was the mug. I should have
socked him there and then because in three weeks' time I lost the job
anyway. I lost it three months after getting it thanks to a bastard
called Mac — may his hair turn into hay.

From the day of the party I couldn't stand the sight of Mr. Hook
and I didn't beat the bush about it. I asked for a transfer and I got it
almost immediately. I joined the Retail Section and that is why I
happened to be on duty at our stand at the Nairobi Show on this fatal
day that cost me my job.

I had just finished my two hours on the stand and I decided to
stroll around seeing other trade stands. I was looking at a revolving
pig on top of a column at the Uplands Bacon Factory stand when a
friend tapped me on the shoulder. We walked down to some army
place where beer was cheap and got ourselves thoroughly juiced. It
was after this juice stuff that I met this bully called Mac at the Uplands
Stand. I don't know how the quarrel started but this Mac told me that
I reminded him of a pig. He said that all Africans stink like pigs and
when I tried to say something he gave me a left punch that connected
with my cheek bone with a bang. I reckon the fellow was drunk too.
They were dishing free drinks at their stand.

I think he still remembers it. I gave it to him Chinese fashion and
punctured a few holes into his neck using a high heeled shoe I picked

from somewhere. He took one week in hospital and came out with
a black patch over one eye which reminds me of Moshe Dayan of
Israel and I got fired the following day.

"We don't train fighters," the Marketing Manager told me as he
handed over my dismissal papers. "I am afraid you will have to try
your luck elsewhere."

I thanked him and walked out. You simply cannot argue with a
stubborn Britisher. The best thing is to walk right out on him and
so I did. I was given two weeks' salary in lieu of notice plus what
I had earned for that month and I hit the road. I am still hitting the
road.

I had rented this bachelor flat and life had gone back to normal.
I was having my normal share of women and drink and occasional
swings at the nightclubs. That was good while it lasted. Real good
and no kidding. I was enjoying myself like the real son of woman that
I am. So what? You can't enjoy yourself all your life can you?

I have my suit on and I am walking towards the Ministry of Lands
and Settlement's offices. I am going for an interview for the post of
Settlement Officer. I don't like the job and I really can't satisfy myself
as to why I am going there. Maybe I'll decline the offer if I am accepted.
I'll only do so if this other job with Unga Limited materializes. I'd
rather work among bags of lousy posho in a Nairobi factory than
in a remote settlement scheme somewhere right out and away from
civilization. Anyway we shall see.

I am walking along Government Road when this old gentleman
wearing a City Council overall confronts me.

"Hey, hello! I haven't seen you for days. How are you?" I look
at him and decide that I have never seen him anywhere. I wonder
what the racket is all about.

"I am fine but I don't recall having met you before," I tell him.

"Oh, I see you around. I am always seeing you. My wife came
yesterday you see. She is all right but the kid isn't. The poor boy has
horrifying pimples that exude bloody pus and the government doctors
are hopeless. Their nurses just give you diluted ointment every time.
Very mean, these nurses. They even help themselves to patients'
rations. As I was saying, the kid is sick. I am supposed to feed him
with vegetables, carrots, tomatoes, fruit and what-have-you and
starve myself. That would be okay if I had the vegetables and things
but I haven't. My boss is an Indian and you know what they are like.
Wouldn't part with a thin cent — not him. Damn him anyway but
there is this shilling that I want. Just one shilling for these vegetables.
Immediately I saw you, my face lighted up because you are not like

64

the bloody Indians. You would sure part with a shilling for a starving child — and I will pray to God that fortune comes your way. Just one shilling."

I look at the fellow and feel sorry for myself. He has spun all that yarn about knowing me and the rest hoping to get a shilling. I feel sorry for him. I feel sorry because I don't have a shilling on me. If I had, I would certainly give him one or two and with great pleasure.

I decide that if I tell him that I am broke, he wouldn't believe me. Not with this nice suit I am wearing. I decide to play it his way. A little subtlety and melodrama — that is the only language that this fellow would understand. I dig my hands into my trouser pockets and pretend to look for something. I pretend to be surprised when I find nothing. I start fiddling with my coat pockets.

"You know what," I tell him. "I had one shiny silver shilling right here in this pocket but it looks as if it has just walked out. It's no longer there. Hey, do you happen to have change for a hundred shilling note?"

"What?"

"One hundred shilling note. That's all I have got. You don't have the change, do you?"

"God forbid. One hundred shillings change. Oh, no! Not this time of the month. I have got only three."

"Ah! You have three shillings then?" I ask open-mouthed.

"Oh no! Certainly not. Did I say that? It was a slip of the tongue. I told you I don't have a thin cent and I have this sick kid. We can get change from that grocery store across the street."

I look at him and spit. "We can get change from that grocery store across the street," I mimic, jeering at him. "You nit-witted beggarly cheat." I spit again. "I have a good mind to slap you for wasting my time and if I remember, I'll get you sacked. Be gone."

I walk away laughing. This sort of thing happens to you once in a while. The fellow is either dying of hunger or he has a sick child or wife. He pretends to know you, tells you a plausible story and then virtually blackmails you into giving him something. Some few cases are genuine but over eighty percent are false. Anyway that's life. If I could get my daily meals through telling funny stories I reckon I'd become a story teller.

I get on to Queensway and into Silopark House where the Ministry of Lands and Settlement is housed. I go up the lift to the fifth floor, ask the enquiries desk a question, move left and knock at a door.

"Come in," a voice says. I go in and close the door behind me.

The English fellow behind the desk stares at me as if I had interrupted his mid-day nap and raises his eyebrows in enquiry. "Can I help you?" he asks.

"Yes sir, but maybe I got into the wrong office. My name is Kiunyu. Dodge Kiunyu. I am due for an interview for the post of Settlement Officer in this room at this time. I have a letter asking me to see Mr. Jones."

"I am Mr. Jones. May I see the letter please. Sit down." He beckons to the chair opposite his. He peruses the letter quickly, raising his eyebrows as he reads and finally looks at me.

"I am very sorry but I don't know anything about this. I had no information that there was a candidate due for interview but of course it is not your fault. The Personnel people should have informed me when they wrote to you. Sorry but this is inefficiency on our part. Gross inefficiency. It's happening all over as a result of this new move they call Africanization. They simply cannot take inexperienced Africans from nowhere and put them into senior executive posts and expect efficiency. You and I are victims of this nonsense. You may not know but the post has already been filled. You have made a useless trip because somebody — Njoroge, a K.P.E. clerk formerly with the Ministry of Agriculture — is now a Personnel Officer and frankly he is all bone from his shoulders up. I am sorry. Africans cannot simply hope to acquire the knowledge and the experience which took us upwards of ten years of patience, in a matter of one year. It is the antithesis of common sense."

"Do I take it then, Mr. Jones, that all the six posts have been filled?" I ask him. Everything that Mr. Jones has said has done nothing to me except offend my ears. Maybe he forgot that I am an African.

"What six posts?" he asks.

"The advertisement said that there were six posts."

"I don't know what six posts you are talking about. As far as I know only one post of Settlement Officer was advertised and as I have already told you, it's already taken."

"There must be some confusion then. Perhaps we are not talking of the same thing. I have a newspaper cutting from the *East African Standard* of three weeks ago if you'll care to look at it please — it might clarify the situation."

He shook his head. "If six posts were advertised, that was done without my knowledge. I should have been informed. There was only one post and as I say it's already filled. There is no end to this crap. There is inefficiency everywhere. Look at you for instance. You

66

want to be employed as a Settlement Officer, isn't that right?"

"That's right," I tell him.

"What agricultural knowledge do you have?"

"I got a distinction in Agriculture for Cambridge School Certificate."

"I know what is taught for School Certificate. It's shallow academic stuff. Do you think you are capable of running a two thousand acre mixed farm?"

"I don't know. I haven't tried."

"Right. I'll be frank with you. You can't. You need some training in farm management. You need to go to an agricultural college for at least two years. That would qualify you. I have been a farm manager for many years both in Kenya and in Australia. I therefore know what I am talking about."

"Did you go to an agricultural college for two years?" I ask him, feigning interest in his boring lecture.

"That's none of your business but as I say you need some training. How can you hope to run a settlement scheme if you cannot run a small farm?" I look at Mr. Jones and decide that he is a lonely fellow. He is very much in need of a companion to act as a receptacle for his grievances and philosophies. I decide that if I was that receptacle I would get very bored. Very bored indeed. In a matter of minutes I am already very bored. Mr. Jones would need a very voluminous receptacle.

I thank him for his kindness and excuse myself. As I open the door to let myself out I say, "Bye" and Mr. Jones says, "Come again". I close the door with a bang and as I walk away, I hiss between my teeth, "Shit".

I go back to the enquiries desk and ask the way to Njoroge's office.

"Which Njoroge?" the girl at the counter asks me.

"The Personnel Officer," I tell her.

"It's the next floor up—fourth office on the eastern side of the left wing."

"What room number?" I ask.

"It's marked Z. Njoroge, Personnel Section. You can't miss it." I smile and thank her.

I walk upstairs and find the room. I knock and peep in. There is a female sitting at the secretary's desk and hammering at a typewriter as if the poor machine had offended her. She does not notice me till I am right in the room and she does not reply when I say, "Hi". Instead, she lifts her limpid eyes at me in surprise and I tell you she is a knocker plus. If you know that innocent beauty that is too shy to know itself, then you know what I mean. The type of girl you'd look at and give up the idea of laying her because she was too good to be laid and thereafter indulge yourself in a lot of wishful thinking. She looks half Masai, half Ethiopian and has Somali teeth. Her voice is soft and seductive and slightly high pitched.

"Can I help you please?"she asks. Gosh! I feel like telling her, "Yes of course. You can kiss me," but instead I clear my throat and say, "I think so. My name is Kiunyu, Dodge Kiunyu, and I would like to see the Personnel Officer."

"Have you got an appointment?"

"Yes and no — meaning you haven't got my name in your appointment book but on the other hand Mr. Njoroge will be pleased to meet me."

"May I please know what you want to see him about?"

"Certainly, but I am not sure that he would like me to tell you. Is he in?"

She doesn't look pleased as she says, "If you'll please hold on a minute, I'll tell him that you are here." She gets hold of the telephone but before she presses the buzzer she looks at me apologetically.

"You said that your name is George Kungu?" she asks, opening her eyes and baring her teeth.

"Kiunyu. Dodge Kiunyu," I tell her.

"Dodge?"

"Yes, Dodge. Do you like it?" She does not answer me. She presses the buzzer and tells the bloke behind the communicating door that there is a Mr. Kiunyu to see him. After a short conversation she replaces the receiver, extends her hands towards the door and says, "He will see you". I open the door and close it after me. Do I get a surprise or do I? This Njoroge fellow is an old buddy of mine. We were both in Northcote Hall at Makerere and we were both in the tug of war team. What a surprise.

"Goodness, Dod! Didn't know it was you. Come in and take a seat. Gosh. Where have you been holed up?"

"Under some concrete slabs in no-man's-land. Hi chum. The same old mighty Zick. I thought you were working with the Economic Commission for Africa in Addis. How come that you've become an administrator in view of your natural aversion to law and order? No wonder your friend downstairs thinks you are a Standard VII clerk promoted to eminence to propagate inefficiency. Who is

68

the bastard anyway?"

"Who?"

"Mr. Jones downstairs. He told me that you are a CPE clerk formerly working with the Ministry of Agriculture and then proceeded to give me a long lecture about the idiocy of promoting inexperienced Africans, citing you as an example."

"What?" Zick asks. "Are you kidding or are you white?"

"White as your secretary's teeth. No kidding. Mr. Jones was very vehement about your inexperience and inefficiency. I of course did not know who he was referring to but what he said would offend a two weeks' old baby!"

"Now, Dod. You are damn well spoiling my mood by talking about that bastard. I know him and I believe you. He thinks that everybody should feed out of his lily white hand. Forget him. His life in this ministry is as short as the life of a fly. We are used and immune to his syphilitic tongue. Let him be, and now on to other business. Business and pleasure if you like but I'd suggest that we postpone the latter to this evening at Tina's Bar. I have a small wad in my pocket which is labelled "Income Tax Refund" and today is Friday. I'd forgotten about it but they hadn't. Let's meet at five, get cockeyed and talk old times. What is your problem businesswise?"

"That is a wee bit fast for my dull head but it's like this in brief. I have been to all sorts of craps but recently I have been working with the Kenya Shell. I got a sack for walloping a Britisher who called me pig and I am now on the roads. This ministry advertised six Settlement Officer posts and I applied. I got a letter asking me to report to Mr. Jones today but apparently he didn't know anything about it. He told me that there was only one vacancy and that has already been filled. He didn't know anything about the ad in the *East African Standard*. Since he was blaming the Personnel Officer for everything, I decided to come up here and have the situation clarified."

"Mr. Jones told you that there was only one vacancy and that it had been filled?" I notice that my friend Zick is shocked. His face is folded and he is shaking his head. His face is full of disbelief.

"Sure. He hammered that point to the boards."

"Are you sincerely interested in these Settlement Officer posts? They don't pay much."

"Any job that pays something is good enough for me."

"Right. We advertised six posts. They will be tenable in the Ol Kalou and Kinangop areas where we are starting a series of settlement schemes. We want to recruit six people, have them work with experienced Settlement Officers and then send them out on their own after — say — two months. So far only three people have responded to our advertisement. The Public Service Commission people are very busy. They would like to select the six at a one-day sitting, but they are not prepared to do piece-meal interviews. They have, therefore, given us authority to employ the officers and their appointments will be confirmed later when the Public Service Commission guys get a chance of interviewing these people. In effect it means that you would be in the service for a few months before you were called for interview. Mr. Jones has been charged with the responsibility of recruiting the officers and sending them to the field. All I do is send him names of the applicants and the rest is his. Three of you were supposed to report to him today at different times and I am shocked if he disclaimed any knowledge of it. I'll drag hell to see that the blinking imperialist goes. His contract expires in two months' time and he thinks that he will renew it automatically. I'll give him a little shock. This is our country, Dod. This is the new Kenya and Kenya is African. Mr. Jones thinks that he is indispensable and that I am nothing. He forgets one thing. He forgets that a cat may look at a king."

"Am I therefore to assume that the jobs are not taken?" I ask.

"Of course, Dod. If Mr. Jones approved of somebody then he'd send him to me for the usual red tape. He does not employ people. He merely recommends them and sends them to me."

"Then he was lying."

"Sure — unless he has devised a new system of employing people without the services of the Personnel Department which would mean that he'd have to pay them out of his pocket."

"So what next?" I ask, shrugging my shoulders. Instead of answering me Zick gets hold of the telephone and asks his secretary to connect him with Mr. Jones. After a brief moment Zick starts talking. I hear everything he says.

"Yes — Njoroge here — oh no. It's about those six Settlement Officers posts — Yes. The three of them should have reported to you already according to my letter. They haven't turned up? — Not any of them? — That's strange — No? Goodness — Did a man by the name of Kiunyu report to you? — No? Well — eh — do you think you can spare a minute and come up here for a moment? There is something we should get right — No — if it's possible — Yes please." Zick replaces the receiver and faces me.

"I want you to be here so that you can watch as the bastard's face turns pink. There will be a private row after this but I am not in danger. He is. Watch it." The door is thrust open and Mr. Jones strides in.

"Will you please take a seat, Mr. Jones. This gentleman here is one of the applicants for these six posts we advertised but it's apparent that he has been giving me false information and I only called you to put the picture right." No sooner does Mr. Jones set eyes on me than he starts to turn pink. Zick was right. The fellow is going real pink and I am enjoying myself. His lips are quivering as he answers Zick.

"Oh yes. I've met him. What seems to be the trouble? I don't have much time."

Zick clears his throat. "Mr. Jones, you have confirmed that none of the three people who were supposed to report for an interview in your office have turned up?"

"What of it?" asks Mr. Jones.

"This gentleman here claims that he did actually call at your office and that he was given the impression that no posts were advertised and that he wasn't due for interview. I find it difficult to believe his story."

"Oh, I see what you mean. I do now recall that the gentleman came to see me about something in connection with those jobs but of course he is not the type of person we are interested in. He read Geography at College and has no agricultural experience. I told him that we had no vacancy."

"So you did interview him?" Zick asks emphatically.

"Not really. You can't interview somebody who has no agricultural knowledge because in the first instance he should not have been called for an interview."

"Were the other two you saw just like him?"

"This is a specialized job, Mr. Njoroge, and the government has spent a lot of money on this project. We can't afford to take risks with people who can't tell the difference between an ewe and a ram."

"None of the three had any experience, then?" Zick asked.

"That's right. There was a chap with a diploma in Agriculture but he knew nothing about farming. An academic qualification is not enough. As long as I am the Technical Adviser, I'll make sure that we only employ the right person."

"You have, in actual fact, seen the three candidates but decided that they were unqualified: am I right?"

"Oh — yes. They will need some basic training in practical farming. Eh — if it's convenient for you, I'll see you at two and discuss this subject further. There are more than six tried and experienced people I have in mind for these posts but unfortunately they are not Africans. It would need going over some of the red tape before they could be employed and I would like to discuss that with you."

"That's fine," Zick says. Jones gets up, excuses himself and walks right out. Zick smiles and shakes his head for a long time.

"See what type of people we've got to work with, Dod. Fancy a man like that working for the Kenya Government and remember, Dod — we've got independence."

"I'd spit at him if I were in your place. I haven't stopped that old silly habit. I'd spit right in his face and call him shit and watch his face turn from pink to scarlet. I don't understand how you stand him."

"I have a big name and I am supposed to be his boss but tell you what — the bastard gets twice as much pay as I do. He says that it doesn't really matter if we are given a bigger mouth so long as they get the bigger money and damn it, he is right. I'd rather have the money myself."

"So far, so good, but what about a job?" I remind him. I am of the opinion that I am taking more of his time than I should and that it's high time I scrammed out of here.

"Oh don't worry about the job. I'll fix you. Mr. Jones was given the privilege of recruiting these people but from today that privilege will be withdrawn. I'll take charge myself. The only way you can work with Jones is by stripping him of all responsibility. That way you wouldn't clash because he'll sit in the office and read a newspaper the whole day long after which he'll go and play golf. I'll take this matter up with the Deputy Director and I'll wise you up at five o'clock when we meet at Tina's. I have to ditch one or two females at four thirty. You know Dod, when I go on a drinking weekend I don't want any blinking females tagging along. You are not free to say whatever you want. I like to drink with mugs who drink, get drunk and start singing. Roaring drunk as you would call it."

"You haven't changed, you know," I tell him.

"A man doesn't change. Only pretenders do. It doesn't matter what you do, you will always be you. Okay, Dod. I'll be seeing you. Five o'clock sharp. If I am a minute late, you ask for a drink and I'll pay for it when I come."

"This is all in my line, but tell me. This secretary of yours. Who the hell is she? I have. . . . " he cut me short.

"She is my secretary, Dod, and you'd better keep your greedy eyes off her."

72

"Oh I see. Secretary in the office and secretary at home — eh?"

"Ask no questions and you'll get no lies. See you, Dod."

"Okay boss. You can call her and start dictating but I warn you — never trust me with her. Au revoir. I'll keep my fingers crossed."

6

Guess what I am, friend? Open your ears and I'll tell you. Zick — most marvellous Zick. Tremendous Zick. He's been very nice to me. Very nice indeed. He bought me beer and all and then gave me this job. Settlement Officer Grade One, that's what I am on account of my academic qualification. Other mugs who can't write B.A. or B.Sc. after their names are Grade II and that means less dough. I am getting good dough and if you want to know, I like it. I have no goddam self-pity as used to be the case when I was a lousy labour officer or when I lost this job with Shell. As a matter of fact, I am feeling real good and I don't care whether you send me a congratulations card or not. I simply don't care. The only thing I care for is this new job because I mean to keep it.

I am working under this very nice English gentleman who is Senior Settlement Officer for the Kinangops. His name is Stewart and he has a daughter called Sue. That's all he's got — a daughter. Never got married, the poor blighter, and I can never figure out how he came to adopt a child. One would have thought that they wouldn't allow a bachelor to adopt a baby girl but as I say, this guy Stewart was allowed. He is a very nice fellow and probably that explains how. He is very nice to us all and to this daughter of his. He's never told her a lie. The only lie he told when Sue became inquisitive about her mother was that the mother died while giving birth to Sue. The truth is that he doesn't know her mother — whether alive or dead. All the same he is a nice fellow, this Stewart.

I think I am a madman. I have only seen this Sue around here for three weeks and I am working out a comprehensive plan with the sole purpose of giving her a tumble in the near future. Gosh! I am a real lustful bastard for Christ's sake. Can't keep my roving eyes still when there is a gorgeous female around. I have laid white women of course but I imagine that this Sue is going to turn out different. You haven't seen her so you don't know what the hell I am talking about. In fact I would not like you to see her just in case you start getting ideas yourself.

This Sue is around twenty two. She left school and joined nursing but a fat matron had her expelled simply because her husband could not keep his goddam eyes off Sue. The poor blighter nearly got himself hypnotized by her waistline and the matron wife virtually had to drag him off. She complained the following day that Sue was acting sexy in contravention of some lousy nursing code and of course Sue got the axe. She had to leave the damn hospital and decided to stick to the farm and keep farm accounts. That's what she'd been doing till they were bought out by the government and their farm dished out to several smallholder African farmers. Their two thousand acre farm was now divided into one hundred and fifty plots and was supporting one hundred and fifty African families.

Sue very much hated the alienation of their farm. She had never been partial to Africans but now she doesn't care. Sue doesn't care any more. There is this handsome hotel manager at Bell Inn, Naivasha, who has been dating her but he has lately given her the cold shoulder. Every white boy she's ever dated has given her the cold shoulder and you reckon that she is damn bitter about this. No wonder she gives me this I-wouldn't-mind-you-for-a-change type of smile, and poor me, she's getting me really nuts. I am not kidding. Sh'e got me going real crazy but I am afraid of old Stewart. He is very fond of Sue. If he was younger, I suppose he'd tell her the truth and then marry her. He couldn't stand a mug like me hovering around with Sue. Oh no. He would not like me to touch her even with a ten foot pole.

What I am doing, I'll tell you. I have three hundred and sixty nine farmers and I have to settle them on these newly demarcated plots. I organized their ploughing with money-hungry contractors, I purchase livestock for them and then I dish out these animals to them against their loan accounts. I have to organize these fellows into a co-operative society and have to organize even the damn artificial insemination. That kills me. I have watched this Vet. Scout performing the artificial insemination act and I wouldn't like to change places with him for the whole world. Oh no, not me. It's really cheating the cows.

74

I have been at the job for weeks now and this Kinangop place is cold and lonely. I have no friends — I mean real friends — but I know a few punks. There is this Stewart and Sue who are only vaguely my friends. Then there is the Agricultural Instructor who is so dumb that he kills me. The fellow doesn't say a thing and when he does, he sounds damn stupid. A very stupid crank, this fellow. He came to my house last Sunday to borrow my tie clip because he was going to church. Fancy that. He'd walked a long way just to come and borrow my tie clip and when I told him that I didn't have one do you know what the mug said? He asked, "Is that true?" God Almighty! I felt like knocking his teeth out right there but I didn't. I don't do things that I should do so I asked him, "What do you think?"

"I don't think it's true that you have a clip and if it's true then you don't. I mean I am not accusing you."

"And what does that mean, for crying out aloud? What the hell do you mean?" I yelled at him. I was so mad I nearly smacked him, only I didn't.

The crank merely said, "Sorry, Sir" and walked away. He kills me he does. Every time I see him I am ready to puke.

There is this other fellow George, the Vet. Scout. He talks too much and it is always about sex. The other day when we were having beer in this off-licence shop at Njabini, he made everybody roar as he recounted how he used to make love to sheep when he was a kid. He swore that he once tried to have it with a chicken but the damn thing started shitting before he got anywhere. He is real queer, this George. A real phony. Always boasting about the different styles he tries on different women. He is a real bore. A pain in the ass. From sex he switches to artificial insemination and cattle diseases. When the blinking bum gets drunk he turns to politics. You should hear him talk. A real pain in the ass, that's what he is. I am not exaggerating.

I am going to have this fellow George expelled from my area. I am going to have him expelled on account of his being rude to me. The other day we exchanged blows. Fancy that. We actually had a fist fight and then George does not seem to realize that I am his boss. He doesn't think that anybody is his boss. He is the boss around here, that's what he thinks.

What happened was we were having a drink at this Bearno Bar in Naivasha. I have my government Landrover and of course there are a few wogs from my settlement scheme that are waiting for me to drive them home. George is among the crowd and he is as drunk as a coot. He doesn't even know his name. He is staggering all over the place calling himself Dr. George. My ass. Fancy that. He even manages to convince one of the barmaids that he is a doctor but she isn't interested in doctors, so George moves over to where I am sitting.

I am handing a nice spiel to this girl at the counter and she gets as interested as hell. I am telling her what a simple homely guy I am and all the sweet crap you can think of. You can tell from ten miles that this dame would like to mother me. She squeezes my hand when mugs are not looking and we decide to go over to my place after she closes the place at eleven thirty. I am feeling very pleased with myself because this dame is not bad looking. She's just left school and I reckon that she is not spoilt. She looks fresh and respectable if you see what I mean. All is well till George horns in on our company. I'll never forgive him on account of that dame. Do you know what he does?

He moves over and gets hold of the girl's hand. He breathes beer all over her and puts on this drunken stupid smile. And you know what he says? Goodness. I could puke. I really could. He says, "Hey, how about giving me a fuck tonight? I am Dr. George." Christ on a bicycle! Fancy that. I am standing right there and this subordinate of mine doesn't even notice me. I've never felt so murderous.

"Keep your dirty hands off her you son of a bitch," I hiss. "Where are your manners?" I am so mad that I have no words for George. Gosh!

"What did you say?" George asks in contempt.

"That you move yourself from here. I don't like your company. Go and talk to sheep. Just disappear. I am not in the mood to listen to your filthy talk."

There and then George laughs. He is laughing at me. He is laughing like a goddam hyena and I am as mad as satan. Then he says casually, "You shouldn't get so cross, boss. I've fucked her before."

I let him have it. I smack him right behind the ear and he measures his length on the floor. The bastard kicks wildly and lands his kick on a barmaid's ass and she in turn smacks him on the head with her tray. He gets up and starts chasing the barmaid all over the place while I am chasing him. I catch up with him before he catches up with the barmaid and I let him have it again. This time I merely slap his goddam cheeks and you can tell that it smarts. He throws some wild ones at me and only one connects. I give him a real hard football kick in the tummy and he folds over. When I say he folds I mean he folds right to the ground. I then get the hell out of there quick in case the cops come. I don't fancy the dingy ill-smelling cells at the police station. What annoyed me was I didn't take my girl and I couldn't go to sleep. I spent the whole goddam night thinking how I'd like to murder George.

Forget all that muck. It's a thing of the past. It's four o'clock and I am walking towards my house. I have had one hell of a field day allocating plots and clarifying boundaries. I have a whale of an appetite because I skipped my lunch. I am always skipping my lunch and maybe that's why I am getting fat. No kidding. At this rate, I'll weigh two hundred in two months and do I like it? You bet your ass I don't. I don't like it one blinking minute. What with fat behind your neck and your manly tits getting larger and you are bursting your pants because your ass is overgrown. I don't like it. Maybe I'll start skipping dinners too.

I don't like dogs. I can't stand their goddam tails. Dogs should have clipped tails which means no tails at all. Only a stub where the tail used to be. I am walking home past Mr. Stewart's house and this bloodhound of his starts barking at me. The damn dog is coming at me. Gosh, I am scared of dogs. I really am and this bloodhound is coming at me. He is scaring the pants off me but I don't want to run. The damn beast will overtake me and start chewing my ass. He runs right past me and then stops. He is blocking my way and I don't like the goddam teeth that he is exposing for my inspection. I hate dogs' teeth.

I am so scared that I am just about to piss on myself. I am as scared as hell. What I do is I pretend I am not scared. I say to the bloodhound, "Hey, dog, move," in response to which he barks louder and moves closer. Right now I think I'll run. That's what I'll do. I just can't stand there and talk to a deaf dog. But I don't run. My legs won't move. I have grown roots so what I do is I speak to the dog again.

"You heard me, dog? Come on. Be friendly. Master Dodge wouldn't hurt you. Out of the way." I try to edge closer and "Wuh! Wuh!" the dog barks. He is wagging his tail friendly-like but he is barking.

"Shut up, man!" I yell and he merely growls. I know why. I know why he is not barking any more. I hear footsteps behind me and I know that it's some dog's friend.

"C'mon Jock," Sue's voice says behind me. I turn back and she smiles at me. I feel like greeting her with "Hello Saviour" but I don't. Instead I say, "Hello, Miss Susan."

"Hello, Dodge. Did Jock bother you?" she asks.

"In a way, yes. I am not used to dogs. I mean they sort of scare me when they are as big as . . . . What did you say his name was?"

"Jock. He is partly deaf."

"I thought so. Wouldn't get out of the way when I told him to. Anyway, thank you very much. How is Mr. Stewart? I haven't seen him for two days. Is he very busy?"

"He was very busy yesterday writing some reports and he went to Nairobi this morning to present them. He'll be back tomorrow evening."

Jock starts nosing all around me and he scares me. I reckon he is going to give me a bite just for kicks and I don't feel so good. Sue notices that I am not at ease and says, "The best way to make friends with dogs is to treat them like humans. They like that especially when you pat them like little kids. Jock wants to make friends with you."

To tell the truth, I don't care for a dog's friendship. I don't care at all. Trouble is I simply cannot treat a dog as a human. I can't simply say hello to a dog — besides, how the hell do I shake the dog's hand? What with his dirty paws soiling my trousers and all. "I guess you are right," I tell Sue. "Trouble is that from the dog's point of view, you may not be exactly right. I imagine that a dog wants me to behave like a dog before we become real buddies. I don't mind small dogs. You can simply ignore them when they bark at you. But look at Jock. You can't simply ignore him, can you?"

"Oh, I do. Most of the time I ignore him."

"But he doesn't bark at you, does he? I wish he'd ignore me. His teeth are too goddam long for my thin skin. To tell you the truth, he scares the hell out of me, he sure does." She laughs aloud. I couldn't figure out what she was laughing at because I'd cracked no joke.

"You surprise me, Dodge. At your age you shouldn't be scared of dogs even big ones. C'mon. I'll walk you home. If Jock notices that we are friends, he will seek your friendship. He won't bother you again."

Sue walks me home. It's not a long distance and we don't say much. She picks small stones and throws them ahead and Jock retrieves them. They are both very happy and are enjoying the game. I decide that the next time Jock barks at me, I'll merely get hold of a stone and hurl it as far as I can and while he goes to retrieve it, I put some distance between him and me.

For experiment, I pick a stone and throw it a few yards in front of us but Jock doesn't make a move. He merely looks at Sue as if to ask, "Who the hell is this crank?"

78

We get to my house — I mean to the gate — and Sue says, "See you tomorrow." She says it suddenly and I sort of look for a word to say and finally blurt out something.

"Tea. Let's have some tea. I have some tea — I mean I would like to invite you for tea."

"Really?" She raises her eyebrows and there is this mischievous smile all over her face and I am beginning to sweat.

"Sure, I have no cook. I'll make it myself."

"Oh, that's very kind of you. I'd like to know how you brew your tea."

We get into the house and I ask her to sit down instead of which she moves over to the book shelf and starts inspecting my books. They are all geography text books and lots of cheap novels. She gets thoroughly involved and as she squats in front of the shelf, she is not minding her dress. It has pulled right back and I am just about to collapse on the floor staring at those white thighs of hers. I am a sexy bastard that's what I am. Nice thighs just about hypnotize me. I mean it really. No kidding. The truth is I have forgotten about the goddam tea. Come to think about it, I have no tea in this place. It's damn inconvenient to a bachelor, this tea business, so I naturally specialize in instant coffee. All you have to do with the goddam coffee is boil water and have it black. You don't have to have milk and I never have milk in this house. Tea needs milk and what-have-you — pots and things — not forgetting the residue. I hate tea especially when I have to brew it for myself.

"You've got quite a collection of books," says Sue.

"What?"

"You've got quite a collection of nice books," she repeats.

"Oh, sure. Eh — of course they are not all good. Some are positively lousy. I like reading lousy books though. Do you like Perry Mason?"

"Not particularly. Those stories are nearly all the same. Perry Mason wins every case doesn't he? I mean it would be more interesting if he lost some cases. If you don't know how the case will end you get more interested don't you?"

"You are right," I tell her, "but I like them all the same. Makes you get inquisitive and in the type of work I am doing I have to cross-examine farmers — I mean I have to subject them to a thorough interview."

"That's interesting. I never thought about it that way. I'll help you make tea." I am cursing myself for having offered her tea. I don't want to take her to my kitchen either. I haven't washed dishes for the past three days and there's last night's left-overs sitting right on top of the cooker. What the hell shall I do?

"Tell you what. I am very absent-minded. I'd forgotten that I finished all my stock this morning. I must remember to buy some tomorrow but do you mind coffee? I have some coffee. Hope you wouldn't mind." I am feeling like the ass I really am. I can't help feeling that she knows I am lying.

"Oh, don't bother," she says. "I don't particularly like coffee at this time. Don't bother unless you want some yourself."

"How about a drink? I agree with you that it's a bit too warm for coffee. A drink will do fine," I tell her.

"It's too early for a drink."

"Oh no. It's never too early for a drink," I protest.

"All right. What have you got?" she asks.

"Whisky, beer, and some Cinzano."

"Do you have ginger ale?"

"Yeah."

"Give me a little whisky and ginger ale." I get very busy mixing Sue this drink and I give myself a big beer. We sit opposite each other and she is looking at me over the rim of her glass as she sips the whisky.

"Why are you not married?" she asks.

"What?" I couldn't believe my ears. She says everything so suddenly.

"Why are you not married?"

"Well, I'll be damned if I know. Why do you ask?"

"I was merely wondering whether you got married once and then divorced or something. You look like you've been married once."

Fancy that. I look like I have been married once. Gosh. What a thing to say. What the hell do I look like anyway? What makes Sue think that I look like a retired husband? Tell me. Please tell me. Me, I don't know. I don't even know what to tell her.

"I don't know what made you think that. I have never been married. Really. I nearly got married once but I didn't. That is the nearest I got. One fine day in the not very distant future, I'll probably get married if I find a nice girl."

"What happened to the girl you nearly married?" she asks.

"What, which one?"

"Are there many?"

"Oh, I see what you mean. Oh no. She's only one. You can't get married to many girls at a time, can you?"

"I suppose not. What happened to her?"

80

"Got married, that's what she did. Got married to a bloody butcher. Really! The fellow was a bloody butcher. I can never forgive her."

"That's not fair. Maybe the butcher had more to offer."

"What has a bloody butcher got to offer? Tell me that. What can a fat bloody butcher offer? I'd like to know. I hate butchers." I reckon I am getting all excited.

"You are prejudiced," she says calmly. "Naturally you would feel bitter about it. I don't blame you. Is that the only girl who gave you a jolt?"

"Oh no, there was this other one who got married to an Englishman. I don't blame her. Trouble is, all my life has been one hell or another."

"Imaginary hell. None of us are satisfied by what we are. We'd rather be somebody else and we'd rather be doing something else. That is the trouble with mankind. We'd all rather be what we are not. What do your parents do?"

"They do nothing. I mean I haven't any. I am what you'd call an orphan. I have been alone all my goddam life. That's why I wouldn't know how to rear kids if I got married," I tell her.

"What happened to them — I mean your parents?"

We go on talking for a long time but you can be sure that I don't tell her that my mother was a whore. I invent this story about my father being a major and how he was killed in the second war while fighting in Burma and how I was a mere kid at the time the lousy Japs bombed their camp and lots of other crap I wouldn't tell you about.

"That is funny," Sue tells me. "I thought they didn't promote Kenya Africans to the rank of Major during the second world war. Sergeant Major was supposed to be the highest rank." Heck! How the hell would I know that. She's either right or wrong but of course I couldn't tell which. Such things never bother me. Trouble is that I am one hell of a liar. I can't help lying. So I have to cover up. "You are right. Dad was the only Major."

I proceed to tell her about my childhood and the story I am telling is ninety-nine percent phoney. The only thing which is true in it is my name. I am enjoying myself. In case you don't know, lying is very exciting. You are always on the look out for possible traps and all and each lie has to support the other lie. If you are not experienced you get caught and of course you've got to be very witty. I am witty. I think I am a witty bastard but maybe I am lying about that too. You wouldn't know.

I learnt lying from this Muganda friend of mine. His name was Chris and he was a real witty fellow. He'd been kicked out of his home by his parents on account of forging their cheques. They'd sent him to America but he'd been shipped right back under guard because he forged some guy's cheque in America. He'd tried one job after another but he'd never stick. He'd pinch something or try to take the boss's wife to bed and of course he'd get the sack.

The first time I met him I didn't know a thing about him. The blighter was jobless but he was driving a car. He told me that he was an Area Marketing Manager for East African Tobacco, Uganda. He told me how he'd risen from a simple salesman in a very short time. The reason he gave was that he had a Masters Degree in Commerce and that he was a real marketing genius. I had no cause to doubt his story. The following day he came to my college — I mean my hall of residence — and brought me ten packs of State Express 555 and told me a lot of crap about meeting the Kabaka, the Buganda king, at his palace. He left in a hurry on account that he was getting late for the Kabaka's appointment but guess what? I went downtown soon after and I found him at this bar they call Gardenia. When I asked him whether he'd had dinner with the Kabaka he said casually, "I found him necking with my fianceé. I've never felt so mad. I didn't say a word. I merely walked out."

Then he proceeded to tell me what a lousy lustful bastard the Kabaka was.

Anyway Chris was nice. A very nice fellow. I thought he was, till he forged my cheque. He apologized like mad but the matter was in the hands of the police. They put him in the can for six months. During the short time I knew him I learnt a lot of lies. I feel sorry for him though. They shouldn't have put him in jail, considering how much he taught me.

It is this Chris stuff that I am handing over to Sue and she is licking it with her tongue. She has taken five whiskies and I have taken three beers. She is giggling like a kid and I am grinning like the rogue that I am. I reckon whisky is good stuff for women. They sip a few fingers and they start giggling. I like giggling girls. It doesn't matter whether they are ugly or not, when they giggle they look good. Sue is not ugly so you can bet she looks like something you'd like to eat. I mean it. I'd like to eat her here and now but how? Tell me that. Just tell me how you'd go about eating a woman.

Sue takes two more whiskies and I turn on the small transistor radio. There is a lousy Swahili record playing and I switch over to

82

English medium and this time I am lucky. Nat King Cole is singing about this fascination which turned to love and I love it. It's a good song but it's goddam slow for dancing. In case you don't know, I am one hell of a good dancer. I used to be a dancing instructor at Makerere. They had this lousy ballroom dancing club called 'Mabada' where we'd do bull dancing twice a week and go to Mulago Hospital to dance with trainee nurses on weekends. I only instructed the bull dancing though. At Mulago the boys and the nurses were left to tread on each other's toes as much as they damn well pleased. It was more of a dating arrangement than a ballroom dancing club. Anyway, I was a damn good instructor and that was great in those days.

Sue is swaying with the music and I ask her for a dance. She gets up immediately and we sort of sway on the same spot because this music is goddam slow. Well, you know what I am going to say next but I'll say it all the same. This swaying from side to side is really raising hell inside me. I am as sexy as the devil and I wish I had the guts to administer a brief kiss on Sue's purpled lips. They are parted and all and I reckon that she needs a kiss as much as I do but I am a yellow coward. That's what I am. A damn coward. I never seem to get started doing things.

We've been dancing and drinking for the last hour. We are now drunk and I am afraid the damn drink is getting out of stock. I have only one beer left and a little whisky for Sue. It's dinner time, but Sue does not seem to care. She doesn't care. She doesn't care because old Stewart is not at home. He will not be home until tomorrow. That's why she can afford to horse around with me. I am of course considering myself a very lucky bastard because next time it will be easier. I swear to God that I'll be brave the next time an opportunity occurs.

We are dancing this very slow waltz and Sue has her head on my shoulder. We are dancing so close that her tits are sort of spread on my chest. God!
Sue moves her head slightly and we are now dancing cheek to cheek. I have my eyes shut and I am dreaming about the glories in heaven. I don't know how it happens but our cheeks automatically move in different directions — very slowly of course and before I know, our lips touch. Just a brief gentle touch like a passing wind and our eyes meet. Again you know what happens. I stand there like a man in a trance completely hypnotized by the blue in her eyes. Gosh, you have never seen such transparent eyes. Our lips touch and the rest is darkness.

It's like a dream. A heavenly dream. We don't even go to bed. We have it out right there on the goddam hard floor. I am wiping sweat off my face and getting my trousers organized when there is this loud knock on the door. She combs her hair like mad and I am wiping the dust off the back of her dress. As I go to the door, I am wiping the dust off my blinking knees and goddam it, they are hurting. This floor of mine is real hard.

I jerk open the door and nearly have a fit. Old Stewart is standing squarely in the doorway and Jock is behind him. There is murder written all over Stewart's face and by Jingo I'd like to run. Gosh! I wish I was eight feet underground.

"Is Miss Susan here?" Stewart asks and I nod. I nod because I have lost my blinking voice.

"Come in," I manage to say. He comes in and fixes his eyes on Sue. There is guilt written all over her face. She can't face him. He spits and then turns over to stare at me.

"You swine!" he swears and before I know it he's hit me so hard that all I remember is hitting the floor. Damn him.

7

Am I lucky or am I? You thought that old Stewart would give me the sack or something didn't you? Well you were wrong. He is my boss but he don't do no sacking. No sir. That is done in Nairobi and this buddy of mine Zick is the boss where sacking is concerned.

What I did, I telephoned Zick first thing in the morning and told him the whole works. It wasn't yesterday, oh no. It was two months ago. I have since been transferred to this new settlement scheme they call Sabugo in Dundori. My Senior Settlement Officer is an African and he has no adopted grown up daughters. I am not likely to get kicked out of here. Oh yes, I was saying that I phoned Zick. You should have heard him. He congratulated me and all and wished he had been in my boots. Trouble with Zick is that he's never laid a white woman. I don't blame him for getting excited. In fact he is always excited about one thing or another. Anyway Zick told me that everything would be O.K.

Stewart was mad like he'd gone crazy. He called Sue all the nasty names you could think of and they had a fight. A real fight. She slapped him when he called her a base slut and he slapped her back and she slapped him again and he slapped her back and she slapped him again and he slapped her back and she slapped him again and again and again. He was crying and she was crying and they were both crying. Crying real tears. I mean it. He was crying for one reason and she was crying for a different reason.

He telephoned the director straight and demanded my immediate dismissal on grounds of gross misconduct. He made it very clear in no vague terms that he would not tolerate me in his area. It was either him or me.

The matter was referred to Zick who ruled that since Mr. Stewart could not substantiate what he referred to as gross misconduct and since Mr. Stewart had stated that he could not work with me any longer the only alternative was to transfer me. I was given one week after which I was to report to the Senior Settlement Officer, Dundori.

Before I left I gave Sue another lay in the bush just to get even with Stewart. We also made a nice arrangement whereby we'd meet in Nakuru at the end of the month and go flamingo watching and do any other damn thing we pleased. Trouble with Stewart is he didn't realize that Sue was a young woman full of sex and that whatever you did she'd have to have it out with some bloke or other. He can be very blind, Mr. Stewart, and I haven't forgotten the blow he gave me right in my house. Never thought the old geezer was so strong. Damn him.

Now I am at this Sabugo place. It's as lonely as hell and the only consolation is that Nakuru is near. It's less than thirty minutes by Landrover and that is where I go for my after-work pint of beer.. What I do is, I drive to town and then hide the Landrover somewhere. It's a government Landrover and I can't simply park it outside a bar. It's an offence to use a government vehicle for private purposes but they are not very strict if you don't park it outside a bar. Usually you get away with it and I do not care to be holed up in that old bleak and lonely house that they have given me at Sabugo. Oh no! Not me. I like to go places. I like to discover places and dames. I have been in Sabugo for two months and I know Nakuru in and out. I can walk the streets blindfold if you believe me which I am sure you don't. If you do, you are nuts.

What I am doing right now is that I am resting on my bed. I've just had a heavy lunch and I am as sleepy as a snail. They are very sleepy creatures, snails. At least whenever I see a snail the damn creature is sleeping or just dozing. I can never tell which. I am staring at the ceiling and wondering why I took lunch. I am supposed to be slimming you know.

A funny thing happened yesterday afternoon. It's another thing I am thinking about. It was four o'clock and I was driving to Nakuru. I had to be there by four thirty because there is this engineer's secretary that I am interested in. I know that if I don't catch her by the time she leaves the office, I shall not catch her at all. I don't know the place where she lives. As I pass the Military Training School at Lanet this woman waves her hand frantically and nearly gets into the middle of the road. I think she is really nuts. When I stop the Landrover she doesn't say a word to me. She merely hops into the Landrover and bangs the door shut.

"Well?" I inquire raising my eyebrows and folding my face like a clown.

"Drive on," she says.

"Where?" I am even more surprised.

"Anywhere. Just drive somewhere. Get me the hell out of here. Just drive somewhere."

"I am going to town," I tell her.

"Drive there then," she hisses. God, if there is anything I hate it is women hissing. I just can't stand a hissing woman. Gives me a pain in the ass, that's what it does. What in the name of the devil does this hissing woman think? That I am her husband or something? Blimey. I face her casually and explain slowly and clearly.

"This is a government vehicle. Government vehicles are not insured. When you are in this vehicle you are not insured. If anything should happen to you while you are in this vehicle, I'd have to stand the responsibility. That is why we are not allowed to give rides to members of the public. That is why I can't give you a ride. I am sorry but I can't take you. There's a bus coming."

"You must be out of your mind," she says, "but if you'd like to know, I am a government servant myself."

"That is no reason why I should give you a ride, is-it? If you want a favour you ask for it politely but you don't have to hiss, do you? I mean you simply cannot command me to drive you, can you?"

"O. K. Drive on please. I am desperate. I want to be far away from here. If you want me to say please, I am saying it and I'll say it again. Just get moving."

I think that this woman is a madman. She doesn't look like a mad woman at all. She looks like a madman. I ease the clutch and we are on

86

our way. I've already wasted precious time but how the hell would I know beforehand that I would meet a madman — or a mad woman if that's what you'd like to call her. I am somehow amused and I start whistling to myself. She looks at me sideways and I reckon she hates me. She hates everything, this madman. I don't like the way she looks at my pointed shoes. When we get to the Nairobi/Nakuru mainroad I am forced to stop because there is a lot of traffic to and fro. My passenger gets very impatient. I ask her what the matter is and I get no answer. I am thinking that I would like to hit her on the mouth. No kidding. I'd like to wallop her just for kicks.

I get the vehicle moving and I drive slowly. I drive slowly because we have five miles to go and I reckon that this dame has a long story to tell if only I can get her started.

"Did somebody bully you or something?" I ask.

"Why do you expect me to talk to you?" she asks.

"Because if you don't, I'll stop this vehicle right here and you can walk the rest of the distance. If you don't want to talk to people then you should not get into their company. You should lock yourself up." I am really steamed up.

"Thank you for the tip," she says. Gosh! I am almost blind with rage.

"You are mad, aren't you? I mean you are a madman aren't you? I mean — oh God, you know what I damn well mean, don't you?"

"No."

"Right. You don't know. Of course you wouldn't know, oh no. But tell me. Why are you like that? I mean why are you not happy? Why are you rude to me? Why can't you appreciate that I am doing you a favour? Surely there's something wrong with you. You must appreciate that." Then she laughed. She laughed outright as if she was a kid and I'd reminded her where she'd hid her missing toy. She just laughed and I nearly went into the ditch looking at her.

"You are all the same. The whole lot of you. Men are just grown up babies. You are all the same," she says.

"And what is wrong with all men being the same?" I ask.

"Nothing except that you can be very boring to women."

"Am I boring you?"

"Figure that out for yourself," she tells me and I don't like it the way she says it. She's damn irritating and the most boring woman I ever met. I am always meeting boring women.

I am tired of this woman and therefore decide that I won't say a

word to her. I decide that I'll tell her what I think of her and that will
be the end of the whole goddam conversation.

"Listen," I say. "You bore me. You are a terrible bore and I am
bored. That's all. I am bored and I don't want to listen to you any more.
Your problem is none of my business. Just tell me where you want
to drop when we get to town but don't say anything else to me."
I sound like a general giving orders.

I drop her by this bar they call Amigos and I proceed to meet my
girl. This girl is Kisii but she speaks Kikuyu perfectly. Most of the
time we talk Kikuyu. I met her at this horrifying movie Dracula
which I was seeing for the second time. She happened to be sitting
next to me. The goddam horror movie really horrified me but it was
scaring the shit off her ass. Every time Dracula opened his fanged
mouth to take a bite at somebody this Kisii girl would turn her eyes
away from the screen and hold me tight. The first time she did it I
nearly screamed. I thought she'd bite me. Anyway we sat there and got
ourselves horrified until I couldn't stand it any longer. I can't stand
horror films for long even if it's the second time I am seeing them.
I had to leave. I told this girl and she told me that she could not stand
it any longer either so we went out together.

It was drizzling outside and so I gave her a ride to the taxi stand
near the market. She told me that her name was Stella and that she
worked for the Town Engineer and that her father was Kisii but her
mother was Kikuyu. Instead of getting a taxi we just sat in the
Landrover and talked. I told her all the lies that you'd normally tell
a girl you'd met for the first time. In the end we kissed and I escorted
her to a taxi.

I promised to meet her the following day which was yesterday
and I did. Nothing happened though. We went to another movie at the
Odeon and I didn't like it either. It was this movie 'Attila the Hun'
where Anthony Quinn acts real primitive. I can't seem to like the
Huns anyway. They are a damn greedy lot. Again I escorted Stella to
the taxi rank and off she went. She didn't want me to drive her home
the reason being that she did not want her mother to see me. Very
corny excuse I'd call it. This Stella is not exactly a baby. I promised
to meet her again today and I am hoping that she'll be waiting because
I am already late. This madman woman I dropped at Amigos is the
cause.

Anyway I don't meet Stella. I look around the Town Hall and
make a few enquiries and I learn that she'd already left. I hang around
and after thirty minutes I decide that Stella will not turn up. I am all
nerves and I don't know what to do next. What I do is I drive to the

88

nearest Agip service station and park the Landrover. I wander to
a nearby cafe and order myself a stiff whisky after which I change
to Pilsner lager.

I reckon that all I'll do is get myself juiced and then drive home
at ten. That would be fine. I go upstairs and start playing darts with
this thin Tobacco man and he beats me two to one. I don't like skinny
guys beating me at any game so I buy this fellow a drink. He is very
nice this Tobacco fellow. His name is Job but I'd like to call him
Joshua. He looks like the Joshua of the Old Testament, this Joshua
who was a follower of Moses. Like him Job follows only one leader.
His name is Tobacco.

At about eight I have swallowed about eight pints and I am
feeling as good as any drunk. I order myself a Masala beef with green
vegetables and if you like to know it's a rotten meal. I ain't feeling so
good after the meal so I get the hell out of there. I walk back to this
Agip service station and drive like mad to the Midland Hotel. The
place is as dull as a wall so I proceed to this Amigos place.

The madman woman is sitting right there at the bar all by herself.
She's drinking out of a big mug and the mug is full. There are no
customers. The place is deserted. There is a fellow talking to a whore
in the corner and I reckon that he is also a whore. He is still wearing
a hat and these dark green goggles. I reckon he is a madman.

I go over to the bar and order myself a Pilsner. I am standing
right next to this woman but I'd sworn not to speak to her at all.
Trouble is there is this bar mirror right in front of us and I can't help
looking at her. She's pretending not to look at me in the mirror and
that suits me fine. I produce a pack of fags and out of habit I offer
her one.

"No thank you. I don't smoke," she says. "Where did you go?"
She doesn't look the same. Drink has done her some good. Right now
she looks like a woman. A real woman, soft and all. She sounds almost
apologetic.

"Places," I tell her.

"Let me pay for your drink," she says. I swear to God that women
are always taking me by surprise.

"No thanks," I tell her. "I still have some bucks in my rear
pocket."

"Please."

"O.K. I'll save my bucks."

"Are you still mad with me?"

"You bet I am."

"With all that drink showing all over your face?"

"Drink makes me very mad."

"Oh, but you are smiling."

"Of course I am smiling. What the hell am I expected to do. Cry or something? Thanks for the drink."

"Cheers."

"Cheers. Here's to you. And what have you been doing to yourself ever since I left you?"

"Getting drunk," she says. Damn it man. When a woman sits by herself in a bar and simply gets drunk you can bet your life there is something wrong. There's something damn wrong. This woman wears a wedding ring and I suppose she should be warming her husband's bed. Women are funny.

"Sorry I didn't get to know you this afternoon. Is it pertinent to ask what they call you?"

"Margaret. Margaret Kunga."

"Is Kunga your husband?"

"He was till this afternoon."

"Say that again."

"He was my husband till this afternoon," she repeats.

"Did he die or something?"

"Oh no. He is alive."

"You got a divorce then?"

"Oh, no. It will not be necessary."

"I don't understand," I tell her. "A guy cannot be your husband one minute and a non-husband the next minute, can he? You just can't stop being married like that; I mean you can't simply unmarry yourself just by wish. You'd have to kill him or divorce him or something."

"I see what you mean but it's not like that. Legally, he is still my husband but we are quits. Don't remind me of it. I could vomit. The filthy swine. Oh no, I can never forgive him. Are you married?"

"No."

"Let me tell you one thing. When you get married there are things you should do and things you should never do. You can't have it both ways. You can't go with other women openly and expect happiness at home. My husband was an absolute pig. A scavenger for women. I knew it all along but I had never caught him. Other people talked about it but I was deaf. I had to get the ocular proof. Then it happened. He gave me V.D. He told me that he got it from some swimming pool where prostitutes used to swim but I knew that was all crap. You don't get V.D. from swimming pools. That was six months ago and I let it go at that. I forgave him." She stopped and

90

took a long pull at her drink. I am enjoying myself and I am also beginning to understand.

"Today was the last straw. I left for Naivasha to go and see my ailing mother. That's where I come from. I got a ride to the main road and stood for long minutes waiting for a bus. There was a strong wind which was undoing my hair and I started looking for my comb. The comb was in my handbag all right but my wallet was not. I'd left it on the dressing table. I cursed and started walking home. I couldn't get a lift. I got home tired and sweating and naturally opened the door with my key. My husband was on duty and we'd given our house-girl an off-duty. Guess what I found?"

"Tell me. It sounds exciting."

"If you think it's exciting, I don't. My husband and the house girl were there right on the bed. They weren't just lying there or playing, they were actually fornicating. You can't imagine it. Not even if you try. They were both in the nude and he was right on top of her. Worst thing they didn't hear me. They didn't suspect my presence. They were too engrossed to hear me open the door. Oh God! It's the ugliest sight you ever saw in your life. They just went on while I looked on glued to the floor. I couldn't scream or anything. I was practically paralyzed. At last it was over and my husband noticed me. God, I'd like to laugh."

"Why?"

"You should have seen him. The girl fainted outright but you should have seen my husband. First he tried to hide under the mattress but that wasn't good enough. Second he went under the bed but came out as quickly as he'd gone in. Thirdly, he tried to jump through the window but there are iron bars. Only a kid can go through but he tried. I bet he bruised his shoulders. It was then that he realized that he was nude and he started looking for something to wear. He went from place to place like a mad person and in the end he yelled out, 'Where are my trousers?' I pointed at the trousers but instead of picking them up he stood and stared at me. 'Get out!' he shouted, but I remained where I was. He picked up his trousers and put them on and then he had the cheek to smile at me. 'How is Naivasha?' he asked. Fancy that. He had the guts to ask me that with the fainted girl lying there right on my bed. He noticed that I was looking at her and he dashed to the bed and threw her right on the floor. She let out a cry and woke up. She got up and on seeing me she started fighting my husband. 'Why did you do this to me, you lecher?' She was cursing. I moved in, took my wallet, my cheque book and our marriage certificate and walked out. You know the rest. You found me on the road and gave me a ride."

"It's rather sad, isn't it?"

"You're telling me. Please have another drink."

"Oh no thanks," I protest. "I've had one too many."

"Oh come on. One for the road. You wouldn't want to leave me here alone would you?"

"What will you do now? I mean I'll have a drink but what will you do?" I ask her.

"What would you do if you were me?" she asks. That hit me. What the hell would I do if I was in her boots. I couldn't simply go back to my husband and ask him to apologize. Nor would you.

"You tell me. I don't have the vaguest idea."

"I have brooded for a long time but now my brooding days are over. I'd have to be like my husband for me to understand him. I'd have to be as bad as he is. At least that would ease my conscience. If dirt is the only food available damn it man, eat it. I am not going to be discreet any more."

"It's rather difficult to change yourself. If you are decent by nature you simply cannot change. It would hurt you and you alone."

"I don't agree with you. Hey, what is your name?"

"Dodge. Dodge Kiunyu and best known to my friends as Dod."

"Are you decent?"

"What the hell do you mean?"

"According to your own standards of decency, do you think you are decent?"

"I'll be damned if I know. I suppose I am."

"Right. I have booked a room in this hotel. Suppose I asked you as a matter of urgency to make love to me over there in room fifteen. Would you?"

"What would you want to ask me that for?" I ask her.

"But would you? Tell me the truth. Would you? Would you help me get even with my husband?" You reckon that this is going too far. Too goddam far for my liking. Is she asking me just for the sake of argument or does she actually mean it? God! What would you say if you were me? Tell me. Them goddam women are always saking me difficult questions. So I say, "I would, but you wouldn't get even. You'd have to get a houseboy. Then you'd have to give him V.D. or something."

I didn't go home last night. I slept in the Amigos place with Margaret. As I lie on this goddam bed of mine in this Sabugo place and stare at the ceiling and curse myself for having taken so much

92

lunch I am also thinking that some men can be mugs. If a punk is prepared to exchange Margaret for a housegirl, then that punk is a mug. She's really got it, by God she has. I nearly asked her to marry me.

It's high time I got off this goddam bed and started doing something. Trouble with me is that I like to lie on the bed and reflect on past events. I met Margaret yesterday, had a whole night with her but I can't get her off my mind. That's my weakness. I can't get women off my mind. I am always thinking about one woman or another. What I can't understand is why I don't think about men. No man I know of is worth thinking about. They are all dull except Zick but I don't think about Zick either. Whenever he comes to my mind that secretary of his also enters and sort of pushes Zick out. I am hoping that Zick will never get to know about it. The only time I don't think about women is when they are ugly and their husbands are handsome.

There is this interesting fellow from the Coast who calls himself Salim Ali. He works for the creameries and draws a good salary. He got some lousy degree from America or maybe he didn't get one. What he says is that he got one but when you ask him what he read he gives you a list of twenty subjects. Very funny, this Ali fellow. During the course of two years he has wrecked eight cars and no insurance company will agree to insure him. He is small in size but he talks as if he was a real big tough fellow. One day he threatened to beat me up if I didn't keep my trap shut. He drinks like a fish and starts fights whenever he can. Most times he gets beaten. Whenever he is beaten he goes home and gives his wife a few blows just to get even with the guy who beat him up. Very funny this Ali. A very funny fellow.

The reason why he beats his wife is that he thought she was a virgin when they got married but she wasn't. To make it worse, they were married only two months when the mother-in-law came up with a four-year-old boy and found Ali at home.

"This is my daughter's child," the old woman says. "I cannot afford to go on looking after him seeing that his mother is so happily married. Take him. He is your son too."

Poor Ali had no words. He asked his mother-in-law to wait a while till his wife came from the market. He couldn't believe it. He couldn't believe that his wife was capable of such dishonesty. He simply could not believe it. The truth was confirmed by his wife when she came in. Hugged the kid she did, and then asked her mother, "Why didn't you tell us you were coming?"

"I couldn't get a kindly soul to write a letter for me and you forgot to send me money for the boy. A boy should grow up with his parents."

Ali walked out. He banged the door very hard. He drove his car like mad and went to Kays bar. He ordered scotch after scotch till the place closed. He drove off to Kiambu bar and drank more scotch. By six thirty he'd taken so much scotch that all he needed was a kilt and he'd start blowing bagpipes. As he staggered to the door he thought that it might be a good idea to go home and beat up his wife but changed his mind on account of her mother. Instead, he went to a nearby cafe and got this very old whore. He drove her to her place and gave her ten quid for a lay just for the heck of it. A very funny guy, this Ali.

When I think about Ali and Margaret I sort of evolve a philosophy. It's a good philosophy especially if you are thinking of getting married. If your wife suspects that you are getting sweet on some other female she'll go some place and ask a mug to do her a favour. You'd better watch out friend. Next time it could be you.

I get out of the goddam bed and trudge to the office. It's thirty minutes after two and I am still sleepy. I wish I didn't have to work, I really do. I wish I could just sleep and get paid for it. That way I'd never get late for work which is what I am always doing. I never seem to get to the office on time.

I get to my office and take my seat. Trouble is that there is not enough goddam work in this office. I did everything in the morning. I just sit there and smoke and read the newspaper all over again. I look at the crossword puzzle and curse myself for having done it in the morning. Truth is that there are lots of odd jobs that I could interest myself in but I am not bothered. I don't feel like doing anything at all.

I get hold of the phone and give Stella a buzz. Says she is not available this evening, that's what she says. I reckon that she isn't interested in Dod. Maybe there is a rich blighter stuck on her and she was merely pulling wool over my eyes. So what? I am meeting Margaret at eight at the Amigos place and Stella can go gold-digging for all I care. Trouble with me is that I am selfish. I don't mind saying no to a woman but it depresses my ass when she gives me the cold shoulder. I am very lucky with some women and very unlucky with others. You can't always be lucky or unlucky can you, friend? The answer is yes and no. It takes care of everything, that little answer. It takes care of everything because it's not an answer at all.

I get hold of the phone again and telephone Jack Back at his farm in Elmentaita. He is an old farmer who is leaving the country and we are purchasing his Guernsey herd for the Sabugo farmers.

94

I have been over to his farm on several occasions discussing prices
and we have made a damn good arrangement. Jack is a rogue. He is a
real rogue. I am not kidding. Also he stinks with money. He's got
sacks of it. He has given me a very good idea but I am afraid I can't
disclose it to you. It's top secret and you might be friendly with the
cops.

"Hello, Jack, this is Dodge."

"Hello, would you pleath wait a thecond." It's Jack all right and
I know what he is doing. He is looking for his false teeth. He had all
his teeth removed on account of some trouble in his tummy and so he
wears a complete set of false teeth. He hates them like mad and most
of the times he just stays without them. He looks very funny then and
lisps so badly you can hardly hear what he is talking about. He comes
back on the phone and I can hear that this time he's got them teeth.

"Hello, young man, what is the trouble now?"

"No trouble, Jack. I just thought I should say hello to you and,
of course to confirm about tomorrow."

"What is there to confirm? I thought everything was confirmed.
Are you getting yellow or what?"

"Oh no, I just rang to say hello."

"Where are you going tonight?"

"Nowhere. I never go nowhere. I mean I stay at home. I am broke
remember."

"Yes, I know. You are always broke. Would you like to come
round for a drink this evening?"

"Sure, I never say no to a drink," I tell him.

"Come along at seven. You can bring a woman if you like but
if you do, please remember me. I can also do with a woman, you
know."

"Not at the age of seventy for Chrissake. What would you want
a woman for?"

"No harm I assure you. I merely touch them and remember how
good it used to be. It gives me lots of kicks just imagining that. Will
you bring some?"

"I'll try. I can't promise to get decent ones."

"I have no use for decent ones. They don't want to be touched.
See you at seven." He hangs up and I hang up. I think this Jack is
funny. Very funny.

8

I ain't no mug friend, I swear I ain't. Never thought I was a mug till this Jack of Elementaita really pulled wool over my goddam eyes. I'll never forgive myself for getting fooled by an old blighter like Jack. Don't confuse this Jack with my old teacher Jack. Oh no. They are not the same person. My teacher Jack was very black and displayed an overdose of negroid blood in the shape of his nose. This other Jack is typical nordic. His hair would be blonde if he had any but he hasn't. Not a tuft. His head is like an inverted copper kettle with ears for handles and nose for a spout. Very funny looking this cheating Jack. He looks even funnier when he's forgotten his teeth.

For cunning, Jack is a fox. I don't mean like a fox. He is the fox itself — that's what I mean. There is this secret I wasn't going to tell you about but Jack has bugged the works. He's left me holding the can. I reckon I'd have to tell you anyway.

There were these three hundred cows I was going to purchase from Jack for dishing out to new African farmers. On account that he is leaving the country he has not been feeding them properly. We agreed on an average fixed price of six hundred shillings per cow and government would, therefore, pay him some one hundred and eighty thousand shillings. Jack gave me an idea. A dirty idea. He told me I was green and stupid and that I did not know how to make money. This is what he told me.

"Listen, young chap, and don't quote me. Suppose between me and you the price is six hundred but between you and me and the government we make it seven hundred. That's a hundred bob per cow and thirty thousand shillings for the lot. A clean thirty thousand over and above my fair share. Suppose we shared this sum fifty fifty and you had a cool fifteen thousand, don't you think that would buy you some toothpaste?"

The whole idea dawned on me and I nearly jumped to heaven.

Of course it could be done. Jack would get his cheque and he'd turn over to me fifteen thousand bob. Gosh. It's good money and if you'd like to know, I don't have a goddam conscience where money like that is involved. It's cheating but so what?

Jack got his cheque a week ago and I have been ringing him every day. First time he said O.K. he was going to make a cheque in my favour and post it. Next time I rang he hold me that he'd already sent the cheque. Third time he told me that he'd used the wrong address and would I please go to his farm on Sunday and collect the cheque personally.

I go to his farm on Sunday and I am told that he went to Nairobi on Saturday and when I ring on Monday, Jack tells me to go to hell. Fancy that. The old rogue told me to go to hell and he wasn't kidding. I have never been so mad in my life. I couldn't believe it. I couldn't believe that the fellow had cheated me of some fifteen thousand just like that. Oh God. A fellow says "Go to hell" and before the words are out of his mouth fifteen thousand is lost. I'll murder him. That's what I'll do. I'll just take this Masai club I hide under the bed and pay him a visit. No preliminaries. He'll open the door and I'll club him. If he can't share the money with me he'll have to share it with the worms. I wish them joy — I mean the worms.

It is a public holiday today and I am again at Thomson's Cafe. I have treated myself to four pints but I can't get Jack out of my mind. I simply cannot stop my stupid head thinking about him. The bastard does not need the money. He doesn't need a single cent. If he squandered five hundred shillings every day and lived to be eighty he simply couldn't finish half of what he has in the bank. What does a crank like that want to deprive me of fifteen thousand for? I can't understand some people. I simply can't. When I think about that dog in a manger story I conclude that Jack is the dog.

I am drowning my sixth pint when Josephine turns up. Josy is this girl I took to Jack three weeks ago when he called me for a drink. Jack gave her ten quid because she let him pinch her tits and later she played with his dead prick. He is very generous this Jack but so is Josy. She knows him and also knows that he is harmless. They call poor Jack "discharged batteries" and while I agree with them, I would not like to be known by that name if I was in Jack's place.

Josy comes over to me all smiles and says, "Hi, Dod" and I say, "Hi". I feel like telling her how she and her lousy old man are cheats but I reckon that I am merely jealous. I am jealous because Jack gave her ten quid for nothing while he wouldn't give me a cent on an even deal. The bastard knows that I can't go to court or raise the issue anywhere.

It's merely one thief stealing from another. I reckon that Josy is O.K. but she is too goddam nosy. She's always asking you to buy her a drink. If you buy her one she wants another one and when you get broke she goes to another mug. That is cheating, isn't it?

I am very clever with Josy. I never buy her a drink outright. I wait till she's drunk from other mugs and then I wink. She always comes over but then she always manages to ditch me. She is always ditching me and following some rich punk who can give her a quid or two for her time. That type of crap gives me a pain in the ass. I wouldn't part with a cent for any goddam girl's time except for drinks. I am like that. Drink and nothing else. Paying a woman for herself is goddam filthy if you ask me. It's ungodly. Some men do it but not me.

Josy sits down where I am sitting and squints at me.

"How about it?" she asks.

"About what?" I retort.

"One Pilsner, large and in a pint mug."

"It's your turn, lady. Today is your turn. Every time it's me and I am tired of it. Let's have a revolution and have you on the chair instead. You must be tired of begging surely." Nosy Josy doesn't like that. The look she gives me ain't even funny. Not at all. You'd have to be very funny yourself to think it funny.

"Are you down?" she asks.

"I am goddam high but I am tired of buying. Every blinking punk is taking me for a ride and I am just about to puke. I ain't buying nobody a drink. Not even you. Try somebody else for a change."

Josy understands me. When I tell her to go look for another mug she actually does. She moves over to this short army lieutenant who is playing darts and casually asks, "Can I join you?"

These army bastards are all alike. They are all hungry for females whether they are married or not. This fellow lets out a smile that would have won the Queen of Sheba and says to Josy, "Certainly. We are playing three-o-one and you can certainly join us."

Josy hasn't started playing before this fellow asks her whether she'll have a drink and she says, "Eh — yes. I think I'll have one. A cold Pilsner in a pint mug." This military man is very obliging. Before he throws the darts he calls the waiter and orders this Pilsner for Josy. I forget his name. It is either Harry or Perry. Anyway, this Harry or Perry is very generous where women like Josy are concerned.

I am thinking that six pints is enough, when you are driving a government Landrover. Six pints is enough. I decide that the best idea would be to go home. Go home and snore my silly head off. I am

98

thinking of decamping when this fellow Job arrives. I don't particularly
like him but the first thing he does is he moves to where I am sitting
and greets me warmly, "Hey, man. Long time no see. How about
a drink on me?"

When a fellow like Job offers you a drink you make sure that you
take it. You are damn lucky if he offers you one and most likely he's just
had a lay with some prostitute but has still got some dough left. Me,
I accept his drink. I accept it on account that if I don't he'll offer it to
some other mug. We indulge in some silly conversation and he joins
the group playing bar football. A very silly game if you ask me but
some mugs enjoy it. I play it sometimes but I always make sure that
my opponent wins. I let him win firstly because it pleases him but
mainly because I can't play the goddam game anyway. That's me. I
never disappoint a friend.

After one game Josy comes over to me and asks, "Have you
seen the old man lately?" She means Jack. She is asking me whether
I have seen Jack. Gosh. I wish she'd chosen a better question. I am
still mad at Jack so I answer her acid-like.

"I've no need to see him. I've got no goddam tits."

"Is something the matter with you, Dod?" she asks.

"Sure, but you can't help," I tell her.

"Woman?"

"Go to hell. If I had a woman problem you are not the type that
would solve it. No sir. Not the nosy Josy type. I like class." Josy
doesn't like that so she goes back to the game. I am feeling pleased
with myself. I always feel good when I tell a woman off. Lets off lots
of steam.

I look at Josy throwing the darts and I reckon that she looks like
a spider. Funny creatures, spiders. They are just legs and belly. Their
mating is very exciting too. The male gets damn exhausted and the
female eats him up. It's goddam unfair of course but it's sure exciting.
I reckon that if Josy had a tumble with this little army fellow, she'd
eat him up. That would be even funnier.

The darts game gets finished and Josy comes to sit next to me.
I don't like it. Maybe the army chap is interested in her and maybe he
can cough up a few beers. He won't cough up the beers if Josy keeps
hopping from punk to punk. Josy rubs her hands on her dress and
says, "Sure you don't want to buy me a drink?"

"That little fellow there has lots of dough. Why don't you get it
off him?"

"He's bought me one already."

"He can buy another."

"I know but I don't like him."

"Meaning that you like me?"

"Something like that."

"And what makes you think that I like you?" I ask.

"I know you. You don't discriminate."

"I see. Eh — thank you very much for the compliment but you can be sure that I ain't going to buy you no goddam drink."

"O.K. tough boy. I am not dying yet. Actually I came to ask you another favour. It may disgust you but I'd like to see Jack. Oh yes, you need not scowl but I want to see him. He's old and useless but I would like to see him about something different. Not the type of thing you are thinking about."

"What is stopping you? You go right ahead and see him. You know his house."

"I can't go alone. He would misunderstand me."

"And what do you want me to do?" I ask.

"To take me to him."

"And why should I do that? What is my cut in the deal?"

"Anything."

"I see. I'd want the whole world. Every hill and valley in the whole goddam planet. You'd have to give it to me, Josy, before I take you to Elmentaita."

"O.K. It's all yours. Have it."

"How about buying me a drink, Josy? You sure have money in that fat handbag of yours. Trouble with you girls is that you never understand the scripture. The scripture says that you do unto others that which you'd have them do unto you. It's give and take but girls are goddam mean. They are always taking."

"Will you take me to Jack's place?" she asks.

"If you buy me a drink, I'll think about it." She opens her handbag and produces a crisp pink fiver. She makes sure I see that there is more where that came from and then she beckons the waiter. She asks for two Pilsners.

My mind starts working fast. I am asking myself what Josy really wants. A woman like Josy here does not buy you beer just because she likes your face. Oh no. Women are damn mean. Every time she buys a drink it is a bribe to do her one favour or another.

I've made up my mind that I'll see what Josy is up to. I am curious and drunk and that's a hell of a combination. I am thinking that it might be a good idea to see Jack too. At least I can tell him what a blinking dog I think he is. I'll not kill him tonight. Oh no. I am too

drunk. That can wait until I am sober. Trouble is I am hardly ever
sober. That's why I am getting fat although my digestion is lousy.
I am always having one type of diarrhoea or another which accounts for
very frequent farting. I like to fart. There is nothing like farting when
you are alone if the damn fart does not stink too much.

After this drink I tell Josy that I'll drive her to old man Jack.
I also tell her that if Jack donates ten quid for touching her tits I want
five and we make it a deal. You might think I am nuts and maybe you
are right. Trouble is you might be nuts too.

I drive like mad and we are in Elmentaita in forty minutes. It's a
murram road but it's as straight as the road to hell. We bounce over
potholes and anthills as we approach Jack's house and I can see that
the blighter has not gone to bed although it's eight. Sometimes he
goes to bed at six but most times he goes to bed at seven. The only time
he stays awake is when he has company or is in town. I am wondering
what type of company we shall find.

We get to the door and I knock. Nothing stirs. I knock louder
and get the same response. I start thinking that Jack went to bed as
usual but forgot to put out the lights. I move to a window and peep in
through a narrow slit between curtains. Jack is there all right. He is
lying on the settee and sleeping like the dead. His false teeth have
fallen to the floor. I tap the window hard. Jack doesn't stir.

I move over to Josy and I tell her that Jack is having his beauty
sleep. I try the door and heck! The door ain't even locked. We go in.

"Wake him," I tell Josy. "Give him a kiss on the cheek."

Josy moves over and gives Jack a shake. That doesn't do any
good so she gives him a smack on the shoulder. Jack is still sleeping
soundly.

There is this bottle of whisky on the table and I am hunting for a
glass. I am looking all over the place for a goddam glass when Josy
comes over and taps me on the shoulder.

"Hey, Dod. I think he is dead."

"What!!"

"Shhh. Not so loud. He is not breathing. There are some tiny
pills in his hand." This should have knocked me out sober but it didn't.
Trouble is I can't believe Josy. I move over to Jack and with one
pull I sit him up. His eyes stare at me and sure as hell they are the eyes
of a dead man. I get hold of his nose and shake it somewhat but
Jack doesn't even know he has a nose. Jack is dead. Dead and cold
I give him a push so that he lies down like before and I turn to Josy.
She is trembling like a reed and her eyes are bulging out of their

sockets. She don't look so good.

"Snap out of it girl," I tell her. "We've got to get the hell
out of here. Looks like he poisoned himself or somebody else
did. I suspect it's somebody else. Somebody who slipped a pill into
his drink and when he died the murderer put those pills in dead
Jack's hand to make it look like suicide. I know Jack better. He
loved his life. He is not the type that would go about swallowing
deadly pills just for the heck of it. Oh no. Jack would never do a
thing like that."

"Shouldn't we call the police?" she asks.

"I hate cops and I certainly don't want to be mixed up in a
murder trap. The police would frame you and probably hang you.
Let sleeping dogs lie like this our friend Jack. He cheated me.
Instead of giving me my money, now it will all go to the Government
as death duty. I can't feel very sorry for Jack."

"What did Jack take from you?" Josy asks.

"I'll tell you as we go home. C'mon. Out we go."

We get the hell out of there but as we get into the Landrover
I remember something. Fingerprints. I must have left scores of
fingerprints everywhere while I was looking for the damn glass.
I tell Josy to excuse me and I go back to the house. I get my
handkerchief and start wiping the whole goddam place. I even wipe
Jack's nose.

I start gumshoeing out of the place and then stop. Something
clicks in my mind. An idea hits me like a ton of bricks. I reckon that
you can get even with a guy even if that fellow is dead. There was this
English king who unburied Oliver Cromwell and hanged the stinking
corpse just for the heck of it and I reckon the fellow was not mad. It
occurs to me that I can go over Jack's drawers and things and see
whether there is some dough in some hidden corner. It is thieving all
right but it's tit for tat. Jack thieved from me.

First I go through his pockets. He has ten fivers in his wallet and
I proceed to relieve him of this. The only loose dough he has is
some seventeen shillings which I also take because Jack has no use for
it. I move to his writing desk and start pulling out drawers. There is
nothing of value except a cheque book which is of course useless to
me. I give that up and move to the steel cabinet on the other side. The
damn thing is locked. I am just about to kick the damn thing open
when I remember those keys in Jack's pocket. I go over to him, turn
him over and pull out the keys. The third key opens the cabinet and
I proceed to inspect the contents. There are lots of papers, agreements,
statements and what have you but it's all useless to me. Something is

102

wrong. I bang the cabinet door shut and then open it. Of course it's sitting right there. The Cash Box. The cash box is sitting right there staring at me.

I look through the keys and pick the right one. I get the cash box open and feast my eyes on dough. Pay day is tomorrow and Jack has already withdrawn the salary dough for his employees. I stuff the whole lot in my pockets and I am cursing myself for wearing a proper coat instead of a bush jacket with them big pockets. I empty the cash box of every cent including a cash cheque for some four thousand three hundred and fifty shillings. I lock the cabinet. Again I dust the whole place with my handkerchief, put the keys in Jack's pocket, and get the hell out of the place. I reckon I am a goddam thief

"What have you been doing?" Josy asks but I don't answer her. I get the vehicle started and fly over potholes and anthills as if I was competing in the East African Safari.

There is only one thought in my mind. I've got to drive Josy to Nakuru, book myself a hotel room, lock myself in and count my dough. That's all I want to do. Once I know how much I have then I can either decide to drive back to Sabugo or spend a night in Nakuru. I reckon I shall have to spend the night in Nakuru anyway. There is this cash cheque which has to be presented to the bank first thing tomorrow morning. When the bank gets wind that Jack's popped off, they'll freeze his damn account. I've got to get there and get the money before they know. Gosh! I never imagined that stealing could be that easy. Maybe I'll turn out a regular thief.

We get to Nakuru and I ask Josy where she wants to be dropped. She tells me to drop her at her house and I do.

"Wouldn't you come in please," she invites me.

"Ehe, no thanks. Not today. I think I'd better get home immediately. I'll drop in another day."

"That's not like you. Come on. I wouldn't rape you."

"I wish you would but not tonight. I've got to get going."

"Say — what is the matter with you? Going to meet some girls?"

"Honest no. I don't want a girl tonight."

"Are you kidding, man, or do you have V.D.?"

"Go to hell," I tell her and I get the hell out of the place. I drive straight to the Midland Hotel and book myself a single room with a private bath. I get into the room, lock it and then bolt it, close the windows and draw the curtains and then move quietly to the bathroom. There is nobody there. I move back and deposit everything on the bed making sure that the coins don't make a racket worth drawing anybody's attention. I start to count.

I sort out the fivers, the pounds, the tens, the fives and the coins. If you'd peeped through some hole I'd omitted to seal you'd have mistaken me for a bloody banker. I got used to thinking myself a banker too. If you'd popped up from somewhere and presented me with a cash cheque maybe I'd have given you the cash.

I count the dough a second time just for kicks and I reckon it's correct. My record reads as follows:

100 shs. notes	327	32,700 shillings
20 " " 148		2,960 "
10 " " 65		650 "
5 " " 401		2,005 "
1 " coins 122		122 "
50 cent " 100		50 "
10 " " 200		20 "
5 " " 40		2 "
Cheques		4,350 "
Total stolen		42,859 "
Less what I'll drink tonight		259 "
Total wealth tomorrow morning		42,600 "

I put the piece of paper in my pocket, count 259 shillings and shove them into my pocket, tie the rest of the dough in a pillow case, shove the pillow case with its contents into the wardrobe, lock the wardrobe, put the key in my pocket, look myself in the mirror and then blow out, locking the door behind me.

I get the Landrover started and I drive it to the nearest police station and ask the cop at the gate to look after the machine. When you don't know where to hide your government vehicle you can always take it to the nearest police station and the cops will look after it the whole night. If anything should happen to the vehicle it wouldn't be your responsibility any more. It's the cops that have to sweat. Anyway, I reckon that today I can afford a taxi and it ain't fair to use government petrol no more.

I walk to a nearby cafe' but they are about to close the place. It's nearly eleven o'clock and this fellow who owns the place loves the law as he loves his kids so he wouldn't let me buy myself a beer. He allows that I can buy myself a whisky and I buy myself a whisky. I ask him whether he would like some and he says yes. I buy him three tots and a ginger ale and he is extremely grateful.

He now allows that I can buy myself a beer provided the other
wogs don't see the waiter girl giving it to me on account that he
is not allowing nobody the beers because of the law. I smile at him
and say it's O.K. for today. There's still tomorrow untouched. He
pats me on the shoulder. He is a very kind gentleman. Very kind.

I finish my whisky and go round the corner to this new place
they call Tours Night Club. The place is right upstairs and they have
no goddam lift. I walk up the stairs and get into the place. There's
stale air hanging all over the joint and it's a bit early for a night
club anyway. Them night clubs don't start functioning properly
before midnight because people like to get drunk elsewhere where beer
is cheap and only come to the night club when all other places are
closed. Well, it ain't midnight yet so the goddam place is empty.
It's empty except for a few gold diggers sipping coca-cola, waiting
for mugs to come and buy them juice and later on give them a
tumbling fee. There are only three mugs and they are waiters.

I move to this group sitting at the counter and say, "Hi, ladies."
They don't have the courtesy to answer but they giggle all right. I
reckon they are all muggins and therefore I decide to order myself
double whisky and keep mum. I have taken so much goddam drink
tonight that I am myself surprised that I can still stand. That stealing
act sobered me up somewhat. My dough pile in the wardrobe tends
to neutralize alcohol outright. It's as if I am drinking water.

These four coca-cola girls look at my whisky and are sort of
envious and so I say to them, "Coca-cola is goddam intoxicating.
Why don't you girls be decent and stick to something mild like
whisky? It's bad when a man gets drunk but it's worse when a woman
does it. What will you have?"

This sort of takes them by surprise and they giggle some more.
Sometimes I like women to giggle but other times I don't like them
to giggle at all. This giggling really puts me off but I buy them
drinks all the same. One takes brandy but the rest take beer. They get
to asking who I am and whether I am new in Nakuru and what I do
and where I am going and where I am going to sleep and whether
I like dancing and whether I am enjoying myself and whether I
have kids and lots of other crap. After which I tell them that they
must be blind if they haven't seen me before because I am the local
playboy. I tell them three lies for every question. They are so slow-
witted that I don't care what I tell them. They can't see through
the most transparent lie. If I told them that I was a woman dressed
in a man's garb I reckon they'd have believed it too. Very funny
girls, these four.

When this one next to me on the right asks me what my name is I tell her John. I don't tell them gold-diggers my right name. Anyway we go on talking and I forget what I told them. I refer to myself as Peter.

"I thought you said you are John," the girl on my left says with a jump.

"Oh no, Mary, he said Peter." They get on to arguing about whether I said Peter or John but of course I don't know myself. I can't remember. When they are worn out they turn to me and ask me what I actually said my name was. I tell them that I am John Peters and that could have said either.

Mary asks, "Peters? I thought you said plain Peter," and I tell her that Peter is also my name because you can't have Peters without Peter. She agrees with me and also asks me to buy her another drink and I do. I buy another round.

Muggins and more gold-diggers are starting to pour into the place and making it lively. The band which has been playing some soft music is now really hitting the drums. The singer who was previously crooning "Malaika" is now all worked up with this jail house rock and putting all the wind into it.

I pick one of the gold-diggers and go for a dance. I jump all over the place with excess energy and the singer fellow sings louder. When the dance is over we go to join the others and my gold-digger asks for another drink. Again I buy a round.

Them females think I am a goddam millionaire. Every one of them wants to get hooked to me. They are all making faces and winking at me when the others are not looking. I reckon that if I wanted a woman today, I'd have no difficulties. Trouble is I don't want any. I must sleep next to my dough and I can't trust a goddam gold-digger in the same room with that dough. Gold-diggers and dough don't go together. You put them together and next minute the dough is missing. You simply can't put them together.

Although I don't want no woman, I reckon that I'll get these girls drunk just for kicks. I'd like to see how they carry on when they have lots of drink in them. The way things are, they will all want me to take them and I am hoping that in the end they are going to fight over me. I simply adore women fighting over me. It's the greatest fun I ever had in my life. They don't really fight. All they do is tear each other's clothes off and you reckon that's damn advantageous if you've to make a pick. I reckon that if four women were to fight each other, it would be lots of fun.

A punk comes and picks one of them. The rest stop showing off.

Maybe they are old buddies but I don't like it. The punk has ruined my plans.

I am left with three and I really feed them on beer. They are a gluttonous lot. They ain't showing no sign of getting drunk either but I have enough dough to give them an alcoholic blackout.

There comes this young English farmer and he takes Mary. She doesn't even thank me but walks after the man like a dog. That's the trouble with our African women. They can't resist white men's dough. Immediately they see a white man they think he is dough itself. It don't matter how much you have but a white man has got more, at least that's what gold-diggers think. Damn them.

I go right ahead and feed these two remaining females and you'd reckon they were drunk. They are so goddam drunk that they even forget I am there. They start this talk about how mean African men are and how they wouldn't give you more than a pound while white men donate five pounds minimum without a murmur. They go on to say that while the African pays less he wants more for his little money and lots of other crap. They start wondering whether they'll get a white man tonight.

I get so disgusted with this talk that I am almost puking. I never heard such stuff. It's goddam mean of them to talk such shit in my presence seeing that I've already spent so much money on them. I get so incensed that I blurt out, "And what the hell are you doing here instead of whoring your dirty asses to pink-faced sons of bitches?" They don't answer. They pick up their drinks and walk out on me. This tall one, she looks back at me and spits.

"Shit!" she hisses. God Almighty! Just fancy that! Me, Dod Kiunyu, I am shit! shit! That's what I am. That's what that goddam whore calls me. I can't stand it. I wouldn't mind if she wasn't a goddam whore but that's what she is. A whore. Goddam it all.

With four long strides I've got her by the hair. I turn her round and smack — smack — smack her cheeks sing. She tries to claw me but I twist her arm and smack — smack — smack — I go again. This other whore she throws whisky right into my eyes and I go blind for long seconds. In case you don't know whisky ain't no good for your goddam eyes. Don't try it. It's not good for focus.

While I am wiping my eyes them whores are hitting me all over my body and I am kicking wildly and I reckon I kicked a man nearby by mistake. I am beginning to see again when this helluva kick lands on my tummy and I fold over. It takes me a second to get my breath back and you bet I go wild. I don't know who's kicked me so I start with the nearest punk. I give him a mean right on the nose and he falls over somebody who kicks him and who I kick in turn before I turn to this other fellow who is coming behind me whose head stops a mighty powerful punch from my left. Before you could wink an eye nearly everybody is hitting somebody else and some whore is tearing off another whore's dress while the cowards are treading on each other's heels down the stairs. It's real fun.

I don't notice the cops until I hear a whistle. I am lying on the floor with blood running from my nose where lots of us got tangled in a fighting heap. I get onto my feet and just stand there. Nobody is moving from where they are. There are twelve cops with batons ready and they mean to use them. The bartender comes along and points at me and says, "He started it all!" The cops don't believe him. They reckon that cne man cannot fight fifteen men and six whores single-handed. They say thanks to the bartender and hustle the whole lot of us out. There are twenty-one people scooped in one haul and we can't all fit in the 999 police car. They marshal us in a single file way down to the police station and the bloody fools lock us up. They didn't make no entries in their daily record book or ask us who we were. They merely emptied our pockets and locked fifteen of us in one cell and the six girls in another cell.

"You will be charged tomorrow," a cop says behind the bars and we are left in this darkness. You can't see your neighbour. Any time you try to move you tread on somebody's toes or some punk is treading on your toes. I reckon nobody wants another fight. There is somebody saying sorry there, sorry here and sorry everywhere as they tread on each other's toes. I can't hear any other goddam word in this cell except sorry.

I decide to look for the corner of the cell and keep out of this toe-treading business. Everybody is thinking the same so you end up by being trod on or treading on somebody else. Blimey! This is one hell of a place. It is strictly police hospitality. Damn the cops.

I grope around in search of a quiet place and I reckon I poke them fingers of mine into somebody's eye. He lets out a yell and I move back. You simply can't help poking your fingers into somebody else's eyes. I feel around and touch the wall. I lean against it and then sit down. This way it's unlikely that anybody will poke their fingers into my eyes. The chances of being trod on are also limited. I am more likely to trip a fellow up instead. Gosh, I am drunk. All I want is to sit here and sleep.

All of a sudden I remember. I remember the dough. God! I'd forgotten all about it. I curse. I am in a cold sweat on account of this dough. How in the name of God shall I lay hands on it if the cops

108

keep me here. Some fellow will go to make the bed in the morning and he'll know I didn't sleep there. If he suspects that I slept there and oozed out in the morning, that will be worse. The cops have taken from me the wardrobe key and the piece of paper showing accounts but suppose they have a duplicate key and they open up the wardrobe. First thing they'll notice is the blinking pillow case and next my dough. My!

If some punk hi-jacks that dough I can't make much of a fuss seeing that it's stolen dough. If they find it and keep it for me that ain't no good either. I'd be highly suspect. Either way I am licked. I curse myself for indulging in whore-fighting. Heck! How I hate whores. I don't blame them though. It's me that is nuts. I must be nuts. How the hell would any sensible person want to hide stolen money in a public place and then go whore-fighting? I am the original madman.

Some fellow starts snoring and he is joined by another. Shortly there are six people snoring. It's the most boring mixture of sounds I ever heard in my life. It goes ghrtoo-grruur-oorgh-gaaargh-iiing-eeerrha and other fine shades that only a pig can imitate. I reckon that a pig would puke if it heard these gentlemen snore. It's a very poor imitation of grunting.

By and by I doze off. I don't know whether I snore or not but I know I dream. It's a wonderful dream in which all I am doing is counting lots of dough and putting it in pillow cases. I am rich.

9

"Stop yelling at me! I can hear you."

"What is the meaning of this?" the cop asks.

"It's not written in Greek, is it?" I ask him by way of an answer. He is holding this paper showing count of my dough

"I know it isn't but what the hell does it mean?"

"If you stop reading the paper upside down you'll understand. It is a mere record of monies for mathematical purposes." He doesn't understand.

"Whose money?" the cop asks. "It says total stolen. Didn't you haul it from somebody?"

"Money that I'd like to have. A mathematical wish."

"You don't already have it?"

"I had it all in my pocket last night when the police locked me up. I was asked to leave it on the counter. Do you think I could have it back?"

"You are kidding aren't you?" he asks, looking very surprised.

"If you want me to stop kidding then ask sensible questions. I want to get the hell out of here. I am a government servant and I can cause some trouble if you keep on holding me here and asking silly questions. I have work to do."

"I have work to do too and I am also a government servant. Would you please go to that room marked number two and sit down. The investigation officer will be there presently to take your statement. Your charge is merely causing disturbance in a public place and if you are wise don't deny it. It works out cheaper and is infinitely less inconvenient for all concerned if you admit the charge. The fine will not exceed one hundred shillings."

I thank him for his wise counsel and move to this room marked number two. The place is completely empty except for a small table and two chairs which face one another. I sit and wait.

What happened was the cops roused us up too goddam early and hustled us out of the cell. They did the same to the girls. There are some hard benches along the corridor and we are asked to sit on them. We have been going to the desk one by one to say who we are and also to identify our belongings and to get ourselves formally charged. This is the second time I have been questioned. The cops seem to have taken a lot of interest in this silly note on which I recorded what I stole from Jack. I tried to explain to them that the note was meaningless but they are not easy to convince. I told them where I was staying and they started asking me why I'd booked myself in the Midland Hotel while I could have driven home easily. I tried to explain to them that where I slept was none of their blinking business but they seemed to think it was. That is the trouble with cops. They make everything their business. Instead of charging me and letting me free they asked me to go back and sit on the benches till I was called again. Gosh! I am only hoping that they will not go to the hotel and start snooping around in my room.

Everybody else has been charged and has left. They were all

110

charged for being drunk and disorderly. I am wondering why my charge is different. It doesn't look so good you know.

This second time they called me they didn't ask me anything much. I am starting to think that they are merely holding me here while they go out and do some snooping. It was very stupid of me to carry that piece of paper with me. The cops have seen through it and they smell a rat. Gosh! What a mess.

I am sitting there and staring at the blank wall. It's one hell of a lousy wall. It's as dead as any other goddam wall.

Mr. Hangover is right in my system. Gosh, I hate hangovers. Right now my tummy is rumbling and grumbling and I am farting three times a minute. I can't fart with force though on account I have diarrhoea. You can't fart with force when you have the goddam diarrhoea or you might fart shit.

I am thinking what a louse I have become. Drinking has ruined my memory. I am trying to remember Pythagoras' theorem and how we used to prove it but I reckon that I have forgotten everything about it. I can't even prove that a straight line is a straight line. What a blinking bloody bastard I have become.

I give geometry up and shift over to physics. I can remember a lot of things in physics. I start by remembering that like poles repel and unlike poles attract. My mind races through heat, pressure, light but I can't remember a damn thing about electricity. I remember this guy Boyle who discovered Archimedes' Principle and I reckon that he was a great guy. Real first class guy. I try to figure out what Boyle's Law actually said but the damn thing eludes my memory. I decide that Boyle was not all that cute after all. I have a vague recollection that it's something to do with an apple falling on Archimedes after which he runs about naked till he drops into a bath where the king has hidden his crown and starts shouting "eureka". He must have been real nuts. Trouble is I can't figure out at all how Boyle comes in. Maybe he doesn't.

I let out a very loud fart and turn my head to see whether some cop heard the explosion. There is no cop in sight. I fart again. A slow hissing fart that reminds me of a stinking fish market. I fan the air in front of my nose and curse my ass. This room really stinks. I start thinking about exhaust pipes and I really wish I had one. That way I could fart right out of the room if the pipe was long enough. I chuckle to myself. I am thoroughly amused. I am amused at the thought of pointing the exhaust pipe at a cop's face while the fish smell was oozing out. That would be interesting. I'd give anything to see it.

I am tired of sitting here staring at the wall and thinking shit.

Whoever is coming to question me is taking a goddam long time and I'll be damned if I stick around any longer. I let out a fart and walk out.

"Where is this investigation officer supposed to spring from?" I ask the cop at the desk. He gives me a blank look and points at the the room where I've been sitting.

"Go back right there and wait," he tells me.

"The place stinks."

"Go back right there and wait," he repeats, wagging his finger at me. He is in no mood for light talk.

"That room stinks and I need my breakfast. You wouldn't have any fried eggs here would you?"

"You are crazy. Go right back into that room marked number two and make yourself comfortable. What's all this nonsense about the room stinking?"

"I wish you'd tell me what it's all about. Smells like a fish market that's what the room does. I hate fish. I really do."

"Are you a vegetarian?"

"Yes," I tell the cop.

"You are lying," he says.

"Of course I am. What the hell do you expect me to say when such a question is put to me. I am a lousy Kikuyu and so are you. You should know that there are no vegetarians among us or what did you think I was? A lousy Indian or something?"

"O.K. You are not a vegetarian. Walk right back into that room and sit down."

"No I won't. I want to plead guilty for that blinking charge and get out of here. There is nothing to investigate. I'll merely pay the fine and that will be the end of the whole nonsense."

"You call it nonsense?"

"What do you think it is?"

"I am asking you for the last time to go back into that room and wait. If there are fish inside there, have your goddam breakfast."

"Thank you," I tell him. I move back into the room, and sit down again. I have been giving the cop the impression that I am not very concerned and that I don't really care one way or the other but I am as concerned as hell. There is more in this than meets the eye. I sit there and think of that pile of dough sitting there in a hotel room and I start to sweat. I mean it. I am really sweating. I've been trying my hardest not to think about that dough but it's futile. Thinking about guys like Archimedes doesn't help. I can't even think straight about the fellow anyway. Gosh! Am I jittery or am I? I am even trembling like Jesus. He was a nice fellow but so what? He's dead.

I stretch my legs and wipe the perspiration off my face with the back of my hand. Some sweat goes into my right eye and I start blinking. I am blinking like a madman. What on earth could have possessed me last night? Why did I pinch Jack's dough? Why did I rob a corpse? Tell me that. Why the hell should I career off with a dead guy's dough? God have mercy on Master Dodge.

I am hoping against hope that they will not discover the dough. I am also promising God that I'll never steal again if I am not caught. I am also promising myself that if I escape I'll give half the money to this school for the blind, at Thika. I am vowing that I'll never drink or smoke again and that I'll start going to church. I'll keep off women and quit cheating. From now on I'll be as straight as a flag pole, that is if the damn bastards don't catch me. Hey, I forgot swearing. I've got to stop that too. I'll stop everything that is ungodly.

I rest my hands on my knees and close my eyes. I think I am going to cry. Honest. My eyes have some uncomfortable warmth. I rinse them and curse. "What the hell!"

I start wondering what I would do if I was another guy. I reckon I would sneak out when the cop is not looking, dodge my way to the hotel, pay my bill, collect the dough, take it to some safe place and then present myself to the cops. They can add any other goddam charge for all I care but the dough would be there to pay the fines. I would be so kind that I would voluntarily offer to pay double the fine just to please the magistrate. That would puzzle the bastard I am sure. The only appeal he ever heard was from guys who wanted a mitigation on their fines or jail periods. I reckon that if I offered to pay double the fine he would think I was nuts and perhaps send me to a psychiatrist. That would be real fun. Fancy that.

I would give this fellow the impression that I was really nuts. Instead of saying "hello doctor" I would say something like "hello brother" and proceed to ask him about the kids and last year's banana harvest. He would be dumbfounded and I would casually tap him on the shoulder friendly-like and tell him that he was cheated by the butcher. That should knock him out cold. I would lay him flat by advising him that he should not trade in cows. Pigs are more profitable if he fed them on cassava juice and asparagus shells. To crown it all I might howl like a wolf. Just a little howl to put his temperature right. No further examinations would be needed. He would ask the cops to handcuff me and take me direct to the nearest mental hospital. How I would laugh! That would be the funniest joke ever played on a doctor.

I perform a double yawn and decide to sneak out. Thinking about doctors and madmen is wasted effort. It's very dangerous thinking. If a doctor believed you were nuts and sent you to a nuthouse you might find it very difficult to convince anybody that you were not nuts. I know a guy who let on that he was nuts at Makerere and they believed him. Trouble was that when he later laughed and confessed that he had fooled them all, they couldn't believe him. They took him to a nuthouse but he refused to enter the goddam place on the grounds that he wasn't a nut. He shouted and cursed and tried the hardest he could, but nothing doing. Everything he said made it worse. They had to drag him by force and lock him up in one of those cells for the violently insane. When he came out after a week he was really nuts. He was mad at everything. To let off steam he went back to Mulago Hospital and beat up the doctor who'd examined him first time. He claimed that the doctor should have known real madness from faked madness. He knocked out two of the doctor's teeth and was of course arrested by the cops again and charged with assault and causing actual bodily harm. He would have gone to jail but he faked madness again. This time they kept him in the nuthouse for a whole month and when he came out, he was a thoroughly confused character. He couldn't tell for sure whether he was really nuts or not.

"I might be a real nut," he told me one day at the swimming pool. He was telling me about this funny incident when his girlfriend came to see him one afternoon. They had a hectic so and so till it was tea time. His girlfriend did not want tea so he got dressed and went to the dining room for tea. After the first cup he wiped sweat off his face. To his horror it wasn't a handkerchief that he'd fished out of his pocket for wiping his face. It was his girlfriend's nylon knickers. Other students saw it and laughed like mad. They made fun of him and my friend walked out feeling an absolute mug. When he told me I laughed my silly head off. Life can be funny. He reminds me of this guy in Chaucer who kissed a bearded woman.

The cop is telephoning and he has his back towards room number two where I am sitting like a mouse. He is telephoning another cop at Eldoret and they are talking about accident reports. I ease out casually making the type of noise that you wouldn't hear even if it was placed right into your ear and presently I am at the outer door. I am not looking back. If the cop sees me and yells at me I'll simply tell him that I am going for a leak. I turn left and walk towards the back where they have parked these derelict vehicles. I put my hands in my pockets casually and walk out through the back gate as innocently as

114

the son of man. My heart is pounding like a million mortars and my mind racing like a meteor. Life is no longer funny.

I have only one thing in mind. To gumshoe to the hotel. Spy around for stray cops that might be snooping and if the coast is clear ease into my room and regain my dough. This has to be done quickly and cautiously. It's jail or freedom. Life or death. If that cash cheque in the loot is found, the cops will obviously get in touch with Jack. On finding him dead and cold they will let all cops loose on my trail. Theft will be the motive for murder and I will surely hang. I'd need a real smart lawyer to keep the noose off my neck. No lawyer would however be able to restore my reputation. In case you want to know, I am really fond of my reputation. I love it. I am sure that some mug or old hag like you would brand me as a son of a bitch but I wouldn't let you get away with it. Oh no. You are a son of a bitch yourself if you say that. My correct and unblemished title is "son of woman" and you'd better remember it. If you think I am a thief you are one yourself. Any bad thing you think me to be, you are that thing yourself. You can't win. It will therefore pay for you to think well of me. Think of me as a sweet lad and I'll promise on my honour not to call you bad names.

I pass the Standard Bank conscious that everybody is staring at me and circle the Midland Hotel cautiously but casually. I can't see a police car. There is no sign of cops. Some American tourists have just arrived in one of these tourist minibuses which are striped like zebras and are happily chatting. The only thing I hear is 'twaang' aang' four waong' oar gaime aar mersai nood nirives'. I decide that I don't know what the hell they are talking about and walk casually to the enquiries desk.

The clerk gives me a once-over look and exclaims, "Hey, you didn't sleep in your room."

"That's right," I tell him.

"What happened?"

"Oh, one of them things. I want to pay and check out."

"Did you have any baggage in the room? I'll have it brought here."

"Don't bother. Only papers. I'll get them myself."

"It's thirty-five shillings bed and breakfast but I am sorry it's too late for breakfast."

"I have already breakfasted," I tell him. "Is the room open?"

"There's somebody cleaning it and spreading fresh sheets."

"Did somebody use the sheets then?" I ask him.

"Oh no. Just routine. You paid for the bed and it's therefore assumed that you used the sheets.”

Out of my last night’s balance I pay this guy thirty-five shillings. It’s just about all I have. I walk fast to my room and jerk the door open. The wog in there gives a start because I reckon I’ve caught him red-handed. His right hand is half-way between the vital pillow case which he is holding with his left hand, and his bulging trouser pocket, and between the fingers are a stack of notes.

“Hello,” I say cheerfully. The guy is mute. He has his mouth open and his eyes peeping out of their sockets and his right hand is still halfway between the pillow case and his pocket.

“You aren’t stealing by any chance are you?” I ask him casually. The wog is still transfixed. I reckon it’s a terrible thing to be caught red-handed. Perhaps I would feel the same if I was in his boots. I sort of feel compassion for this guy. He looks a good guy you know. His uniform is spotlessly clean and his fez is straight and red. He is wearing new canvas shoes and even his broom, which is resting on the bed, looks like it’s well looked after. He has a benevolent face and I reckon that this is probably the first time he’d ever tried to steal.

I move over to him and tap him on the shoulder. That puts some life into him. I reckon he thinks that I am going to murder him or something. I shove him onto the bed.

“Empty all your pockets onto that bed and make it snappy.” He complies. He turns all his pockets inside out.

“Is that all?” I ask him.

“Yes, Sir,” he answers timidly.

“How long have you worked in this joint?”

“Three years, Sir.”

“Have you ever indulged in stealing acts?”

“No, Sir.”

“I mean why were you stealing my money?”

“No, Sir.” This guy is real daft or pretending to be.

“Listen, this is my money. When I came in you were stuffing it into your pocket in a manner that was highly suspect. Your aim was to sneak away with it and make it your own. That is stealing, isn’t it?”

“No, Sir.”

“What is it then? What were you doing?”

“No, Sir.”

“What do you mean, ‘No, Sir’, you dumb pickpocket?”

“Nothing, Sir.”

“For Chrissake stop saying, ‘No, Sir.’ I want the truth. If you tell the truth I will not report you to the authorities. You were stealing, weren’t you?”

"No, Sir." Gosh! I never met a waiter who was so dumb. I am wasting precious time with this guy, which is very stupid of me. I am very stupid at times.

I pick up the dough and stuff it into my pockets. I do it casually so that this guy does not smell a rat. After I've emptied the pillow case my pockets are bulging to heaven. You can see the notes in the gaping pockets. I start for the door and then remember the cleaning guy. I turn to him and give him one sneer just for keeps.

"You are very stupid," I tell him. "You are also dumb. If you weren't, I would report you to your boss but now I won't. If you were sacked you couldn't get a job elsewhere. Hide your face and cry." I bang the door after me and walk briskly along the corridor.

I walk the way I came and cross the street. I go into the Rift Valley Grocers and buy myself a bag for baby nappies. I ask the fat Indian whether I can use their toilet and he says yes. An African guy escorts me and shows me the can. I thank him. I lock myself in the loo and proceed to empty my pockets into the bag. I am taking great care not to drop the coins and after a brief discussion with myself I tear Jack's cash cheque into nothingness and toss it into the toilet. Then I piss on it and flush the toilet just to keep the record straight. I walk out, buy a pack of fags and some deodorant and get the hell out of the place. I am feeling lighter.

I get into the post office and make a reverse charge call to my office at Sabugo just in case somebody is looking for me. My typist/ secretary tells me that everything is O.K. and I tell her that I'll be there within half an hour. Then I get an inspiration. I fish more coins from my pocket and telephone the police. I tell them who I am and that they might be wondering where I am and that I am having breakfast and will be at the police station in ten minutes. I hang up before the guy says anything and walk out of the post office. I seem to be walking in a dream — happy and sad. Trouble is that I do not have time to think. I am doing things purely by animal instinct.

I walk to the market and start looking for a taxi. I am going to Sabugo first thing. It's hot and I am sweating. I am looking around when I meet this girl. She isn't a girl really. She is a woman but she is a girl at the same time. My immediate reaction is to say hello — long-time-no-see but I realise in a flash that I don't really know her and I can't remember where I ever met her and yet she looks familiar. I stand there and get puzzled half staring at her. As if by a signal she also stops and stares at me. She's puzzled too.

For want of a better thing to do I shrug my shoulders and walk on. After two seconds I turn my head and notice that she is standing in the same place staring after me. I get too goddam curious and walk right back and say hello. She says hello.

"I've been trying to think but I can't remember where we met before. Your face looks familiar to me," I tell her.

"I've been doing the same thing for the same reason. I am Mrs. Njenga. Tonia Njenga. What's yours?" There's something about her name that rings a bell in my dome. Something distant and far, yet familiar and real.

"I am Dodge. Dodge Kiunyu and best known to my friends as Dod. Does that mean anything to you?" She ponders over it and then I see her face light up. She starts beaming all over. She puts out her hand. I get more puzzled.

"Of course you are Kiunyu. Sure you are. What a break. Don't you remember me? Don't you remember Tonia? We used to play together when we were kids." We shake hands vigorously. Of course this was Tonia. Young Tonia grown into a woman. A married woman. She reminds me of my youth. Something I try hard to forget. But I am mighty pleased to meet her. It's difficult to believe that little cheeky Tonia could have grown into such a beautiful woman as the one in front of me. We are both talking at the same time and talking fast. It's as if we are kids all over again. Tonia is laughing and talking and asking a million questions but I can't answer them because I am also asking her questions. Out of the blue she asks me about the baby.

"Which baby?" I ask.

"I thought you were carrying baby things."

It was then that I became conscious of the bag in my hand. The bag containing the loot. I've got to do something about it. In fact I've got to get out of town as soon as possible.

I explain to Tonia that I have got to get a taxi and report in my office as soon as possible and I ask her how I can get in touch with her should I come to town in the afternoon. She tells me that their house is behind the stadium in the freehold section of the town but that she will not be at home in the afternoon. She was looking for a bus to Thomson's Falls. Her husband was away in Nairobi for some refresher course in telecommunications and would not be back for two weeks. She was therefore going to Thomson's Falls to stay with friends for two or three days. She was lonely.

We talk some more and finally agree that we can ride in my taxi up to Sabugo and that Tonia can get a bus from there. I get the taxi and we set off.

We pass the army camp at Lanet and Tonia gets all excited about these large fields of majestic wheat swinging with the breeze. There is

118

wheat as far as the eye can see. Some patches are green, some patches are yellow, some patches brown and other patches are other colours. Looks like a gigantic variegated carpet mantle spread over the goodly earth to protect the worms from heartstroke. It's simply gorgeous.

The old Ford crawls up Dundori hills in second gear farting grey smoke from its exhaust. I should have hired a newer car. This one is just a beat-up rusty heap that limps like an old woman. I hate old cars. Tonia is telling me how her mother died when we get to the turn-off to Sabugo. I'd have to leave her on the main road so that she can catch a bus but I'd like to hear about Miriam first. I invite her to come to my house and promise that I'll walk her to the road later. She says O.K. and we go.

We get to my house, I pay off the driver and get in. The place smells mucky.

"It's a nice place you've got," Tonia says.

"I wouldn't call it nice. It's just big and empty. I have six bedrooms but I only need one. I reckon one day I'll start rearing chicken in the other five. I have a feeling that the goddam place is haunted."

"How come?"

"Hair-raising owl-like squeaking sounds in the dead of the night. Banging doors and windows and howling winds rustling through curtains and under the doors. The place scares me. I only come to bed when I am drunk."

"Then how do you happen to hear the noises and sounds when you are drunk?"

"I don't hear nothing. I have a good imagination and that's how. Don't believe it."

"Believe what?"

"That ghost stories are true. But that doesn't stop you from telling the stories."

"You like to dally with words, don't you?"

"Sure. It only happens when I am gay."

"Are you gay now?"

"Very much so."

"What's the inspiration?"

"You, my dear Tonia. You are the oldest friend in my memory. I remember you as a naughty, demanding, mischievous little Tonia who thought that little me was standing between her and nice things. You remind me of those old days. Funny enough I have been to Eastleigh several times but I could never find where we used to live."

"Those old slum houses were demolished a long time ago."

"So that's why. Now tell me about your husband."

"There's nothing to tell. I am happily married to one of the nicest men a woman ever came across. Gentle and kind, understanding and loving. I know that a man like you would not want to hear how a wife was loved by her husband because you'd rather have it the other way round so that you can pity and paw her but it happens to be the truth in my case. We have a moderate income and I believe that he will get some promotion when he comes from this course in Nairobi. Then we can afford to have children. I don't intend to look for paid employment. I am quite content to be a housewife. I've nothing really to grumble about."

"I envy you. I have everything to grumble about. Do you love your husband as much as he loves you?"

"What a question, Kiunyu, of course I do. What did you expect?"

"Again I envy you but to tell you the truth I wish it was otherwise."

"But why?"

"Look, Tonia. You've grown into the prettiest girl I've ever seen. You have grown into the ripest womanhood and damn it you've got lots of S.A. Pardon my bluntness, but flattery aside, I'd marry you tomorrow if this other guy had not beaten me to it. I wouldn't have to think about it. I would know that we could be goddam happy. I would have no misgivings whatsoever. None. I wouldn't even think about love. That would be unnecessary. I would simply understand that I was made for you and you for me and each for the other."

"What makes you think that I would feel the same?"

"Because you would. You'd simply meet me and want to be my wife."

"I don't want to sound rude but that sounds very vain."

"Oh no, it isn't. I know it is true. I know that if you were not married and we met like we did, you'd not think twice. I wouldn't even have to ask you to marry me because I'd know that you would and you'd know that I knew that you would. Your thinking is biased now because you are already married and you can't figure out how you'd have reacted had we met when you were single. I know I am right."

"You take too much for granted, don't you?"

"But I am honest with myself," I tell her.

"I am glad to hear that. If you will escort me to the main road please, I'll be on my way to T. Falls."

"Not so fast, Tonia. I haven't annoyed you, have I?"

"If you did you wouldn't know. You must come and see us one day but really I must be on my way."

120

"Forgive my bluntness again but this is one hell of an anticlimax. What are you in so much of a hurry for? Is my company so base that you'd insist on walking out on me before you had rested for ten short minutes? I am sorry if I am the cause of your haste but you will please excuse me for one minute. I will merely rush to the office, make sure that everything is O.K., make a telephone call and come back to you. It's not very far to the main road as you noticed. I wouldn't be a minute."

Before Tonia can protest I bolt out at a run. Very shortly I am in the office and at my desk. There are only four letters and they are not urgent. I put them back on the tray. I learn from my typist that there have been no telephone calls and that everything is O.K. When she asks me what happened to the Landrover I tell her that it developed carburettor trouble and that it's in the garage. I was going back to Nakuru after lunch to fetch it.

I get hold of the phone and dial Nakuru Police Station. I tell this same cop at the desk that due to other pressing matters I was not able to report and that right now I am on my way. I hang up before he asks questions and walk out and jog-trot to my house. Tonia is sitting in the same place with a book in her hand.

"That was not a minute, it was five," she says playfully.

"As you see, I carry no watch. I can tell time better without a watch. It helps me to be patient," I tell her.

"Sorry but I was curious about the baby things you had in that bag there. You shouldn't throw money about like that." If I'd been white I'd have coloured like hell but I am not white. I am as black as niggers go but if you called me a nigger to my face I'd smash your ugly face in several places. That's what I would do. Smash your face. I am a careless cuss. I should not have left that dough sitting there but so what? I tell her that it's salary for settlement workers and she believes it. I sit down and cross my legs.

"I am getting married," I tell her. It's a goddam lie but I can't think of anything better to say right now.

"You are kidding, Kiunyu. You told me that you have no girlfriend."

"As a matter of fact I do have a girl. Her name is Silvia. Silvia Gathoni. Her father is a rich farmer in Eldoret and she is coming out of the Nairobi University at the end of this academic year. She is a real nice piece of work. She took lots for herself when God was dishing it out. We are getting married in five month's time."

"Rich fathers always ask for a fat dowry. Have you sounded him?"

"I knew the old geezer before I met Silvia. We were having one of them meat parties at Njoro and we got to like each other. We talked a lot and I was surprised at the wisdom in the old fellow's head. I flattered him somewhat and after a few pints of hooch he was cursing because he did not have a son like me." Tonia laughs.

"Poor man," she giggles. Her chest is heaving. "You must have taken him for a real long ride for him to wish that you were his son. Unlike you, I am not surprised at the wisdom in the old fellow's head as you so nicely put it. He needs a mother."

"And a son-in-law, don't forget the son-in-law. He needs a son-in-law," I tell her.

"How did you meet the daughter — eh — Silvia. That's her name, isn't it?"

"I was invited to the farm and there she was. The most . . . I reckon that I'd rather not go into that but she has . . . she has plenty, to put it simply. We discussed geography which is what I read at the University and which is what she reads and got on fine. I had no time for the father. Silvia has preoccupied me ever since."

"Are you still preoccupied?" Tonia asks. I notice that she is damn annoyed with Silvia or myself, or both. There is ice in her tone.

"I can't get her out of my mind. Looks like she's taken away my silly heart and left me nothing. She haunts me. My blood thins when I think of her."

"It hadn't occurred to me that you were capable of such strong love. It now appears that I was in error."

"I don't usually love, Tonia, but when I do, I love most horribly. Silvia has got me that way."

"Are you faithful to her?" I cock my ears.

"What was that again?"

"Are you faithful to Silvia?"

"If I was unfaithful to her, I would be unfaithful to myself. Since she became mine and me hers, I have never touched a woman or beguiled my thoughts with desire for other women. To her I am as pure as a baby eunuch and to me she's all those flowers in heaven which God alone is allowed to smell. We intend to remain pure."

"That is very commendable but I doubt if you will keep to it. Any man who drinks like you say you do is bound to be overcome one day. You should go to church more often."

"I have sworn, Tonia. I'll never touch another woman. My eyes are closed. My feelings are locked and sealed. I cannot, except with Silvia."

Tonia is sitting next to me. She is relaxed on the settee and she

122

starts talking about old days and how our teacher Jack married a white blind woman. As she talks she keeps moving her knees in and out, exposing and hiding her thighs and watching me. I am listening to her but I am not feeling very comfortable. I don't like that movement. It's too damn sexy. I have a feeling that she is doing it on purpose. She wants to see whether I can succumb and break my vow with Silvia. That is the trouble with women. If you tell them that you love another woman very much they feel insulted and they retaliate by breaking you down. They make sure that they get you. You are a challenge. They expose their charm and since most guys are weak, they give in.

I am one hell of a weak guy. No sooner do I see good thighs than I start panting and swallowing. Tonia is showing me them thighs of hers and she makes sure that I see them. I am sitting directly opposite and therefore I can't help it. I can no longer listen to what she is talking about. She is reminding me of that boy I nicknamed Master Roundhead who got run over by a bus in the early days of our first year in school. Right now I am not interested in Master Roundhead. No sir, and you can guess what I am interested in.

I can't bear it any more. I shift awkwardly in my seat and she also shifts into an even more provocative position. Her pants are yellow and she doesn't care whether I know or not. She is still talking but this time I am deaf. I am stone deaf. No kidding. I am as deaf as a stone.

I stand up. I move over to the settee and sit beside her. I don't say a word. I just relax and rest my hand on her lap. She knew I would. She doesn't protest. She pretends that my hand is not there as she goes on talking.

"You saw the races didn't you?"

"What?" I ask.

"The races. The Nakuru motor races last Sunday. Were you there?"

"Yes. It was marvellous. Oh yes. Wonderful. I like races. They excite me. Very exciting especially when there are accidents." All the time I am moving closer. I put my hand on her tit stealthy-like and go on talking about motor racing.

"Yes, very daring. Makes my blood crawl. That's what it does. So fast. It's like lightning. I mean it's very fast." I move my hand along her thighs. "They make a horrible noise, those racing cars. A horrible noise. Oh, yes I don't like noise." I am now stroking freely her everywhere. I am holding her thigh in my hands. I am still talking.

"I like excitement. Real excitement." She's holding me tight.

"Tonia, I like excitement. Real heavenly excitement. I like to get excited. I like to yield to it. Tonia. It's me. Yes me." We are now rolling on the sofa. She is scratching my back and searching for my lips. I am doing one hundred things at once.

"No," she says softly but again I am deaf. That is the only word she says. I don't even hear it.

We are quietly putting our clothing in order and kissing little kisses when she says, "You shouldn't have done it."

"I know," I tell her, "but I'll remember it for ever."

"Silvia will murder you if she ever gets to know about it. She may want to take out my eyes."

"Which Silvia are you talking about?"

"Your fiancée, you goon."

"Oh! That? I am sorry but I just made it up. Silvia does not exist." You've never seen a woman go mad. Tonia lashed out and slapped me across my face and then hurled her handbag straight at my belly.

"You cheating swine! You made me do that on the strength of your lies — you filthy pig. How dare you?" That reminds me of the young old days when she used to wallop me and blame me for everything. I used to hate her for that. I am just about to strike back at her but I check myself. I relax my nerves and rub my smarting face. I am very calm.

"I didn't make you do it, Tonia. It was the other way round."

"But why did you cheat me about Silvia? I wouldn't have allowed you to touch me."

"What has Silvia got to do with it? She doesn't exist. It was just a story."

"I feel absolutely awful."

"I feel fine."

"Swine!" She collects her things in a hurry and storms through the door. I stand perplexed and then decide to follow her. She doesn't look behind. She is still the proud Tonia that used to annoy me when we were young. I hate following her but I find myself doing so. I catch up and walk alongside but I don't say a goddam word. I simply walk beside her towards the main road. Then all of a sudden I get annoyed. I was not to blame. No man could have resisted being so tempted. So I let her have it.

"What the hell are you so glum about? It isn't the first time you have been unfaithful to your husband is it?"

"For heaven's sake, Kiunyu, please leave me alone. I can walk to

124

the main road on my own."

"I know but I am catching a bus too. I am going back to Nakuru. I have a date."

"What?"

"I have a date. I am already late."

"How I hate you." (

"Look, Tonia. You don't have to act high and mighty with me. I try to understand people but I don't pretend to understand you. You are acting all too strange. That's all you are doing — acting. Why don't you come down to earth?"

"If you were kind, you'd please leave me alone."

"What does it mean then? Are we enemies or friends?"

"Nothing. We are nothing. We didn't meet. We didn't do anything. Remember that. We haven't met since we were kids. You've merely had a dream. You dreamt you saw Tonia. You haven't seen her since you were a kid. You merely dreamt. A vivid dream. A very real dream but a dream all the same. You have been dreaming, Kiunyu. Remember that. You have been dreaming. You have not seen Tonia since you were eleven. That was a long time ago in Eastleigh. Your mother had just died and you were staying with Tonia and her mother. You were a kid. Then you went away. You have never seen Tonia since. She might be dead. You merely dreamt that you saw her. You have been dreaming, Mr. Kiunyu."

By God, she nearly hypnotized me into believing that I was dreaming. I pulled my hair and scratched my chin and damn it man, I couldn't have been dreaming. I grabbed her hand and she slapped me. "You are dreaming, Kiunyu." I wish she'd call me Dodge.

We get to the main road and wait for buses. We are going in different directions and it will mean different buses. I wish my bus would come first. Tonia is still harping on this dreaming theme and it gets on my nerves. She is now spreading her fingers in front of my face and saying:

"A wonderful dream. That's what it was Kiunyu. A dream in which you saw Tonia, a dream . . ."

"Oh shut up for Chrissake with this dream nonsense! I have just given you a lay and that was no goddam dream. It's different in dreams. In dreams you collapse before you get anywhere."

"A very vivid dream. You are still dreaming. You are not awake. You are sleep-walking and dreaming. Your mind is confused. You are confused. Very confused. You. . . ."

"You are mad, Tonia," I interrupt. "Stark raving mad. I can't be dreaming."

"You are confused, you . . . ."

"For crying out loud stop harping on this nonsense about. . . ."

"No, Kiunyu. I am not harping. You are confused. You have never seen Tonia. You dreamt. You are still dreaming. You are confused. You don't know where you are. You don't know where you left your money. You don't know where you are going. You do not know who I am. You don't know what you'd like to do. You are confused. You are dreaming."

At the mention of the word money I bolt like one posseessd towards my house. I left the money sitting right there and I didn't even remember to lock the place up. That at least proves that I am not dreaming. If you are dreaming you can't remember your money can you? You'd probably catch a bus in your dream and forget the money and when you came back the money would be gone. Dreams are very tricky.

I burst into my house and look around. I must have hidden the dough somewhere. It's not where I left it. I dash here and there pulling things apart but I see no dough. I look under the table, under the chairs, under the settee, I look everywhere. The dough is gone. I can't think that any of my workers would have come to my house in my absence. It's not possible. I sink on the settee and screw my face trying to figure out how. Could I be dreaming? Am I dreaming? Is this real? Have I really lost all that dough? Oh no. Never. I must be dreaming. Gosh! I am sweating too.

An accidental fart makes dolorous sonorous music behind me and I start fanning my face. It really stinks. Then all of a sudden it hits me. As I fan my face and inhale rotten air it hits me bang and nearly lays me flat. Tonia of course. She collected her things in a hurry and with them my money. Now that I think clearly about it I reckon I actually saw her take it and put it in her big bag. That was after she hit me with her bloody bag.

I run as fast as a hunted hare towards the main road and on the way meet a police patrol car. On seeing me they stop the vehicle and make a sign for me to stop but I don't. I run past them and I can hear them cursing behind me but their curses don't worry me and I don't even look behind. I figure out that by the time they have turned the vehicle on that narrow road tract, I will be some distance away but I am mistaken. Two cops are chasing me on foot. Their heavy boots are going paipaipai-paipai behind me but I am faster. I have lighter shoes and in case you have forgotten, I was an athlete. I am enjoying the race but then the damn cops blow a whistle. They keep blowing

the goddam whistle as they chase after me and I don't feel so good.
People are peeping out of their huts and some are even joining the
chase for the heck of it. Gosh. It doesn't look so good. Some punk
has let his dog loose and the beast is barking some hundred yards
behind me. I keep on till I reach the main road. There is no Tonja. She
has disappeared. Over to the left I can see a cloud of dust and a bus
moving towards Thomson's Falls. She must have taken the goddam
bus. I don't move. I wait till the cops and their retinue of farmers and
their dogs get to where I am. I am staring after the bus as they
surround me. Like me they are panting.

"We have a warrant of arrest for you, Mr. Kiunyu." He doesn't
finish speaking before the police car pulls alongside and I am hustled
in. Before you can wink an eye the vehicle is reversed and we are
again moving towards my office. This cop next to me asks me where
my house is as we get to the office and I point the way. In other
circumstances I would have used delaying tactics for the heck of it
but we are outside the goddam office. My clerks are coming out of
the office and staring at us.

The vehicle moves forward and stops outside my house and the
cops just about burst in. They don't ask a thing. They get into the
house and start pulling everything to pieces. They move into the
bedrooms and really wreck the place. They are at it for some ten
minutes while I stand there guarded by the Luo inspector who is
proudly holding a cane. He faces me squarely.

"Where is it?" he asks me.

"At the police station," I tell him.
"Where?"
"At the police station. Didn't you see it sitting there?"
"What in the name of God are you talking about?"
"About it."
"What does your 'it' refer to?"
"Same as yours," I tell him.

"Listen, Mr. Kiunyu. We are wise to you. You can't take us on a
wild goose chase. I want the whole works and all in one piece. The
whole lot. You can make things easier for yourself if you tell us where
you have hidden it."

"I didn't hide it. I drove it there. I left it under the charge of the
cop on duty. He promised to look after it. I believe he is still looking
after it or whoever relieved him is."

"Wait a minute. You are too fast. Who do you say you gave it
to?"

"I didn't give it. I left it there under the charge of the policeman on duty."

"What do you mean by saying that you left it there?"

"I parked it."

"You parked what?"

"The Landrover of course. I drove it there last night."

"For crying out loud, man, I am not talking about the goddam Landrover. I am talking about the money. The money that you hid in the Midland Hotel yesterday evening and which you collected from the hands of the cleaner this morning. The money that you hauled from somewhere. That is the money I want and I want it quick."

"Do you dream, inspector?"

"What?"

"Do you ever dream?" I repeat.

"Out with the money, Mr. Kiunyu. Sooner or later we shall lay our fingers on it with or without your help. Either way it's going to be tough for you unless you spill the beans. I want the truth."

"Since I am under the impression that you are dreaming, inspector, I am unable to help you. I'll have to wait till you are fully awake. As for money, I wish you'd lend me some. I am really broke."

"What were you running away for?"

"Did I run?"

"Of course you ran till you were caught and don't be silly. What was the cause of your flight?"

"Was I caught?"

"Stop playing with words. You were running from justice. When you saw a police vehicle you took off, didn't you?"

"Did I?"

"What did you do?"

"I merely continued doing what I was doing before."

"Why were you running?"

"Since you are inquisitive, inspector, I will tell. Of late I have decided to keep fit. I do various physical exercises in bed but from today I decided that I'll run to the main road and back once every day to improve my knees. You fellows insisted on giving me a ride back but to tell you the truth, I'd have preferred to run back. Do you do any exercises, inspector?"

"Why did you sneak out of the police station?"

"That is the wrong word, inspector, I did not sneak. I walked to the desk and saluted the constable on duty and then walked out."

"What?"

128

"I saluted and nodded at the fellow at the desk. It is not my fault if he did not see me. He had his back towards me."

"Very clever, aren't you?"

"Thank you very much, inspector. I am starting to respect your wisdom. Did you go to university?"

"Now, now," he signalled his cops. "Take him out. Lock this place up and you, Onyango, will have to remain to guard the place till you are relieved." He addressed the other cops. "Make sure that Mr. Kiunyu is locked in a cell by himself and that he is not allowed to communicate with anyone till I return. I am going to interrogate the clerks in the office and will expect you to be back within thirty to forty-five minutes. On your way."

"You are a fast worker, inspector. They should give you an extra pip. I'll see you when you see me and thank you for the ride back to Nakuru." The inspector comes for me but I am wise. I get into the police vehicle fast, curl myself up in the right hand corner of the rear seat and start raising the window. He'd have to yank the door open before he can punch me but he is wise. He doesn't try it. He knows that he has all the time he needs to do whatever he likes in respect of my person and I know it too.

"Off with you, driver!" he orders. "Knock out his teeth if he becomes fresh."

I don't say a word. The driver eases the clutch and the Ford Zephyr starts to move backwards and then forwards and off we go. I curl up in my corner and smoke silently.

All the way to Nakuru I am farting like an over-loaded donkey. I am making it very loud when I can. The two cops beside me on the rear seat are having one hell of a time. All the windows of the car are open but they can't escape the smell. I am enjoying myself.

At the police station I am booked and locked in. The cops are positively hostile but that is only natural. I have never met a friendly cop. They are very suspicious fellows. They even suspect kids. I have learnt one thing though. Jack's body has been discovered but one thing does not click. They did not find any pills or the bottle of whisky. He was found in his bed by the cook and the cook telephoned the police. The latter figured out that he died of a heart attack or some such sudden malady but the doctor will find out. There was no talk of theft.

I sit in the dark cell and think. I am thanking Tonia for having pinched that money although I think I should strangle her for having done so. I am not going to admit that I had any money. It will be my

word against that of the waiter. The waiter cannot prove that I put
the money there or that it was mine. I found him with it. Tonia cannot
testify. She is a thief. The police can't touch me. They cannot prove
robbery because nobody has been robbed. No robbery has been
reported. If I had the money it could just as well have been truly mine.
There is nothing criminal about having large sums of money in cash.
Nothing.

The police are not justified in locking me up at all. This is false
arrest. Gosh! If I didn't have some guilty conscience and if
circumstances had not played against me, I should not be here. I am
not guilty. I am only guilty of one thing: I sneaked out of the police
station. But they cannot prove that one either. I telephoned them
twice and said I was going. I was not cheating them. I meant to go
back. They had no business coming chasing after me as if I was a
thief. At least they didn't know that I was a thief. Injustice! This is
goddam injustice. I might lose my job. Hell's bells! I am as mad as
bells. They are ringing in my head — bells, I mean. That is what they are
doing — ringing in my goddam head. I let out a fart and lean against
the wall. Life can be funny. Positively funny. But sometimes it isn't.

10

To a bachelor of two and a half score, I have only one word of
advice. Marry. Get married you silly blighter. You are wasting your
goddam life. If I was married, I wouldn't have landed myself into this
bloody mess again. I would have stayed at home watching my wife
do her knitting. How I hate myself. Another thing. Never steal. Even
if it's a pin or a banana, just keep your itching fingers off it. If I'd
observed that, I wouldn't be in jail again. Heck!

What I am doing is I am biting my fingernails. They are dirty and
long. I am looking at my bare feet. I haven't worn shoes for the last
four months. That's how long I have been here. Here at Kamiti, the
largest prison in this goddam country. I should have been jailed for
several years but I reckon the magistrate was just merciful. He only

gave me a year. He should have given me seven but I guess he liked my face. Sometimes a magistrate can like your face. Who knows? Maybe the blighter was homosexual.

Never trust a woman. Where secrets are concerned never trust any of them goddam women. Their will is too weak. If it wasn't for nosy Josy I wouldn't be here. She spilled the beans. She was too eager to tell the truth. Damn her, she is in jail too.

What happened was that Jack's death appeared as one of the headlines in the local paper. Josy read about how Jack was found in bed and how the doctors found out that he had died of alcoholic poisoning. Josy smelt a rat. We had left Jack lying on the settee and there were those goddam pills all over the place. I reckon Josy had a soft spot for the old bastard so she marched to the police station and told them that there was something fishy. That interested them plenty so they pumped her. She gave them the whole works but it boomeranged back on her. She was charged and held for failure to report a body and I was held on the same charge.

The money business was forgotten. It was no longer important. There was evidence that Jack had withdrawn a large sum of money and that the said sum was missing but it was not possible to connect it with his death since he wasn't murdered. The doctor said he wasn't murdered. I think the blighter was murdered anyway. The doctor who performed the post mortem may have made a mistake but I wouldn't know. Anyway, I saw Jack's corpse and I didn't report to the police and that's why I am in the can.

I'll be in the cooler for another eight months. No. Seven. I think they will knock one month off. I wish they'd knock out two. I am tired of this prison business.

I found out about Tonia. She is not Mrs. Njenga. She is Mrs. Everybody. She was just pulling my leg. She is what you'd call a hard core prostitute specializing in army guys at Nanyuki. She did not live in Nakuru either. Some army guy from Lanet brought her to Nakuru from Nanyuki but could not take her to the barracks because he was living in single quarters. He'd kept her at Amigos for three days and nights and I suppose he got tired of her. When I met her she was actually going back to Nanyuki through Thomson's Falls. She told me all that sweet stuff about her husband because she did not want me to get wise to her. She was damn clever about it — the bitch. I haven't forgotten that she slapped me for spinning a yarn. Very clever. One day I'll get my claws into her. Trouble is they are not sharp — I mean my claws. I've been biting them all along but I don't swallow. Maybe that's why I am hungry. I am always hungry in this goddam jail. What

131

they give you would not satisfy a one day old baby even if the baby had belly ache. That is why I am biting my fingernails.

I have great respect for this guy Macharia who is trying to organize the prisoners to stage a hunger strike. It's one hell of a good idea as ideas go. I'd hate to starve to death but I wouldn't mind fasting for a day or two. As things are we are just about fasting every day. A fasting Moslem is better fed than we are. The only difference is that we are allowed to swallow saliva and goddam it man, the saliva isn't all that sweet. Mine tastes like raw avocados.

There is a small lizard moving on the rafters and occasionally it looks at me suspiciously. It fascinates me quite a lot seeing that I have no friends. I am looking at it when all of a sudden it darts out its elastic tongue and grabs a fly. It chews slowly and deliberately and then swallows. Gosh. That makes me feel hungry.

I smile at the lizard but it only looks at me suspiciously. I decide to talk to it.

"Hello, little lizard." The lizard gets tense as if to ask: "What?"

"I only said hello." I wish I could hold it in my hands and play with it. I might kiss it for a bang and then put it inside my prison shirt just to warm its cold blood. When you have no friends a lizard looks lovely. I wish it could talk to me.

"Hello man," I say. The lizard bolts off through the rafters and outside into the glorious sun. How fascinating. I start wondering whether a lizard would obey the scientific law which says that bodies expand when subjected to heat. I can't remember what the goddam law says but it's something to that effect. There is this corny word inversely or conversely or directly etc. which is mentioned in the law but I can't remember which one it is or where it fits. That is beside the point though. What I am wondering about is whether my little lizard will expand in size after it has been subjected to the heat of the sun for some time. The more I think about it the more I get convinced that it must expand. After all it's a cold blooded creature. I wish I knew.

I shift my ass to the right and sit up and cross my legs. I try a Buddha posture but I am too stiff. That guy Buddha must have been very flexible. He beats me. I wonder whether Christ would have sat like Buddha. I wonder what they would have said to each other if they'd met. Of course they wouldn't have said a goddam thing. They couldn't have understood each other. They would just have sat there, talked with their hands pointing at heaven and then saluted one another. They would, of course, smile at each other and probably shake hands. It's a funny thought. There would be nothing funny on the other hand if Christ met Mohammed. I reckon that these two would come to a physical showdown. That is the way I see it. They would have it out there and then and their apostles or disciples or whatever they are called would have a fling at each other just for the heck of it. That would spark off a holy war and damn it man — I would take a fling at some other prisoner just for a bang. I think I would get a real bang. I need a bang. This prison life is goddam boring. It's lousy.

There is this lousy fellow who's been in the quod for five years. He sleeps at the other end of the dorm. He doesn't like me because I have been sick this last week and I don't go out to work. That is why I am here all alone. Anyway, this fellow, he strips his clothes off after work and walks about in the nude fingering his little man. He is goddam impotent and therefore swears that it's not a prick. It's a wart. He has been whipped three times but he wouldn't stop the practice. The reason he does it is that no woman has ever seen him in the nude and that he is giving us men a treat. Such filthy bastards are my daily companions. You can imagine how I feel.

The doctor has been very kind to me. He is a Kisii fellow with very smart hair and he just got married. I guess he must be having it nice with his wife and that's why he is so kind. He went to Makerere too but he doesn't remember me. He was in New Hall while I was in Northcote Hall and fortunately we were never friends. He was too proud for my liking. Anyway this guy is the doctor here. I don't even remember his name. It sounds like a Luo name.

I am due at the prison hospital at eleven thirty. I will have my eighth injection and more bitter pills. That's what I have been taking these last few days. No wonder I am so goddam hungry. At least they should have the decency to feed prisoners better.

I am suffering from chronic malaria, ulceration, and I have this big boil on the right armpit. The goddam boil has been exuding some jelly-like sticky fluid but it's drying up now. It's itching like mad but I daren't scratch it. I would only open it up again.

I don't really mind being sick in this place. It's better lying here on the bed with a pain here and a pain there than going out early in the morning for hard labour every day. Sometimes there is no useful work to be done but the goddam warders make sure that you sweat anyway. They really do. You are always sweating if you are not sick.

I am not letting the other prisoners know that I am a graduate and all that. No sir. If they knew that I am a graduate, I'd be in trouble. They'd mistreat me just for the heck of it. They think that

it's the educated who are having everything and oppressing the poor,
If there weren't educated people to run the government these guys
wouldn't be in prison anyway. That's the way they look at it. I am
letting on that I am a big time crook. I let on that I have done lots
of dirty things in the past and that I have been jailed some six times.
There was this gang that hauled lots of dough from the City Council
some two years ago. I tell the mugs that I was the brain behind the
whole works and that I don't care who gets to know about it. They
think that I am one of the very tough and brave thieves and that I live
like a millionaire. I tell them about this eight bedroomed house that
I own in Nakuru and my dairy farm in Kitale and they are so dumb
that they swallow all the crap. They know that my I.Q. is above
average and they therefore respect me. I enjoy telling lies especially
to morons who are themselves great liars.

I have to be escorted to the goddam hospital whenever I go
there. It's either one of these two funny warders who does it. One is
very thin but has an enormous head. I call him Fathead. The other
has these classic bushman buttocks and I call him Fatbottom. I don't
know whose turn it will be today. I prefer Mr. Fathead on account
of his sense of humour. Boy, is he funny! All he has to do is nod or
shake that big head of his and you start laughing. He looks like a
football on top of a reed. I expect him to topple over himself every
minute.

Well it turned out the guy who escorted me was Mr. Fatbottom.
This guy says nothing but he likes to whistle. He doesn't whistle any
particular tune but he whistles all the same. He depresses me. You
take a guy who doesn't say anything but is whistling all the time and
he'll depress your ass, that is if it's not already depressed.

We got to the hospital and a funny thing happened. The hospital
assistant gave me this injection and I started feeling funny. My knees
didn't want to hold together. I felt as if I was folding over. I wanted to
sit down. I really did. I knew if I didn't sit down I'd hit the floor full
length. I started seeing fading fifty cent pieces floating in front of me
and my head was very hot. Darkness was approaching. I grabbed the
hospital assistant as I fell and that's all I remember. The rest is quiet.
Heavenly oblivion.

It's two weeks hence. I am at Kenyatta National Hospital. I
gather that I have been delirious since they brought me here. I have
been saying horrible things in my sleep. The doctors think that it's
this chronic malaria business but I tend to think otherwise. There
must have been something wrong with that bloody injection. It was
either the wrong injection or whatever it was, it was poison to my body.

134

I am as weak as hell. I am practically an invalid. I have not opened my mouth for these two weeks. They have been feeding me with this stuff which they are injecting into my system through my big toe. I don't mean right bang on the big toe. No. It's between the big toe and the next toe. There is some soft skin there and that's where they have punctured a hole to let the feeding juice in. The bloody bottle is halfway gone and it's hanging right before my eyes. I don't like the look of it.

There is this other guy on my right and they are feeding him through the nose. I don't know how he manages to snore but he does. Maybe he is snoring through one nostril. What I really meant to say was that it looks damn nauseating — I mean feeding a guy through the nose. If I had anything to puke I reckon I'd puke. Trouble is I am as empty as a vacuum. I can't puke nothing. I wish they'd move this guy out of my sight. How in the name of holy Jove can I sleep with a snoring guy next to me who's got this beat-up face and bandages all over with a goddam tube right through his nose. Gosh, there are bubbles in the tube too, and I suppose the guy is eating them too. They move up and down as he breathes. God, it's nauseating.

On my left is an old short fat fellow. From his breathing I reckon that he has asthma or chronic T.B. His breathing is very funny. It goes *beea biii borrea* — *biii* and sometimes it stops for a while and then comes out forcibly but with a lot of difficulties — *borr-bi!* He is also driving me nuts. I am really nuts. I can't figure out what I have been doing or thinking these two past weeks. I don't know what I have been saying. It was only yesterday that I got fully conscious.

There is a prison warder between me and the old guy on the left. I wonder whether he is guarding me or the two of us. Maybe the old guy is a prisoner too. At least he looks like one. You take a fellow who breathes like this guy and you know he is a prisoner. He has resigned himself to fate. He doesn't care how he breathes and he doesn't care what you think about it. All he knows is that he must breathe and he jolly well does it. He is breathing now. Gosh! I wish I had a cigarette.

The breathing guy turns over onto his right side and faces me. He smiles at the warder.

"How are you feeling now, Mr. Kiunyu?" the guard asks. I am just about to answer when the old man interrupts.

"I am feeling rotten."

"You will be all right soon," the guard says. "It's only a minor chest trouble."

"I wish I could be certain. I feel so weak. Lately I've been tasting blood in my mouth. I don't want to recover. I'd like to die here and now. I pray that it comes quickly. I pray. I don't want to live."

"Listen, Kiunyu," the warder says. "You have several years ahead although you will be inside. It's better inside than dead, Kiunyu. You must pray for health." At this juncture I can't contain myself any longer. The warder is confusing names. I never heard of anybody else called Kiunyu except myself. Not anywhere in the whole wide world.

"Are you sure you are not confusing names?" I ask the warder. "I am Kiunyu." This sort of surprises the guard. He advances towards the head of my bed and reads my name on the chart.

"Dodge Kiunyu. Of course you are the educated prisoner. This man here is also Kiunyu. He has been a long time with us. It's just coincidence."

"Is the young man called Kiunyu?" the old man asks weakly.

"It appears so," the warder says.

"Uh," the old guy grunts thoughtfully. I notice that his face is contorted with some pain and that he would cry out if he was a kid.

"Where is your home, young man?" he asks me.

"Here. Right here where I am housed. This is my home." I don't like it when a guy like this starts calling me young man and starts asking me questions. I hate it. The old guy moans. In a way I feel sorry for him. I don't think he has long to live. Take a guy that's just about dying and he wants to know where the hell you come from. That's not even funny.

"How did you get that name, sonny?" the old guy asks. It's annoying enough to know that the old fellow is called Kiunyu like myself. It don't worry me where the hell he got his name. It doesn't worry me one little jot. Why should he worry about mine? I tell him that I got this name like other people get theirs. I just fished for it.

He doesn't like that. He moans some more. I reckon that it's a real effort opening his mouth. It doesn't improve his breathing. Then he asks me this silly question: "Who is your mother?"

I feel like getting out of bed and clouting him on the dome except that he is dying. You clout a dying fellow like this guy here and straight away he dies. You go to the cooler for manslaughter. I couldn't clout him anyway even if I wanted. I don't have the strength to get out of bed. That way he is lucky and so am I. I answer him between my teeth.

"She's a woman and that's none of your business. For Chrissake relax. You need all your energy to stop yourself from dying. Please don't talk to me."

136

"Young men are impolite these days. In our days we respected the elders."

"You are not an elder, are you? You are a jailbird like me. I don't have to respect a jailbird, do I?"

"They are all the same—the young men of today. I have lost touch with the real world. I have been in jail for too long. If I have any future, that will be in jail too. I was only curious about your name. There aren't many with that name. For me it was a nickname. They nicknamed me when I was a kid. I liked to lick salt. That's how. It became my name. I only know one other Kiunyu but I don't know whether he is living or dead. That's my son. I never met him. I was in jail when he was born. That's why your name intrigued me."

"And where was this Kiunyu of yours born?" the warder asks him.

"It's about thirty years ago. I was going to get married to a woman. Her name was Theresa. Theresa Ngendo. She was already pregnant. That's one of the reasons why we were going to get married in a hurry. Everything was arranged but unfortunately I killed that old Kamba taxi driver in self-defence. They booked me for manslaughter. A life sentence. Ngendo saw me a few times after the kid was born and told me that she called him Kiunyu after me. Whenever she visited me in the prison she never brought young Kiunyu. It really drove me crazy because I wanted to see the boy. Now I know I'll never see him. I'll die in prison."

All the time he is speaking my mouth is wide open. I never heard such stuff in my life. Of course Theresa Ngendo was my mother. That's all I remember about her now. Miriam used to call her just Theresa and when she was drunk she called her Terry. I don't want to remember all that. I don't want to remember anything. All I know is that if what this old man says is true, then he is my father. Fancy that. After all these long years when a father means as much to me as the dinosaurs mean to you, I meet a dying jailbird who is my father. If you expect me to be overjoyed you are not my type. If you expect me to rush to him, give him a kiss and then sob on his chest, again you are not my type. Trouble is I simply can't get interested in fathers. I think they are very cruel people — fathers I mean. They are either killing someone and getting jailed or beating up their wives and scaring the hell out of their kids. Most times they are unfaithful as hell.

I feel sorry for my father. It isn't exactly honey to spend all your goddam life in a prison just because you smacked a soft skulled taxi driver on the head after he called you a pig after which he decides to pop off. Maybe the fellow would have died of sunstroke or something anyway. I really feel sorry for my father.

Trouble with law courts is that they don't make an allowance for age. If you are twenty and you manslaughter an old geezer of eighty, it ain't fair to jail you for life. The old geezer would have lived some three or four years before he died of old age naturally and that should be the maximum sentence if you manslaughter such a guy. This guy here has had it the tough way. That's why I feel so sorry for him. Maybe I should wake and kiss him after all. No kidding. If I had the strength I'd do exactly that.

The Kiunyu family if you may call it so, has had it tough all along. So this guy was going to get married to my mother? Gosh! I am confused as hell. I think I am going to cry. Really. My eyes are all moist. We've had it real tough. I shouldn't have hated my mother so.

The way I see it is that she loved this guy and all, but he gets booked for life. She knows that she'll never get him. Life for her just becomes an amorphous nebulous mass in which she floats from nowhere and goes nowhere. There is no shred of light. It's all darkness. She doesn't know which way to go but she gropes in the darkness. She cries and frets and beats her chest to a state of hysteria. She doesn't know herself any more. She gropes here and there and everywhere till she is weary. She is exhausted. She can't love again. The pain of her first love nags and nags and her heart is worn out. She surrenders. She surrenders to fate. Life has no meaning any more but she has to live. How she lives is immaterial because life is meaningless. She merely exists. She had no feeling for the things she did. Her life had died when her man went to jail. Poor mother. Oh God! I wish I could see her again. Just one little glance. One soft smile. One brief touch of her hand. Oh me! Why did you die, mother? Why? God rest her. At least I should have loved her a little. For that I am to blame.

"Why are you crying?" the warder asks me. I have no words for him. His presence is redundant. The old man is watching me too. He is wearing a puzzled face. His suffering is more than he can bear. I wish he'd live. Gosh! He is my father.

"What has moved you so that you beguile your cheeks with unchecked tears? Leave it to the women. They feel with their eyes." He said it so weakly and hoarsely that I just about gave up the ghost. This hot torrent of tears comes rushing down my cheeks and my nose is in a mess. I manage to say through my nose, "She was my mother. Theresa Ngendo, she was my mother. She. . . ."

"Then you are . . . you are Kiunyu my son. You are my son. You

138

are Kiunyu." He leaps out of bed with some unknown strength and literally comes flying almost into my bed but he doesn't get there. His foot gets caught by the rail of his bed and he goes crashing onto the hard floor at the warder's feet. He lies still. I am inspired by some unknown power and I get out of bed like lightning. I am bleeding at the place where the feeding tube entered my body between the big toe and the next toe but that is nothing. The feeding tube is dripping onto the bed.

I kneel by my father and hold his head in my arms. Some nurses haul me away and they lift him onto his bed. Blood is coming through his mouth and through his ears and his eyes are shut. I push the nurses away, weak as I am, and stand by his bedside. I hold his arm but it goes limp on me.

"Father. It's me father. Kiunyu. Your little son. Don't die. Please don't. Don't die. It's me." He opens his eyes once. A long three seconds. He fixes them on mine. Three painful seconds and then his whole body sags into peaceful oblivion. His eyes continue to stare but there is no life in them. Deep inside me I know he is gone. He's gone and left me. I am all alone. Alone like Cain but banished by fate. So soon we met and so soon parted. Who said that God was merciful? Gosh! I could whip Him.

I move my hand and close his eyes, then I kneel down and cry. I am crying for mother too. When she died I was too young to know. I am crying for forgiveness for the wrong I have done my parents in my heart. I was full of hate and unschooled disgust when I should have forgiven and loved. It's for this that I cry, for in their hearts I know they loved me.

I am lifted by unseen hands and laid on my bed. There are people all over the place — doctors, nurses, patients and others. I can't see them properly. I don't want to see them. I don't want to see anything.

Everybody is asking what happened. The warder is struck dumb and is of not much help. There is somebody asking me what happened but I am merely looking at him without seeing him. He puts his stethoscope into his ears and starts putting it all over my body.

"Treat him for shock," he tells some nurse. That's all I heard. I reckon I fainted or something because when I woke up it was the following day.

I wake up suddenly. I must have been dreaming. I was saving a drowning kid when this crocodile comes from nowhere and starts nosing us in a very friendly way. The crocodile didn't bite us or anything. It just kept nosing around but it scared the hell out of me. I tried to swim away like mad but the goddam crocodile was always

there nosing around. It went under and I imagined that this time it
was really going to take a bite. I let go the kid and swam for my life
but I didn't swim far. The bloody crocodile was right in front of me.
That scared more hell out of me and I reckon it's the reason why I
woke up. I am in a sweat. They have the goddam feeding tube fixed
to my toes again.

There is a nurse looking at my chart and taking my temperature
and she smiles at me when I come to. It only takes a few minutes of
reflections and adjustments to remind me where I am, what I am
doing and who I am. I take in everything and doze off again. This is
sleep. It's not any goddam swoon.

It's about eight in the evening when somebody wakes me up.
I open my blinking eyes and keep on blinking on account of this
bright light above me. When I focus I see the doctors — I mean the
Kamiti prison doctor. He is arguing with another doctor. There are
some three prison officials and two warders.

"Are you awake?" the Kamiti doctor asks me. I wish I knew his
name.

I wink at him in the affirmative.

"You are coming back to Kamiti. Your father will be buried
tomorrow in the prison cemetery. The nurses will dress you."

The news doesn't excite me any. I am sort of half dead if you
want to know. If the doctor had told me that they were going to
chuck me into the sea I would have felt no different. If he'd told me
that I was going to meet God I would have felt no different either.
I have no feelings. If they'd dragged me by the feet instead of
chucking me at the back of a prison van I wouldn't have cared. I
wouldn't have bothered to forgive them or damn them. I would have
been simply indifferent.

The burial of Kiunyu Senior was simple and according to prison
procedure. I attended but I was on a stretcher. I couldn't walk. I tried
to but I couldn't.

Word had gone around of how I met my father and how he died
trying to jump to my bed. Everybody was sympathizing with me.
I hate sympathy. Every lousy prisoner is saying sorry for what has
already taken place and two of them actually wept at the grave.

It's all very nauseating. I mean old guys snivelling all over the
place and saying what a nice fellow Kiunyu Senior was and how sad
I must be and asking the Almighty to have mercy on us all etc. That
type of stuff doesn't go down well with me. What I need is just quiet.
All I want is to rest on this goddam bed and think. I am sick.

140

11

I have been trying to interest this guy sitting next to me with several lines of conversation but he is a lousy conversationalist. He just says yes or no and then keeps mum. He is looking out of the window as the bus passes this dry stony landscape of Murang'a District just after the township before we reach Sagana. There is nothing interesting about the landscape. It's all barren and dry as hell. It takes a queer fellow to go on staring at landscape like that unless he is some sort of a geologist which this fellow isn't. I doubt that he knows the difference between granite and clay. If you told him that you just noticed some quartz on the rock face he might think that you are talking about some wild animal. Anyway this guy is sitting next to me and we are both going to Nanyuki.

I am travelling on donated proceeds. I got it from Zick. He is no longer working for the Department of Settlement. No sir. He is Deputy Permanent Secretary to the Ministry of Housing. A big shot. He is understudying some expatriate old-timer who is getting the axe. Zick complains that the old guy doesn't teach him a goddam thing. He agreed with me though when I pointed out that the old guy ma, have nothing to teach. Take a guy who doesn't know anything about housing. Right. How the hell can such a guy teach you anything about housing? But so what? Zick and his outgoing expatriate are the tops in that ministry and are drawing handsome dough. What they know about housing is practically nil but don't forget the dough. It makes everything else immaterial.

I only wanted to borrow five quid from Zick but he gave me twenty. Fancy that. He didn't even lend it. He gave it to me. Just like that — the way you'd snap your finger. One of these days I must do something for Zick. Guys like him are rare.

What I am doing is I am going to Nanyuki. I am trying to trace

Tonia and my dough. I don't expect to find the dough though. Oh no.
I know it's all gone. The reason why I am going is that I want to kill
Tonia. I mean it. I am going to give it to her if I find her. Then they
can give it to me in turn but I shan't worry. If you don't want to live,
for God's sake, there is no reason why the rope should scare you.
It's like being your own hangman.

Don't get surprised, my friend. Don't. Prison didn't change me.
It hardened me. I am as hard as steel but I hate prison. I'd rather hang
outright.

I came out a week ago. I hitch-hiked to Nakuru and went to my
bank but there were no funds. I found three hundred and two shillings
and that's what I've been living on till yesterday when Zick gave me
this other dough. When that goes I'll start begging. No kidding.
I am not going to look for work. If I can exist through begging why
the hell should I work? At least I wouldn't have a job to lose. That's
a consolation. I know you don't agree with me but so what?

Some people disembark at Nyeri and more come in. The bus
conductor gives us ten minutes of rest and I move to the tea kiosk
and buy myself a cup. It's almost lunch time but I don't feel like
eating anything. I am not hungry. What they have at this kiosk is not
appetizing anyway. Cold samosa and the like. Filthy stuff.

My dumb bus companion approaches me exuberant-like and
guess what he says.

"It's a bright fine day today," he says.

"Sure," I tell him. "It's what I've been telling you all along.
It's a bright fine day. Those were my exact words."

"Are you going to be in Nanyuki for long?" he asks. I think it
rather funny that this guy should all of a sudden open up after he has
been so glum and boring. I would like to pay him back but I reckon
I am the talkative type. When I don't want to talk to people I don't
just shut up. I talk about things they don't like to hear about or things
they don't understand. I speak as if I am bored or as if I am jeering at
them or indulge in plain irrelevancies. That puts the other guy off.
He keeps mum. If I want to infuriate him I just go on talking even
when he is not listening. I smile and laugh at my own clownish jokes
which makes the other guy thoroughly mad. I might then proceed to
bore him with some stuff on seed dispersal and soil conservation
measures for the control of erosion and such crap after which he is
ready to puke or wants to thumb me if I do not keep my big mouth
shut. I never let him burst his top though. Oh no. When I observe
the right signs I sort of tell him that I am very glad to have met a

142

person like him who could intelligently discuss such a wide variety of interesting topics. It works but not always.

"I'll be there for a long time," I tell this guy.

"You live there?"

"I am going to live there. I'll be there till the end."

"You mean — eh — what do you mean?"

"There is only one end isn't there? I mean you can't end twice, can you?"

"Probably not, but. . . ."

"Oh no. There is no probability involved. It's a definite end. What I mean is — eh. When you are not ended you can't be ended, can you? Or rather when you end there is no probability that you are not ended, is there?"

"Well I suppose not but suppose. . . ."

"Oh no. Supposing breeds an argument. You could argue on how a man would behave if he became a cow. That is an argument based on a supposition. You might even follow the point and discuss how he would behave if he didn't become a cow. I mean a perfect cow. The point I am trying to make is that a man would make one hell of a cow even if it's only supposed. My original idea was about a definite factual ending without probabilities and suppositions. A definite end."

"I suppose you are right. An end has to be definite."

"And factual. An end is a fact."

"I suppose so — yes."

"And non-recurrent."

"What's that?"

"Non-recurrent."

"Oh, I see what you mean."

"Do you?"

"Yes, sure. An end has to be non-recurrent."

"What do you do? I mean how do you earn your living?"

"I am a teacher. I teach at Nanyuki. My home is in Kiambu and I dashed there yesterday to straighten things."

"What do you teach?"

"Physical training."

"You mean drilling the pupils and all?"

"Yes, that's just about it. I drill them and I teach them. I train them too. It's very interesting."

"It must be if you say so. I've enjoyed talking to you. If you don't mind I'll now excuse myself."

"Hey, wait. You didn't tell me what you do."

"You didn't ask me," I tell him and I walk back to the bus. I sit and relax.

Looks like all my life I am privileged to meet stupid guys. Take this teacher fellow for instance. He has a handsome face and what have you but he is goddam stupid. If you told him that strictly speaking he wasn't a teacher but a businessman and managed to convince him that he did not understand himself well enough he would end up by supposing that he agreed with you. It isn't even funny, is it?

The bus doesn't move after ten minutes as the conductor said. It moves after thirty-five minutes. I am all impatient and jittery and if I was invisible I would definitely move and give the conductor fellow a bang on the mouth. I reckon that would surprise the bastard all right. He would probably look around and give the nearest guy a bang. If I gave him another — say from the back — then he'd think that everybody was fighting him and start fighting everybody. He'd swear under oath that he was being hit from all directions. I think it's very fascinating — being invisible. You sneak up on folks and see what they do in private and all. Very funny. There are lots of things I could do if I was invisible.

To begin with I'd ride a bicycle or a horse or something. Then I'd go round the world several times having lots of fun on ships and planes, touching girls' tits or pulling their dresses or something. I'd take cigarettes out of people's mouths or take their drinks from their hands or just bang their heads together. I'd eat from their plates, drink from their glasses and pour water on anybody I didn't like. I'd be real mischievous and I'd get a real big bang from it all. I'd keep away from dogs though. They might nose me. Anyway I wish I was invisible.

It's thirty-seven miles from Nyeri to Nanyuki and the bus takes exactly one hour seven minutes. What I am going to do is I will go to all the bars where military men go and find out whether I can find Tonia. I will live on soft drinks and buttered bread and that gives me a whole week of comfortable living. After that I'll start begging as I told you before. Maybe you didn't believe me. Anyway, I can always book myself in at an hotel and sneak out in the morning. I am hoping that I will have found Tonia before the week is out.

The first place I go to is the Sportman's Arms. It's some distance from the town but this teacher friend of mine — I have forgotten his name — told me that this joint is very popular with army top hats. Tonia would go for top hats.

It's after hours for liquor — or between hours if you think of it that way — and the bloody bar is closed. The bartender is actually closing. He is just putting in the padlock.

"Hey friend!" I sort of rush to stop him. "Is there a chance of getting a drink. I mean one cold drink just before you close?" He shakes his head but I persist. "Hey, wait. How about a coke?"

"You can get that from the restaurant bar." He clicks the lock in position.

There are several white guys and their females having their last drink but they are not military men. They are tourists. They are German or French or Italian or something because I can't make out what the hell they are saying. They might be Greeks or a mixture of the lot but they are not English. You can always tell an English tourist or an American tourist from a mile off. They make sure that you know that they are English or American tourists but they wouldn't like you to confuse English for American or American for English. They are very similar in their differences or different in their similarities, whichever way you'd like to look at it. Anyway you can't mistake them and they make sure you don't.

I pass these people and move to the restaurant bar. I order myself a cold coke with ice just to show the guy at the counter how sophisticated I am. I sit down on a stool and start sipping slowly while I try a line of conversation with the fellow on the other side.

"This place looks somewhat deserted today. Where have the people gone?"

"We are never full during the lunch break. We only get people crowding the place after five."

"Lots of women come here these days?" He looks at me queerly.

"Want a woman?"

"Oh sure. Every man wants a woman."

"Not every man. I for one hate women."

"How do you manage? I mean what do you do when your body requires the services of a woman?"

"I do nothing."

"You must do something. I mean you are just about my age and if you are physically fit you must need a woman. I mean you can't live all your life without touching a woman. Once in a while the body needs sex."

"Not mine. Do you want a woman?"

"I said yes."

"I could show you one. Not in the evening. Right now after

I've closed this place. She is Somali and very beautiful. She's only a kid really. About nineteen — no, eighteen at the most. For a night she'd charge twenty or thirty or forty bob depending on who you were and what time of the month but if you want a quick fling during the day, five will do. I could show you if you are interested but I'll want my commission. It's only five shillings so the total cost to you will be only ten. That is very moderate for a young Somali girl even if it's only for one fling. Are you interested?" I nod. I am not really interested but it might be helpful. I can pump this guy and he'll give me all the information I want. I screw up my face.

"Hey, do you know this girl called Tonia? She is as beautiful as hell but she's approximately thirty although she looks twenty."

"Who doesn't?"

"You know her?"

"Of course I do. The men are missing her terribly."

"And why are they missing her if I may ask?"

"Because she is in jail, my dear friend. I am telling you about a young Somali of sixteen and you start asking me about a whore like Tonia. The number of men that have given Tonia a lay could line the road from here to Mombasa. This Somali girl is really nice. Do you want her?"

This guy is just a go-between. I suppose whores pay him to get them customers. He is also a goddam liar. This Somali girl keeps getting younger by the minute.

"I sure didn't want a whore like Tonia. I only met Tonia once and I didn't even take her to bed. She's not my type. What happened was that I had some money in my coat pocket, just a few pounds and the lot disappeared when Tonia disappeared. I suspected her. If I met her I'd tell her what a goddam thief I thought she was."

"That's like her," the guy says. "She's always pinching somebody's something. She didn't get jailed for stealing though. She hit an army officer with a full beer bottle bang on the head and just about killed him. He was in hospital for two months and he'll never grow hair on some patches of his head. They booked her for six months only. They should have kept her in for two hundred years."

"Did you know any of her friends?"

"Now tell me. Do you want the Somali girl or no? I've got to know. Tonia's friends are lousy anyway."

"For heaven's sake have a heart man, I have told you two thousand times that I want the Somali girl but that doesn't mean that we can't discuss other women, does it?"

146

"I hate women and I don't like to discuss them."

"What is then so interesting about the Somali?"

"My commission. I get five bob and that's half the bargain. That's what interests me. If it wasn't for that, I wouldn't even discuss her with a one-legged blind and deaf and dumb with a hump on his back and webs between his fingers. She is nothing to me. I am allergic to the female sex."

"That is very interesting indeed but when do we go to meet the Somali?" I ask him.

"Right now. I've only got ten more minutes to go. You'll have to give me my five bob in advance. Like another coke?"

"On you?"

"Oh no. On yourself. You can't simply sit there for ten minutes doing nothing."

"Why not? I am waiting for you."

"It's not done. You don't go to a restaurant bar and just sit there. You have to order something." I order myself another coke. I give him a ten shilling note but when he hands back the change it's five shillings short.

"I have taken my five bob," he says.

"Oh no, you don't. Not till I have met the Somali. How do I know that you will not close the place up and sneak through the back?"

"Because I can't lock you in. When I lock up, I lock the whole place." I don't argue. I don't know all that I would want to know but this fellow here is some sort of a fanatic. He has a one track mind. Now that he has his goddam commission I suppose he won't mind if I talk about other women.

"Hey," I say, "when was this girl Tonia put in jail?"

"That whore? I don't know. It's about five months ago or thereabouts. I can't get interested in women leave alone whores. If she gets the usual one month remission she should be coming out right now and if she came out, this is the first place she'd come to. What I can't figure out is how she's managed to stay five months without a fuck. That beats me. She's one whore with number one lust. If she can't sell the godddam thing she'll give it for free."

"Where did she live?"

"In a whorehouse. Where else would you expect her to live? I understand that they are better housed at Langata prison. If I had a gun I would just go about shooting whores. What is the use of keeping her in a prison where she's feeding from public funds. We pay taxes and what do we get? Do you know what happens to that tax? It's used to feed whores in prison. If I had a gun I'd shoot them all.”

“Are you certain that she is at Langata?”

“Why should I be? Why should I be certain of a thing like that for Chrissake? Grow up man. I know she’s there but I am not certain. Some of the other whores go to see her there and word spreads around. That’s how I know. You’d better finish your coke. I am locking the place till five.”

He comes round the bar and asks these other folks who are sitting at the other bar to leave. I don’t know how they get to understand him but they drain their last drinks and start walking out. I walk out too and the bar guy follows, locking the doors behind him.

We take a bus to Majengo and then walk a short distance. We are right in the slums. You’ve never seen such lousy filthy slums in your goddam life. You’ve got to walk with your eyes on the ground or else you’ll step on somebody’s shit or sprain your ankle in a scum-filled drain. The place smells like a million sweating guys pissed and shitted all over the place last night. It isn’t a place for Christians to see.

We get into a Swahili type of house where you have to bend along the corridor or else you’ll hit your head on the roof and my companion knocks at a door. We are let in.

There is a Somali woman all right but she looks sixty. She has wrinkles and folds all over. She has about ten coatings of make-up and wears two hundred bangles on her right hand. She is as thin as they come and is about six feet tall. She smiles like a crocodile, exposing her gold teeth and extends her hand to me. I don’t feel like shaking that wiry hand with two hundred bangles, claws and what-have-you, but I do it all the same. The hand is as coarse as sandpaper.

“Five bob,” my companion says to the old hag. “Five bob a throw.” He walks out. I look at the woman and bolt out too. I catch up with my companion and grab him by the neck.

“Is that the beautiful unspoilt young Somali of sixteen?” I am as mad as hell. I am going to beat up this guy.

“Don’t get fresh, my friend. She says she is sixteen. I wasn’t there when she was born. How do you expect me to know when she was born? Go and ask her. She’ll say she’s sixteen.”

“Right! I don’t want her. I want my five bob back.”

“Let go of my shirt!” he yells. “You wanted a woman and you got a woman. What difference does it make. You can close your eyes when you are at it.”

I smacked him twice and let him go. He didn’t try to fight back. He merely cursed me as I walked away. I didn’t even bother to look

148

back. I had to look down or I'd step on somebody's shit.

I hang around town and in the evening I hop into the train. I am on my way back to Nairobi. I want to go to Langata Prison and see Tonia. She couldn't have spent all that loot within a few months. I want to know when she gets released. I will be right there when she gets released. I'll escort her to wherever she goes and I'll get my dough.

At nine o'clock the next morning I am at Langata. This female guard at the gate won't let me in. I have told her lots of fibs about being Tonia's brother and all but she is not playing. She has this list that she is perusing and she tells me that Tonia is being freed at eleven and that arrangements have already been made to transport her to Nanyuki which is her home. She also tells me that according to the records Tonia has no relatives. She knows I am lying.

I tell her that the records are correct because Tonia believes that I am dead. I tell her that I have just come from the Congo where I've lived for five years and that somebody I'd lent my driving licence to got killed and everybody thought it was me. I tell her about the Congo and the pigmies and how they drive on the right and how I was a personal friend of Lumumba and lots of other crap. She swallows it. She has her eyes wide open and is full of smiles. I tell her that she is nice and that if she was my wife I'd take her to the Congo only that they speak French there and she wouldn't understand. Gosh, you should see her. She's jubilant.

"Do you speak French?" she asks.

"Oh sure, everybody speaks French."

"How do they speak it? Say something in French. I'd love to hear you say something in French." I don't know a goddam thing in French. Not a word. I round my lips and say: "Je voo sey pare le ma si. Ghay var twar buku si si. Signor es te te." I am smiling all over.

"What does that mean?" she asks me. "Tell me."

"It's rare that a man meets a nice woman and when he does she doesn't like him. That's what it means in English. French is a beautiful language," I tell her.

"It sounds wonderful. Which is the word for girl?"

"Si. It really means teenager. A mature woman is sisi."

"Very nice. I am not si. I am sisi. I am twenty-four. What is the word for man?" she asks.

"Peti-eh — before I forget could you get in touch with whoever is organizing transport and tell him or her that I will organize Tonia's transport? That should be some help." She calls me peti and gets onto

the phone and starts cracking jokes to whoever is on the other end.
Then she gets talking cold turkey and says a lot of crap about me.
They talk for a considerable time and then she suddenly turns to me.

"Do you have a car?"

"No. I'll ring for a taxi." She talks some more over the phone
and then hangs up.

"It will be all right. You can take her home."

"Thanks." I sit and wait. This female guard wants to know a lot
of things about Congo women but I am not in the mood. My mood
has just changed and besides I know nothing about Congo women.
She eggs me on because she thinks I am shy on the subject and I
finally tell her that Congo women are rather ugly and that I couldn't
get interested in them. That seems to please her. She is not very good
looking herself. If a woman chooses to be a prison guard then she has
to be ugly.

Just before eleven I ask this guard to telephone Archer's Cabs
for a taxi but she says no. That is not official. I tell her that I'll pay for
it and she says no. I make some more French sounds all aimed at
praising her and she says yes. She telephones Archer's Cabs and asks
them to bring a taxi to Langata Women's Prison in ten minutes' time.
I thank her profusely in my French. She nods her head all over the
place. She points at herself and says, "Me sisi — you peti. French is
nice." I tell her yes.

At eleven-thirty Tonia is sitting next to me on the rear seat of the
Mercedes and the driver is whistling Malaika as we pass Wilson
Airport towards the city centre. Practically no words have been
exchanged between me and Tonia. When she came out and saw me
the hard expression on her face did not change. We merely shook
cold hands and I escorted her to the taxi.

What I have in mind is we'll book a room in a cheap hotel where
Tonia can bathe off the prison dust. Then I suppose I'll buy some
cheap dress for her. The one she's wearing doesn't look so good.
Looks like she was doing some cleaning job at the time they picked
her up. Then she can have a proper lunch and after that we'll talk.
We'll talk cold turkey.

Looking at her I feel almost sorry for her. She looks forlorn
and woebegone. She looks like I did when my dad popped off. There
is something nagging at her. Something eating deep right into the
undercurrents of her personality. A feeling of shame. A determination
in the soul to disclaim the past. Grim determination that is furrowing
her face as she fixes her eyes on the road ahead. She doesn't look at
me or question my presence. It's as if I and everything else are in

150

another world. She is not part of us. She's withdrawn from the world around.

I ask the taxi driver to take us to the Terrace Hotel and he does. I pay him and we go upstairs. She doesn't question anything. She doesn't say one goddam thing. She just follows me looking as sad as Mary Magdalene when Christ was crucified. She doesn't object to me holding her hand and leading her. It's as if she was a mere shadow.

I book a double bedroom for Mr. and Mrs. Gathongo and pay in advance. I am not in the mood for telling hotel people my own name. Some waiter shows us the room, the bathroom and the toilets and I thank him. I usher Tonia into the room. She sits down on one of the beds and supports her cheeks with her hands. She looks very sad. I am starting to get worried. Somebody should say something. I sit on the other bed and face her.

"Well," I say, "aren't you glad to be out?"

"Should I be?"

"Who wouldn't? I certainly would."

"Why did you come for me?" she asks. That is one hell of a strange question. She should be thanking me.

"Guess."

"I have done so already."

"Then you know the answer."

"I could be wrong. I want to hear it from you."

"I am a friend, aren't I?"

"I hadn't guessed that. Why did you come for me?"

"Because I want my money back."

"Suppose you can't have it?"

"I'll kill you. I mean I had thought of killing you."

"Do you think the same still? Will you change your mind?"

"Not until you've talked me out of it."

"How much was it?"

"What?"

"Your money. Do you remember how much?"

"Yeah."

"I haven't touched it. It's all there as you left it."

"I didn't leave it. You took it. You had no goddam right to hoodwink me into. . . ."

"Hold it. I said I've got it all. It's hidden somewhere in Nanyuki and I know I'll find it there. I am sorry I took it. I didn't really mean to keep it. It was a practical joke. I wanted to give you a jolt for the way you took advantage of me. I was going to return it but they jailed you."

"Where is it?"

"In Nanyuki. I've already said that once."

"Are you prepared to give the whole lot back?"

"Why? Yes. It's yours. I have no need of it. From now on I have no use for money. I have lived the better part of my life prostituting myself for it but now that's all over. Money is not everything. I had to go to jail to find that out. I am therefore pleased that I did go to jail. I have been a slave all my life. I have slaved for money. Now I am free. Money will not be my master any more. I'll be my own master."

"What will you do? I mean if you are not going back to your old profession, how are you going to earn your living?"

"Like other women do. Women who are not prostitutes."

"Did you have money of your own — I mean did you have your own savings? If not, I can let you have some of mine."

"Thanks a lot but I don't need your money. My savings are nothing to me. Your money was stolen. I wouldn't touch it with my toe. If you are desperate for money I can let you have some of mine too."

"I don't pretend to understand you but listen. Let's order ourselves lunch after a cold bath and then go out to town for some shopping. You could do with a new dress. Tomorrow morning we go to Nanyuki and after I've got my money then I can take my leave. Is that O.K.?"

"It's all fine except for the dress. I don't need it."

"What is the matter with you, Tonia? Have you become a Christian or a nun or something? Why all the holy airs? Why the self-denial — simplicity — sadness — open-mindedness etc.? I was expecting you to tell me one of them stretchers like you did the last time I met you. You made your husband so real and poor me so mad. You aren't planning to give me the slip or something — I mean you wouldn't tell me about dreams and then disappear woula you, Tonia?"

"Rest ssured, Kiunyu. I leave the past behind me like a cow leaves ite droppings. If you'd not come today at the prison I'd have searcheu everywhere for you till I found you and gave you back your money. I would not have rested till I was sure that the money was in your hands."

"But what are you going to do? You can't just sit at home all your life. You've got to do something."

152

"I'll join the Church."

"You mean a nunnery or monastery or convent or a cloister or...I don't know how many types of such institutions there are but is this what you mean?"

"Yes. That's what I mean."

"They wouldn't accept you. By God, Tonia, you are about thirty. They wouldn't touch you. Not with a ten foot pole."

"They will. I've already been accepted."

"Then you have talked to them?"

"Yes."

"Wonders are many. I'll have none—I mean the convents or the monasteries or whatever you call the places. You must be crazy. What the hell would you want to go to a nunnery for? The ordinary nuns are virgins anyway. At least one would expect them to be. They don't have the vaguest idea of what they are missing. I mean sex. They don't know a goddam thing about it and therefore they don't miss it. They have become what you would call defunct on those lines. Look at yourself, Tonia. You couldn't live all your life cloistered in a nunnery for Chrissake. You'd be craning your neck at men. You'd have the urge and. . . ."

"Thereby you do your thinking injustice. Don't worry about me. I'll be alright. I know what I'll miss. It's the price I've got to pay."

"Pay for what? You have no price to pay. I'll not have you shut yourself from daylight into the seclusion of a nunnery. Convents don't interest me and neither do nuns. I'll not have you become a nun. Oh no."

"What have you got to do with it? My mind is already made up and you are not my father, Kiunyu. You can't stop me. You are out of it."

"I can't stop you physically but it's one hell of a decision you've made. What you need is a man and a home and kids and perhaps a few chickens to keep you busy looking after when your husband is at work. That is what you need. You just can't move from hell to heaven overnight. You are too good a woman to waste and I am sure you would love kids. They are lovely creatures. You watch them grow up from tiny helpless sweet yelling bastards to people like ourselves. They would fulfil your dreams. They are the missing link in your life. You don't know what to do with your love. You have given it to men and pleasure but that's not

what you were looking for. You have found that out. Men are
no longer attractive. Now you want to love God. You want
to love all humanity. After a time that will not be attractive. You can't
love humanity all your life. Sometimes you must love yourself. You
will get fed up but it will be too late. You will stay in but regret the
day you went in. Kids are what you want. You will love them all the
time. Forget your old man. You don't have to love him but you will
sure love kids."

"Suppose I can't have them?"

"What do you mean — suppose you can't get them? Of course
you can get them but it takes two. A man and a woman."

"I know all that, Kiunyu. I can also see the way your mind works.
There's one thing you are overlooking but couldn't possibly know
anything about. I cannot have kids. My uterus was taken out years
ago after I had an abortion. No honest living man would want my
type. I've been a prostitute for too long. I am known by too many men.
My presence would always be too humiliating for my husband. You
surely wouldn't want to know that whenever you were in a social
gathering at least a few men there had taken your wife to bed, would
you?"

"Confound it all. If they took you to bed before you got married
that is immaterial. Nobody is a virgin these days even at the age of
fourteen. What matters is not what people think. They can go to hell.
They can think till their goddam heads burst but so what? What is it to
you what they think? What matters is what you think. The same
goddam people who think so much about you would not give you a
penny if you were dying of starvation. Why bother about what they
think?"

"That's all very kind of you, Kiunyu. In a way you are right. I
wish there was something I could do about it, but my mind is made
up and a decision reached. That way I can see a future. Your way has no
future but a great vain hope for a future. You don't pick husbands
like flowers. I cannot have one by wishing and besides I know with
absolute certainty that he would get miserable in the long run. I do
not wish to make anybody miserable."

"You talk like a goddam saint."

"You are forgetting my reputation. I am an old whore."

"But you are going to change. You will not be a whore, will
you?"

"This is getting us nowhere. I'll go take a bath. I need it badly.
You can't make me change my mind."

154

"I can. I mean I can marry you. You wouldn't have to worry about anything." Then she laughed. For the first time since I picked her up she laughed. It made me laugh too. We looked at each other and laughed. There was nothing really to laugh about but we laughed all the same.

"Would you please say that again? Marry me, is that what you said?"

"Why not. You are a woman aren't you?"

She laughed again. "It's the greatest joke of the season. Don't say it again. I am in no mood for jokes."

"Look, Tonia. Is there any earthly reason why one jailbird could not get married to another? We'd have lots in common. At least we'd both be trying to lead a respectable life to make up for the past. In any case, we can try it for an experiment."

"You don't know what you are saying. You don't know what it would mean. You would never forget my filthy past. You would nag me. You would tease me. You'd never try to be good because so far, the respect you have for me is zero. You would never be proud of me. You'd never feel like other husbands. Worst of all you'd never trust me. If you couldn't trust your wife then you'd be damn miserable."

"For Chrissake stop preaching to me. I know all these things. It's what everybody says. It is what everybody thinks. But is everybody always right? I mean is it conclusive? Does it mean that if I married you, we'd have to do what everybody expected us to do? Oh — stuff and nonsense. There is nothing like just one way in life. Come to think about it I could marry you just for the heck of it."

"Are you serious?"

"To tell you the truth, I wasn't really serious when I said it the first time. I just said it. It just came out but now I mean it. The more I think about it the more convinced I get that it can work. I have known prostitutes who've turned into the best of wives. They have had so many goddam men that they don't want any more. They just want their man. They daren't be unfaithful to their husbands. It would remind them of their filthy past and it's the last thing they want to remember. It works."

"So what?" she asks.

"Right," I tell her. "Here is my plan. I have just hatched it. It's a mad plan but it is a plan all the same. This is what we do. We go to Nanyuki and collect everything. All the dough you have and all the dough you've kept for me. Take all your personal belongings. I have none myself. That is tomorrow. We come back by the night train and

we shall be here in the early morning. We buy two second class
tickets to Mombasa and take the six-thirty train that night. We shall
be in Mombasa the next morning. Have you got me so far?"

"I am listening."

"Right. Nobody knows either of us in Mombasa. We don't know
anybody there. Right. Then . . . eh tell me. Roughly how much
money have you got?"

"You can have the whole lot," she says.

"That's not what I am asking. I want a figure."

"Approximately three times what you are worth."

"That's splendid. We can even donate some of it to the Thika
School for the Blind. I think we should. At least I'll donate some of
mine. That will ease my conscience somewhat. Anyway, what we do
is we book ourselves in a hotel there as Mr. and Mrs. Kiunyu but only
for a while. The thing to do is buy ourselves one of those beach
cottages — one that is not very expensive. We recuperate there. We
stay like that for about two or three months and if we decide that we
really like one another then we get formally married. It will give us
time to think. If after the three months probationary period we have
decided that it wouldn't work then we shall sell the goddam cottage
and go different ways. You can always try anything once."

"What about kids? I told you I couldn't have any."

"To hell with kids. I don't want kids. If we got kids they might
get wind of our filthy past and that wouldn't be good for them. Even
if you could have kids we'd have to practise goddam birth control.
I hate birth control. Rubbers and sheaths and coils and pills and
God knows what. There is even something else they call coitus
interruptus or some such hideous name. It's all very nauseating.
Horrid. There is no end to these silly devices which are all aimed at
making sex boring. We shall be cured of that nonsense."

"So far you have done all the talking, Kiunyu. Have you finished?"

"No, I have not. I hate contraceptives. That's what I was
saying. You are ready for a fling and your husband goes groping all
over the place for a rubber and by the time he gets it he is all droopy
as hell and you don't want the goddam fling any more. That's what
I can't stand. Someone might as well castrate me for Chrissake."

"Don't get worked up about it. It's just a way of life. You've
said quite a lot but you haven't asked for my views. In the first
instance you'd be rushing the whole thing too much even if I had
accepted your proposals. I don't. It's tempting but it's not for me.
It's the convent for me. Even if I was going to get married to you I

156

wouldn't be your mistress for three months just for you to find out
whether I was the woman for you or not. Don't look at me with wild
eyes. I can't accept you just because you suddenly decide to ask me.
Even I have some pride. I don't want any favours from you. I don't
want favours from anybody."

"I am not trying to do you any goddam favour for Chrissake.
All I am trying to do is stop you going to the goddam monastery or
convent or whatever you call it. It's a waste of humanity pining away
cloistered in a convent. It's against reason. Such places should be
abolished. I don't want you to go to a damn convent. That's what I
want to prevent. I love humanity. I'd hate myself if I witnessed you
condemning yourself to that type of hollow life where you pray every
day although you don't know what the heck you are praying for.
You are a real nice price of a woman and it would be a hell of a
waste if your womanhood was locked up somewhere. That is the only
reason I want you with me."

"Very selfish isn't it?"

"A guy has to be selfish sometimes, hasn't he?"

"Would you marry a woman you didn't love?"

"Why not? I'll marry any woman provided we are good
companions and there is mutual understanding of our exclusive
togetherness. It's all nonsense — I mean love and what have you.
When people have been married for five years or more love naturally
fades. They learn to tolerate each other and to depend on each other
and to exist together. During that time they have shared so many
personal secrets that they are practically one. It's not love that keeps
them together. Oh no. If love was absolutely necessary for marriage
then nobody would be married for more than five years."

"Very pessimistic, aren't you?"

"It isn't that. You don't try to understand me. Take a guy of
fifty who is married to a forty-five year old wife. They have been
married for twenty-five years. Right. What alternative have they but
to remain married? Film stars are different. They are mad anyway,
but take normal human beings. They are scared as hell if anything
threatens their married life at that age because separately they have
no identity. Don't tell me that you will be in love with your husband
when you are forty."

"At least they start by loving each other. They couldn't possibly
get married if there was no love between them, could they?"

"Of course yes. Look at Indians or Moslems. They get married
first and love later. As a matter of fact some never get to fall in love

even after marriage but they live goddam happy lives."

"You interest me. Your way of thinking is very strange. Tell me. Do you by any chance love me?"

"Goodness gracious no! How in the name of the holy mother do you expect me to love you only two hours after coming out of prison? Not only that — I mean you just don't love by wishing. I know I may love you later but that's only by the way. If you told me that you loved me I'd walk right out of this room. You'd be cheating. We've been bad people in the past, you and I. All I want is for us to come together and see whether two bads can produce a positive good. It's worth trying even for the heck of it."

"How do you know that I am not your sister? The way our mothers went about, it's probable that we might have the same father."

"Not a goddam chance. I met my father and I know that you couldn't possibly be his daughter. Not a chance. I am his only son."

"You met your father? Where is he? Tell me. Where has he been? I mean how did you find him? How did you know it was him?"

"Those are too many questions. I met him when he was dying, and he died. We shall talk about that later. Now tell me one thing yourself before I go any further. Do you want the monastery — I mean convent — do you want the convent or me?"

"Are you proposing?"

"I am asking you."

"In a very cold way — I've got to think."

"I don't want you to think. Just tell me. If you choose the goddam convent, please yourself. You'll cry later. You will cry bitter tears. Very bitter. If you choose me at least there's some hope for life. At least a glimpse. An opening that could open wider. You've got to make up your mind. I am not going to tell you soft flattering sweet nothings. We are both thirty. To indulge in that would be like walking backwards. What will you have? Me or the bloody convent?"

She started biting her fingernails. She bit them for two minutes. All the time we are staring at each other.

"You. I'll have you. I wish the circumstances were different. I am a woman, remember. This is like making a business policy but, here I am." She spreads out her hands and shrugs her shoulders.

"From now on we are friends, companions. It's like a dream though, giving yourself to another person's will but that's the way it is. It's a relief in a way. I don't have to think. You'll have to do all the

158

thinking. It's difficult to imagine. I can't even convince myself. I don't know how it will end. I don't want to know."

"And that's very sensible of you, Tonia. Now go and get washed. After lunch we go shopping. To hell with convents."

"Shall we drink to it?" she asks.

"Now you are talking. I've kept off goddam beer for a million years. I am sure you didn't get any in prison. I'd like to crown this with something terrific but perhaps we'd better not. Let's just be sad and understanding. It might be a good idea to fast. It gets you meditating and what-have-you and I reckon that it's good for the inner soul. Let's punish ourselves in joy and pay for a fraction of the past. Let's fast until tomorrow morning. We couldn't simply die by then."

"What about saliva. Shall we swallow it?"

"Yeah. We are not Moslems after all. We can't go on spitting all over the place. It's bad manners. We shall swallow saliva and take soft drinks and water and milk but no food. We shall just fast and meditate and be sad. Prayers are not necessary."

"Shall we love? I mean can we kiss?"

"Oh no. It's against the rules of fasting. We shall merely look at each other but of course we can smile and hold hands. Now be gone. Run to the bathroom."

"Will you come and scrub my back? It's really filthy."

"Oh no, I can't. It's against the rules of fasting."

"To hell with fasting. Do come please."

I let out a loud fart and she hurries to the bathroom. She is cursing me and my ass. I like that.

So there you are. You know all about me. Like mother like son. My mother was a whore and I am getting married to a whore. Honest, no kidding. I am going to marry Tonia just for the hell of it. Why shouldn't I? I am not kidding about the beach cottage either. We are going to buy one. We shall live there, go out swimming on the beach, go to movies, go to parties, go to Malindi for fishing, cook our meals, plant some flowers in the garden, join charitable societies, go to church on Sundays, go to night clubs or simply stay home and fuck. That will be fun too. When the money runs out it's all we'll be able to do anyway. I'll write some poems for Tonia too and try to get them published. If you know any other easy ways to keep the dough flowing in, send your ideas to me. Just drop me a line. You can bet your bottom dollar I'll be needing them. But nothing that will land me in jail. No sir, I'm not interested.

www.ingramcontent.com/pod-product-compliance
Lightning Source LLC
Chambersburg PA
CBHW070550100726
47907CB00004B/1328